Going Bicoastal

ALSO BY
DAHLIA ADLER

Going Bicoastal

DAHLIA ADLER

WEDNESDAY BOOKS
NEW YORK

Published in the United States by Wednesday Books, an imprint of St. Martin's Publishing Group

GOING BICOASTAL. Copyright © 2023 by Dahlia Adler. All rights reserved. Printed in the United States of America. For information, address St. Martin's Publishing Group, 120 Broadway, New York, NY 10271.

www.wednesdaybooks.com

Designed by Devan Norman
NYC skyline art © chuckstock/Shutterstock.com
Palm tree art © Champ008/Shutterstock.com

The Library of Congress Cataloguing-in-Publication Data is available upon request.

ISBN 978-1-250-87164-0 (hardcover)
ISBN 978-1-250-87166-4 (ebook)

Our books may be purchased in bulk for promotional, educational, or business use. Please contact your local bookseller or the Macmillan Corporate and Premium Sales Department at 1-800-221-7945, extension 5442, or by email at MacmillanSpecialMarkets@macmillan.com.

First Edition: 2023

10 9 8 7 6 5 4 3 2 1

For my parents,

the fiercest proof that the best successes

can be found in forging your own path

Going Bicoastal

Chapter One,

in Which Natalya Has a Decision to Make

What would you say is the appropriate amount of time in which to have to decide which parent you love more than the other?

Because my parents seem to think that twenty-four hours ought to cut it, and while I'm not what the kids call a "whiz" at math, that feels a little short.

"Let's go through this again," Camila Morales says with the focused dedication of a girl who already has both her love life and future career in order. "Pros of staying here for the summer. Obvious number one: I'll be here."

"I don't know if you can count your presence in Manhattan when you'll be visiting your Abuela in Puerto Rico for an entire month, but okay." I yank a handful of grapes from the bunch we brought with us on our picnic to Central Park—because nothing helps us make big decisions like people watching—and put one between my teeth, letting them pierce the skin slowly. About ten feet to our right, three girls who look a few years younger than us sit together on their own blanket, each one glued to a cell phone, and to the left, a couple is babying a cat so big and fluffy, it looks like the world's comfiest pillow. "Obvious number two: it means not ditching my dad, plus not packing."

"Okay, but obvious number two is canceled by not seeing your mom, though I will give you points for the packing thing. You're horrible at packing."

I can't even be offended. I absolutely am horrible at packing. If you invite me to a pool party, you can be certain I'll forget my bathing suit. In fairness, my absent-minded gene is so clearly inherited from my dad, I can hardly be blamed for it. If it weren't for his various TAs and author's assistants over the years, and the fact that he's one of the most brilliant math professors Columbia has ever seen, he would have been out of a job decades ago.

"Fine." A throuple walks by, the man in the middle wearing a baby in one of those carriers while the parents on either side of him each have a pinkie in the cooing infant's grip. It's impossibly cute and reminds me of my easy number three, though I'm not going to say it aloud to Camila.

Unfortunately, my best friend knows me at least as well as I know myself, if not better. "Obvious number three: the Redhead."

"The Redhead is not a reason to stay," I argue weakly, even though she absolutely is, because we both know she occupies an absurd amount of my brain space. But to be fair, she is obscenely cute, and also ridiculously hot, and impossibly cool, and it's not easy to roll that all into one person. "Besides, what if she's not here for the summer?"

"Okay, but what if she is?" Camila counters. "What if she's wandering the Upper West Side all summer wondering why she's stopped running into that cute blue-eyed brunette everywhere? And then, because that cute blue-eyed brunette was the last thing keeping her in Manhattan, she leaves town and moves to Nebraska?"

"I don't think they have punk girls in Nebraska."

Camila rolls her eyes. "Yeah, I'm sure there are no punk girls in the entire state of Nebraska. I forgot they've completely banned nose rings over there, and I hear listening to Bad Religion can get you exiled to Kansas."

I stab another grape with my teeth. "Now who's being ridiculous?"

"Still you, Tal," she says, yanking out her ponytail holder and immediately putting her thick black curls in an even higher and tighter knot. "Always you."

"Says the girl who thinks random run-ins at bookstores and cupcake shops are the last things keeping the Redhead in New York."

"You know what I mean." She stretches out her legs in front of her and flexes her toes back and forth, fuchsia pedicure winking in the sunlight. "The universe is clearly smashing you and the Redhead together. You've been crushing on her for almost the entire year, and you haven't even managed to get her *name*. This is the summer you finally introduce yourself and ask her out. I'm convinced."

"Or, point for going to my mom in LA: no pressure to make a fool out of myself to the Redhead, who may or may not even be queer, let alone interested in me."

"Didn't you say she wears a rainbow pin on her backpack?"

"Yeah, but maybe it's an ally thing. Maybe she's got queer parents."

"Maybe she has a bisexual best friend who absolutely cannot get up the guts to ask out anyone of any gender, despite the fact that she would be the world's greatest girlfriend and anyone would be lucky to have her," Camila says pointedly.

Whoops—I accidentally crushed the last couple of grapes in my hand. I shove them all in my mouth together to avoid acknowledging Camila's jab, sweet as it may be, and immediately regret it when one goes down the wrong pipe. She has to whack me on the back, and eventually it dislodges. "You talk big for someone who's practically married," I shoot back. "You haven't had to deal with dating since before we were old enough to date." That part isn't even an exaggeration—Camila's and Emilio's moms are both nurses at New York Presbyterian and bonded immediately over their parents being from the same city in the Philippines. Their kids bonded just as quickly the first time they met, and their friendship morphed into romance the second hormones hit. They've been "Camelio" for as long as I can remember. "Let's tone down the judgment, please."

"That was a compliment *mixed* with judgment, thank you very much." She helps herself to some of the grapes, then reaches for her phone when it chimes with a text. Judging by her sappy smile, it's Emilio, which fascinates me because it feels like a person should not be able to still have that effect on another person after this long.

Then again, I don't have much to model it on. You know those couples who split up and everyone is all, "Oh no, why? They seemed so happy!"?

My parents are not that couple.

My parents are the couple who make you say, "What were they ever doing together to begin with?" And they'd be right there with you in asking it.

In their defense—or, at least, as they tell it—finding another Jew at a grad school Christmas party in Durham, North Carolina, seems like the kind of scenario for which the word "bashert" was created. Between awkwardly declining shrimp cocktail and crab puffs at every turn and faking knowing the words to carols they'd only ever heard on TV, Ezra Morris Fox and Melissa Rina Farber exchanged numbers. Then they went on way too many group dates to realize they didn't actually like each other when it was just the two of them, eventually figured it out on their honeymoon, but *also* realized they'd gotten pregnant on their honeymoon, and voilà—then came me. Cue three years of trying to make it work with couples therapy, four years of trying to keep it together by throwing themselves into their jobs and avoiding me as much as possible, and finally, a weary, inevitable divorce that was just amicable enough to work out shared custody.

Until three years ago.

When Melissa got poached from her marketing firm to join Cooper Frank in LA as an executive vice president, she couldn't say no—but I could. And my refusal to move to LA meant I was now in full custody of one absent-minded pro-fessor and spoke to my mom approximately once a week. So it could be nice to actually get to spend the entire summer with her.

Or it could be awkward and miserable, lonely for my dad, and just generally an ill-advised mess all around. Who can say, really?

"Maybe LA will have its own version of the Redhead," Camila suggests, her daggerlike nails catching the sun as she unscrews the cap on her coconut water. "Los Angeles definitely has punk girls."

"How do you know what LA has?" I challenge, watching a corgi do a series of tricks for a bone-shaped treat and willing it to toddle over so I can pet it. "You're always complaining that you've never been west of Chicago."

"First of all, LA is huge—I'm pretty sure they have liter-ally everything. Second of all, my mom's brother lives in Eagle Rock, so we're *going* to visit at some point. We just have to, you know, actually get there."

"I don't think that makes you an expert on the city, Cam."

"No, but you could be." She takes a swig of her water, and it's a good reminder for me to hydrate, but of course my Nal-gene is empty. I grab another couple of grapes instead. "Go to that all-romance bookstore. Do a zillion sketches of the beach. And my uncle would be very happy to make Filipino restaurant recommendations, since he never shuts up about them."

The corgi flops onto its belly, exhausted, and accepts a treat happily. "Maybe you should go instead of me. Melissa probably won't even notice. I doubt she even remembers what I look like."

Okay, so I'm a little dramatic about her move. But I've earned it. I understand them splitting up, and I was all for it, even at seven years old. Leaving your daughter behind as you move three thousand miles away for a *job*, though? A job she already had—albeit at a lower level and in a firm she hated, with a boss who absolutely sucked—in New York? When she never even tried to look for another one here? That part, I can't understand.

I don't know if I wanna have kids when I grow up, but I sure as hell know I wanna live on the same *coast* if I do.

Camila rolls her dark Bambi eyes; she's used to my drama by now. "Or maybe spending time with your mother will help fix things between you and you can stop making excuses to avoid her calls and actually tell her what's going on in your life. You know your mom would be very happy to talk you through college applications and not knowing what you wanna do with your life."

Sometimes I really hate how well Cam knows me. Though it's easy for her to act like having a conversation with my mother will be the fix to everything; just like her relationship, Camila has known for years what she wants to do for a living—follow in her mom's footsteps as a labor and delivery nurse.

"So basically, we're back where I started. Obvious pros, obvious cons, and no closer to an answer." I huff out a breath. "What would you do?" I ask, even though I already know.

"Oh, definitely LA, but I like trying new things. That's not really your MO."

"So you think I'm gonna stay here." Am I offended? I can't tell.

"I think you're gonna stay here," she confirms. "You like what's comfortable. There's nothing wrong with that."

"There isn't," I agree, but the words don't feel like they carry as much weight as I want them to. I don't want everything to be exactly the same this summer, do I? But how uncomfortable do I have to get to shake things up? "I don't know. Maybe I need a change of scenery to finally make some decisions."

"Maybe you could use a different sounding board, too." She gets to her knees and starts gathering up her stuff. "It's almost five and I promised I'd make dinner for the kiddos tonight."

The kiddos are Emanuel and Esperanza, Camila's twelve-year-old brother and nine-year-old sister, who get seriously hangry after 6:00 P.M. We clean up quickly and part ways with our usual double air-kiss, and I go on home with my head still swimming with possibilities.

What does it mean that I don't like being thought of as someone who doesn't take chances? It's not like Camila's wrong—not by a long shot. I haven't taken a risk since . . . well, I'm sure I'll think of an example eventually. But do I want to? And is spending a potentially horrifyingly awkward summer with my mom the kind of risk I want to take? Not all risks are created equal, is for sure.

"Tally? Are you okay?"

I blink when Adira Reiss snaps her fingers in front of my face. I didn't even notice her getting out of the elevator, but I guess I've just been standing at the door to my apartment, key in hand, afraid to go inside and be confronted by my father for my decision. "I'm okay," I say with a sheepish smile, meeting the concerned brown eyes behind her round-framed glasses. "Just spacing."

"Still trying to decide about LA?"

"Mm-hmm."

"And avoiding your dad because you still don't know?"

God, why do all my friends know me so well? In fairness, as my across-the-hall neighbor for the last billion years, Adira sees a lot more than most people, but still. "You don't know my life."

She cracks a grin and opens her front door. "Shabbat leftovers for dinner?"

"Yes, please." I abandon my apartment and follow Adira into hers, my mouth already watering at the thought of her potato kugel. When my dad and I do Shabbat meals together, it's always takeout from the Kosher Emporium or, if he's feeling fancy, one of the many kosher (or kosher-style) restaurants in the area. But the Reisses have us over at least once (usually twice) a month, and both Adira and her mom can seriously cook. Dr. Reiss keeps telling me she'll show me how to make bourekas and stuffed chicken myself one of these days, but she's one of the most in-demand pediatricians on the entire Upper West Side, and honestly I'm not even sure when she makes her own food, let alone when she'll find time to teach me.

Maybe that's another thing that can go on the summer to-do list if I stay.

Learn how to make a Shabbat meal by myself, from challah to dessert, so my dad and I can have home-cooked Shabbat dinners without relying on the Reisses.

Not a risk, but a change. A good change.

I take a seat at the small round table in their kitchen while Adira makes us plates that'll go right in the microwave. I've tried to help a million times before, but she always says not to bother since she's got this down to a science. And she does, always portioning out the perfect amounts of garlicky chicken, fluffy rice, oniony potato kugel, and whatever roasted, steamed, or sauteed vegetable is on the menu that week. (In this case, string beans that drip with soy sauce and minced garlic—my favorite.)

"Do you want soup?" she asks, taking one last look in the fridge to see if she missed anything. She doesn't need to specify—it's chicken soup with matzoh balls and a healthy heaping of carrot and parsnip every Friday night, which was Adira's father's favorite, and is still their tradition nearly five years after his death. But while they have it fifty-two Shabboses a year, I can't bring myself to have soup in the summer.

"No thanks—just a plate is perfect."

Once our food is steaming from the microwave, we dig in, and Adira tells me all about the day camp she'll be running this summer with her best friends, Chevi and Becca, in Chevi's backyard. (Unlike Camila and me, who go to public school a few blocks away on West End, Adira goes to a private Jewish school down by Lincoln Center with lots of kids from Jersey and the suburbs—backyards aplenty.) It's obvious she's giving me some space from talking about the Summer Dilemma, but it's impossible to clear my brain from it. Finally, she asks where I'm leaning, and I ask her the same question to her I posed Camila, though I'm far less certain of her answer: "What would you do?"

"I don't know," she says, and I appreciate having someone else in my life who doesn't think it's a no-brainer. "Being near the beach in the summer sounds a lot nicer than being in the city, and LA's got a ton of great kosher food. Plus, no getting on subway cars with—surprise—no AC or walking over grates blasting hot air. . . . New York in the summer is kinda gross."

"Okay, but it's also kinda great," I argue. "Random free concerts? People watching with ice cream in Central Park? Hanging out on the High Line? Movies in Bryant Park? Yankees games? Shakespeare in the Park? And I know you've never been to Pride, but trust me when I tell you it's one of the best parts of the summer."

Adira laughs, showing off teeth made perfect by two separate rounds of braces. "I'm pretty sure LA has Pride celebrations too, but you don't have to sell me on the city, and you know I'd be happier if you stayed! I just think it's cool that you have options. But anyway, we're only talking places. Going to LA also means leaving your dad, and I know you guys are really close."

Close feels like a funny word to describe what we are, like I run and tell him all my secrets or whatever. Our relationship isn't like that, because he's not that kind of person. When I told him I'm bi, all he said was, "Dating rules remain the same—don't bring anyone home who can't do a basic algebraic equation."

But we *are* a unit, and I absolutely hate the thought of leaving him on his own. He's not incapable of taking care of himself or anything, but he's spacey in that way people are whose brains are always occupied by work they're passionate about, and it's not unusual for him to realize as he's going to bed that he hasn't consumed anything other than coffee all day.

Of course, if he got even a whiff of the fact that taking care of him factored into my reasoning to stay, he'd put me on the first plane to LAX.

My phone beeps with a text, and I look down to see a message from the professor himself. **Café 84 for dinner?**

Whoops. I've devoured 90 percent of what's on my plate already, and I'd been eyeing the babka on the Reisses' countertop, but if I'm even potentially bailing on my dad for the summer, I'm definitely not bailing on him for dinner.

Even if this is the dinner where I'll have to make my choice.

"Sorry to pig out on your food and run, but apparently my dad wants to do dinner." I start to clean up, but Adira tells me to leave it.

"I got it," she says. "Just tell me what you end up deciding. I'm dying to know."

"Me too," I respond with a shrug. "Meeee too."

Chapter Two,

in Which Natalya Really Needs to Make That Decision Already

On a long list of places I'd miss if I went to LA, Café 84 is definitely near the top. The food is perfectly average—typical quiche and pasta and fish and whatever—but the real magic is in the massive menu of desserts, and, in the summer, twelve different kinds of lemonade. Plus, the sidewalk dining setup is beautiful, studded with small trees wrapped in fairy lights.

"What are you thinking?" Professor Ezra Fox, aka Dad, asks, the hand that isn't holding his menu tapping a beat on the glossy table.

My skin prickles in a cold sweat. I didn't think he'd *start* the meal by asking the all-important question. "I, uh . . . I'm not sure yet."

"Really?" He raises his bushy graying eyebrows. "Last time we came here, you talked about the butternut squash ravioli for hours afterward."

Oh. He wants to know what I'm thinking about the *menu.* Still a huge choice but not quite on par with choosing a parent and city. "I don't think I can do pasta right now," I hedge, the pounds of food I consumed at the Reisses still sitting heavy in my stomach. "Maybe eggs. Like a Denver omelet, hold the ham." We're not as strictly kosher as Adira and her mom are, but we do forgo all things pig. "I'm feeling adventurous."

He looks like he wants to laugh at the idea of an omelet with some vegetables passing as "adventure," but he very politely says, "And I assume you'll be getting an adventurous lemonade as well."

This is a good point. I usually stick to the delicious fruity ones—raspberry or strawberry or pomegranate. But there's a section of plant-y ones I never dip into, like basil or lavender, and judging by my conversation with Camila, it's time I mix that up. "Yes, in fact," I say firmly. "I'll have the . . ." My eyes scan the list. "Limonana." I'm not sure what that is, but it definitely sounds adventurous.

"Oh, limonana." My dad's voice takes on a wistful tone that suggests some long story from his past is about to follow. There are three eras to said past—the good ol' college days at MIT, the master's program he did at Technion in Haifa, and his PhD program at Duke, which doesn't get quite as much love because, well, my mom. "There was this place by the beach in Netanya that made the most amazing ones, and we used to go parasailing and then chug 'em." Master's program, then.

"I think I'll join you in that. And in an omelet, too—sounds good."

Of course my "adventure" involves a few bell peppers and a new flavor of lemonade and my dad just randomly drops something about flying through the air. I make even math professors look cool.

We place our orders, and I ask for my omelet to be delivered with some hot sauce. There, that's something. Or at least it would be if my dad didn't add an "Ooh, that sounds good too. Tal, you're really hitting every nail on the head tonight."

Is this really who I am? I don't *feel* this boring. Would going to LA change it all? Or is staying and making the most of NYC the best move?

How do I *still* not know?

I ask my dad how the book's going—he's working on a second edition of his best-selling textbook on algebraic topology—and he immediately gets excited talking about the new exercises he's adding and all the supplemental materials he's been discussing with his editor. "Animated diagrams, Natalya!" he says with not a little bit of joy in his voice. "Imagine *Intro to Algebraic Topology*, second edition, with animated diagrams!"

Well, now I know what my dad is thinking about when he makes goofy noises in his sleep. I guess that's better than the alternative.

As always, his descriptions start to get far too technical for someone who doesn't have at least an undergrad degree in math, and I let my gaze wander to the other diners. There's a young couple with a toddler who's absolutely giddy with sugar from a half-eaten cupcake, her face smeared with berry-pink icing the exact color of the bows securing her adorable tiny Afro puffs. On the other side of them, an older white woman in an awesome feathered hat is sitting in a wheelchair pulled up to the table, an aide in aqua scrubs helping her with a plate of plain salmon and undressed broccoli. And then my view is obstructed by a server in khaki shorts and a black T-shirt carrying a tray of tall, frothy green drinks. "What do you think *that* is?" I ask my dad, immediately feeling bad when I realize he was still talking. "Sorry."

He smiles. "I'm aware my work isn't quite as scintillating to you as it is to me. But what do you mean?" he asks, and I realize the server is coming right to our table. "Didn't you want a—"

"Limonana!" The cheerful ginger server places one huge glass in front of my dad and the other in front of me. "Enjoy! I'll be back with your omelets in a few minutes."

He waits until the server's out of earshot and then says, "You had no idea what a limonana was, did you?"

"I did not." Green is not my favorite color of drink, but I did order it, so, time to give it a shot! I take a long, noisy sip, and . . . it's mint. Mixed with lemon. And while it is clearly delicious to my extremely delighted father, I could swear to God I'm drinking grass. I push the glass away from me so quickly, it nearly tips over.

"More for me, I guess! But first . . ." And I know my dad is going to say he needs to go to the little boys' room before he even does it.

The number one rule of our father-daughter dinners is no phones at the table, but without a drink to sip, my hands need something to do. I pull my phone out of my pocket and start scrolling through photos and videos with the volume on low when suddenly it starts ringing and *Melissa* comes up on the screen, *Mom* in small letters beneath it as if it were the name of her business.

Crap.

I'm not ready for this. The last time we spoke on the phone was when she called to tell me that she'd worked out a paid internship for me at her company, and if I wanted, I could spend the summer at her house in Beverlywood and have a job all set, but I had to tell her ASAP. The internship was only available because an executive's kid had bailed at the last minute to follow his dream of doing stand-up, and if I didn't grab it, then some other employee's kid definitely would. The whole thing sounded shady as hell, but Cooper Frank *would* be a killer name on my otherwise very empty résumé.

And it's not like I'm leaving gainful employment behind. I applied to a bunch of places—bigger chains like Barnes & Noble and Michaels and smaller shops like OcCult Fiction and the Silver Wrapper Bakery—but weirdly my complete and total absence of retail experience wasn't desirable. So all I've got going for me this summer on the work front is ten hours a week shelving books at the university library. And yes, I got the job because of my dad, so no matter what, we're looking at shameless nepotism.

I mean, *I* feel some shame about it, but you can bet Ezra and Melissa don't.

The thing is, I've decided what I'm gonna do. And I'm at least 80 percent certain about it. But if I pick up that phone call, I'm gonna have to be 100 percent there. Except when my dad returns for the Conversation, I'll have to be 100 percent there anyway.

So.

One hundred percent time.

My thumb hovers over *Answer Call*, and then I make my choice.

Chapter Three,

in Which Natalya Makes a Choice

I gnore.

I'll call her back. I will. At some point I need to tell her that I'm not coming, but my dad deserves to hear it first. Besides, truth be told, I haven't decided if I wanna be nice about it or point out that it is waaaay too little, too late. I mean, a last-minute internship? So glad I could be an afterthought to you in this and in everything else, Mom.

I go back to scrolling, liking Camila's shot of the chicken adobo she made for dinner, one of Emilio's billion photos of his family's golden Lab, and my friends Lydia and Leona's selfie, hashtagged #twinfie. Then a shadow passes over the table and I slide my phone back into my pocket as my dad sits down across from me with a "What'd I miss?"

No point hiding it. "Mom called."

"Oh?" His eyebrows rise, and I know he's trying to look casual. "What'd she have to say?"

"I didn't pick up, so the world may never know." I meet his eyes over our bright green drinks. "I'm staying, Dad. I'm gonna stay with you this summer."

Ezra Fox is not a big smiler, as anyone in the math department at Columbia can tell you, but this is a good one. "You sure?"

"I'm sure. I barely even know Mom at this point. I don't need to spend a summer playing catch-up. Besides, my friends are here, I have the library shelving job, and you're here. It's an obvious choice." As soon as I say it, I know I'm making the right move. Because it *is* obvious. This is a way more comfortable choice, and comfortable choices are my jam. Why would I throw away everything I've got here for a summer of the unknown?

"That's great, Tal. But if you're staying, we're gonna need to implement a few rules."

"I'm very familiar with the 'immediately text me with the medallion number whenever you take a cab' rule, Dad."

"That's not what I mean." He takes off his glasses, cleans them on his shirt, then replaces them. "You're going off to college next year, and I have to admit, I'm a little worried about you. I'm thrilled you're staying, of course, but a part of me was almost hoping you'd take the path less traveled for once. And I don't think I'd be doing a good job as a parent if I constantly let you make the easiest choices."

Well. Way to roll all my fears up into one ball there, Professor Fox. "Okaaay," I drag out. "So what does that mean?"

"It means you're going to try some new things this summer. If you're going to stay here, you need to get another part-time job, and you need to get it on your own; nothing affiliated with the university."

Honestly, my pride kind of demands that, so I nod. "Deal."

"And until you find one, you'll be working as my assistant on the book. This one *and* the next one."

Ugh. Math. "Yes. Fine."

"And I want to see you taking some chances in your personal life." He removes his glasses again, but this time, he leaves them dangling from his fingers, like he needs me to be a little blurry for this part.

Which makes sense when he opens his mouth. "I'm not getting involved in your dating life, but for the love of God, please just get the Redhead's actual name so you can stop discussing her with Camila like a character in *Portnoy's Complaint*."

"I don't know what that means," I tell him. "For the millionth time, I'm really not interested in movies from last century."

My father isn't big into praying, but I swear he closes his eyes and does it just then, and I take advantage of him not watching to give the drink another shot. Welp, still tastes like sour herb grass. He opens his eyes in time to see me make what I'm sure is the most repulsed face known to man.

"Not a fan?"

"Not really," I admit weakly. "But back to more important things. Can we please make a deal never to discuss any crushes I may or may not have ever again?"

"I would like that very much. As soon as I say this one

thing." I brace myself for something hideously embarrassing—if he knows about the Redhead, what else does he know?—but all he says is, "Nat, your mother and I may not have been bashert—"

"Understatement of the decade," I mutter. Maybe somewhere in the world my parents do have soulmates, but they certainly weren't each other.

"But at least we took a chance. And we got you out of the deal, so it wasn't all bad."

"That could *not* have been worth it."

He smiles wryly, and I'm not sure I like the implication. "I just want to make sure we haven't destroyed your ability to believe in love. I know divorce can have lasting effects on children—"

"I'm fine, Dad. I promise. This isn't about you and Mom scarring me for life. I just don't know how to talk to attractive people. Or unattractive people. I must've inherited extreme social awkwardness in at least half my DNA," I say pointedly.

"Ha. But speaking of your DNA, I have one more condition for this summer, Natalya."

Full name. Never a good sign. Especially when paired with that face.

People always assume I'm Russian because of my name, and while there's definitely some in the Ashkenazi mix that makes me up, the real story is typical for my parents: my mother wanted Natalie, after her aunt who passed away shortly before I was born. My father wanted to name me after a powerful biblical woman, but not one of the more commonly used names like Sarah or Rachel. And so, in maybe the one compromise they have ever made, they combined Natalie with Atalya and came up with Natalya, a name neither one ever calls me unless they need my full attention.

Oh, and for those without a biblical background, Atalya— Athaliah, in English—was a woman who killed her entire family in order to become queen and was later murdered when her one surviving descendant, who'd been hidden by a maidservant, came of age to be trotted out as king. So. Confused feelings all around on that one.

(Also, I looked it up once, and Natalya means "born on Christmas," which is just a hilarious choice for a Jewish girl born in February, but that's another story.)

"Drop the hammer."

"I want you to communicate with your mother more. At least a few times a week." I open my mouth to argue—he and I barely communicate a few times a week—but his eyes are doing that thing that absolutely forbid you to even attempt to reply. (Mention of that look appears *frequently* on ReviewThe Prof.com, and I'm pretty sure it's why his rating is a 4.7 rather than a full five stars.) "I don't care if you're texting one of those pictures—"

"Emojis or memes?"

He pinches the bridge of his nose. "Please stop." He exhales, eyes his limonana like he wishes he'd gotten a beer. "You didn't make the decision to stay here immediately. That means you were at least considering spending the summer with your mother. Which means seeing and speaking to her every day. There's no good reason you should abandon that just because you're not staying with her."

"Is this a punishment?" I ask, narrowing my eyes. "Because I didn't choose you without a second thought?"

"Of course not." He sounds like he means it, but . . . "Your mother and I never intended for you two to drift this far apart when she took the job at Cooper Frank. It's unfortunate, and we're not going to discuss blame, but we *are* going to fix it. At least one of these communications per week is going to be a phone or video call; the rest is up to you."

"Did she put you up to this?"

"She doesn't know, and you're not going to tell her." His face softens just a little bit. "Your mother lost something big when she moved, Tal. She knows it and I know it and you know it. She's trying to get it back now, and the least we can do is make some space. Especially if it's space you were already preparing to make."

Ugh, my father is so rarely soft that it's impossible to say no when he is. And he has a point—part of me was anticipating letting my mother back in this summer, at least a little bit. So I can do this.

Besides, he didn't say the "communications" couldn't be two-second texts.

"Fine."

We shake on it just as our food arrives.

❊ ❊ ❊

When we get home, it's time to get the very first phone call over with: the one in which I deliver the decision. It rings three times, and I'm so used to waiting for the "You've reached

Melissa Farber" message that comes on with her voice mail that I don't even realize she's on the other end of the line until she says "Nat?" for what's clearly not the first time.

"Hi, yeah, sorry." I clear my throat, wishing we could just skip this part and knowing we can't. "And also, I'm sorry. I made my decision. I'm going to stay here."

"I had a feeling," she says, and I can hear her sad smile through the line, forcing a twinge in my gut. "Well, I had to try. There's even gonna be a new kid working here who's around your age. The company decided they didn't like the optics of having their only new intern be a nepotism hire, so they picked up one of the program applicants. He's cute, or at least what I'm pretty sure a seventeen-year-old girl would think is cute."

My mother is a strange woman, but my dad is right—a part of me wanted to be around that strangeness this summer. I'd wanted to understand her better, not just to understand how she could so thoroughly leave us behind but because I truly am confused by her far more often than seems normal for a girl to be confused by her mother.

Like now—I don't think she means for her mention of me being a nepotism hire to sting, but it does. Am I supposed to envy the other kid, who got there on his own merits and has already impressed my mom with his looks, sort of? Because, so help me God, I kinda do. And anyway, "I had to try"? As if I'm some campaign she went after at work even though she was underqualified? That's what I get? And this is the woman I'm supposed to communicate with multiple times a week?

This is about the length of our usual phone calls, so I mumble something about how maybe I'll come out for the High

Holidays (even though we both know I won't, because school will already have started and I can't afford the time to fly there and back) and prepare to say my goodbye, when she surprises me.

"I was thinking that it'd be nice if we talk more this summer," she says, and it still sounds like she's discussing work, but I can also hear her catch herself and try to change that. "Like maybe it'd be fun if every couple of weeks we bought the same book and had a little book club. Is that too often? Are you still reading a lot?"

"I am," I assure her. "Mostly because I read thrillers that keep me up way too late."

"Ooh, I haven't read a good thriller in a while," she says. "That sounds like fun. I also thought we could strike a deal where you can buy one new art supply a week, as long as you send me a picture of what you did with it."

She's speaking my language so fluently that I'm starting to wonder if she and my dad are in on these plans together. But truthfully, it's really, really hard to imagine them having a civil conversation about anything, let alone this.

So I decide to go with it. Besides, those are two easy communication options, and already I'm feeling a little pressure off my chest at having to come up with how to talk to her as often as my dad wants. Maybe having little prompts is exactly the way to go.

Is that a normal way to have to talk to your own mom? Maybe not. But we've never been normal.

"Deal," I say. "And since, as far as I know, you haven't picked up any artistic hobbies, maybe you can do the equivalent—

every week, tell me something you did at work that you're really proud of." I think back to the last time my mother visited and how we went somewhere new for dinner every night. Granted, she mostly had salads, but at least she was somewhat adventurous about where she had them. "And maybe the best thing you ate that week."

"Deal," she says, and even though it's a completely unfamiliar sound to me, I know there's a trace of a smile in her voice. "Go to the bookstore tomorrow, pick something out, and let me know what to get, okay?"

I already have a shopping list ten books long of stuff I'm dying to read—no further browsing necessary—but I never need to be told twice to go to a bookstore. "Okay." I'm smiling too now. And then I think of one more thing. "And, Mom?"

"Yes?"

"The work thing—it can either be something you were really proud of or something that really sucked. Either one."

I want to know who my mother is, and if I've learned anything from social media, it's that we don't really get to know people from just their highlight reels.

"I like that," she says, her voice a shade quieter than before. "Looking forward to it, Nat."

"Me too," I say, and I mean it.

Chapter Three, Again,

in Which Natalya Makes a Different Choice

"Hi, Mom." I'm outside, but I keep my voice down, partly so I don't disturb the other diners and partly because if my dad surprises me on his way back, I absolutely do not want him hearing this conversation. "I'm actually out to dinner with Dad. He's in the bathroom," I add quickly, before she can snipe, "And he's letting you use a *cell* phone at the *table*?" "Can I call you back right after?"

"Sure, Nat." But she doesn't hang up, and neither do I, and I know what she's waiting for, and I need to say it to *somebody*, so.

"I'm coming," I say quickly. "To LA. I just . . . haven't told him yet, and I need to do that in a minute, and I'm a little nervous about it."

"Oh!" She laughs, but it sounds genuinely happy, and I

hadn't even realized my shoulders had been hunched up around my earlobes until I heard that sound and let them go. "Fabulous! Okay! I'll get things going here, and I guess I'll see you next week! And great news—there's actually gonna be another intern around your age at work, so maybe you'll even make a new friend. He's cute, or at least what I think a seventeen-year-old girl would think is cute. You still like boys, right?"

"*Yes*, Mom, ugh, please do not attempt to set me up this summer. Okay, Dad's coming back. I gotta go. I'll talk to you later." I put the phone away without waiting for her response, but it's too late—my dad's already seen me.

"Camila?" he asks.

I'm so tempted to lie, but there's no point pushing off this conversation any more. Time to rip off the Band-Aid. "Mom," I admit.

"Ah." He takes his seat. "And did you tell her what you chose?"

"I did. I'm—I'm gonna try LA for the summer. Not because I don't wanna stay with you," I add quickly, because even though my dad isn't the emotional type, I am. "I just think it would be good for me to make a change. See somewhere that isn't Upper Manhattan."

"You know you always have my permission to go down-town, as long as you stay above Houston." He looks a tiny bit sad but not mad. Not at all mad. I wish I could give him a huge hug, but the table's in the way, and also he's not much of a hugger.

"Is this okay?" I ask tentatively. "If you tell me it's not, I'll stay. I swear I'll stay."

"I know you would, Tal, but I think it's the right move. You should get out more. See some new things. Prove that someone in the Fox clan is capable of getting a tan."

A *tan.* God, I didn't even think about how hot I'm gonna look with an LA tan. Okay, yes, I'm feeling good about this choice. I reach across the table and squeeze his hand, which is, as always, faintly stained with ink. "Thank you."

The waitress arrives with our food, and we quickly break up the sappy moment and dig into our respective dishes, the scent of fried egg and sweet pepper far too delicious to ignore. Before the waitress leaves, my dad asks her to bring a strawberry lemonade, and like that, my heart ping-pongs the other way.

Am I making a mistake? My mom would never pay close enough attention to me to notice that I hated my drink, let alone know exactly which flavor I want to replace it with. Do I really want to spend the summer with a woman who's basically become a stranger?

"It'll be good for you to spend some time with your mother," Dad says between bites as if he's reading my mind. He splashes some Tabasco on his eggs, reminding me that I've forgotten I was going to add hot sauce to my own, but I decide going to LA is a big enough risk without scorching my taste buds. "We never intended for you two to drift this far apart when she took the job at Cooper Frank. It's unfortunate, and we're not going to discuss blame, but I think it's a good thing that you're giving her a chance to fix it." He takes another bite, chews thoughtfully. "Your mother lost something big when she moved, Tal.

She knows it and I know it and you know it. I hope you open yourself up to letting her get some of it back."

I don't really know what to say to that, or *what* I feel open to; I just know I couldn't get my friends' words out of my head. Camila and Adira don't have much in common besides me, but if LA is the path they would've both chosen, I can't help but believe that means something. Besides, how exciting is the summer ahead of me here? Camila's volunteering at the hospital for three weeks before disappearing for a month, I have zero dating or even hookup prospects, and they'll replace me for that library job in about four seconds—which reminds me, I need to let them know I'll be abandoning said job. Whoops.

"I guess" is all I say. Not that I'm already questioning my choice. Of course not. That would be ridiculous.

Right?

Right.

This is good. This is change. This is giving myself a chance to shake things up, to reconnect, to have new experiences. I have to admit, it's tough to think about going a whole three months without even the possibility of bumping into—

"It *is* a shame," Dad says, cutting into my thoughts. "I was looking forward to seeing if you ever got the nerve."

"The nerve for what?"

He flashes a wry smile. I'm seeing so many new sides to my father tonight, I swear. "To introduce yourself to the Redhead."

Oh no. What is happening? I want to die. "How do—"

"A father knows" is all he says, and though he's wrong—many, many fathers would never, and my mother certainly doesn't—I keep my mouth shut. I wonder, too, if I might have finally gotten up the nerve this summer, especially with Camila out of town and my need for entertainment even more dire.

I guess we'll never know.

❈ ❈ ❈

"Okay, I know I said this is what I would've done, but I can't believe you're actually *doing* it." Cam's perched on my bed, watching me make an absolute mess of my suitcase while she noisily sips from a smoothie. "I really thought you were going to stay, and now I'm kind of pissed."

"I'm going to remind you *again* that you will not be here for half the summer! And the half you will, you're going to be all wrapped up in your volunteer work and Emilio anyway." I examine a T-shirt covered in pineapple print and another covered in lemon print and consider taking both. Camila shakes her head and points to the lemon one, eagle eyes on me until I reluctantly return the pineapple shirt to the drawer.

"Ahem, *we* would've hung out with Emilio," she corrects me, "and Lydia and Leona and Isaac and Elijah and Nate. Please do not make it sound like we constantly third-wheel you."

"Fine," I mutter, even though it sure feels like it when they're being ridiculously cute. "But anyway, this is good, right? I should do this?"

"Yes, you should do this." She puts down her cup and goes over to my closet, quickly selecting three dresses she declares I must bring. "You should spend time with your mother, and you should meet new people, as long as you don't like any of them better than me."

"How could I possibly?" The dresses join the collection of tees, tank tops, shorts, jeans, and leggings already filling the suitcase nearly to the brim. "I don't even know how to make new friends. My mom did say there's gonna be another intern our age—a cute guy, according to her—but who knows if that can be trusted."

"Well, she found your dad cute once upon a time, so that tells you her taste."

"Camila Maria Christina Morales, you are gross."

"I'm just saying! But you better text me immediately with a report. If he's cute, I expect full details and at least one stealth pic."

"He's not going to be cute. I do not have that kind of luck. He's probably just Jewish. My mother thinks every Jewish boy on the planet is cute. It's like a biological imperative." I sigh. "What am I forgetting to pack? I feel like I'm forgetting something big."

"Hmm." Camila's intense gaze roves over the clothing spilling over the brim. "The good-butt jeans?"

"Check. Definitely check."

"Bathing suits?"

"Got the purple tankini and the flowered bikini."

"Bras and underwear?"

"Of cour—oh. Oh, God. No. Crap. I don't think I have enough room left." I *would* somehow forget the most important things, which of course sets off a spiral of us realizing I also forgot toiletries, my laptop charger, a toothbrush, and glasses for days I don't feel like wearing my contacts. Together, we dump out the suitcase, get stricter with what makes the cut, and refold and pack. "My mom will probably have stuff I can use, right? I didn't pack shampoo or anything like that."

"She's a human person with her own house. I'm pretty sure she's planning on sharing her shampoo if she's having you stay with her all summer."

"You don't know my mother," I mutter, which is only half true. They definitely crossed paths plenty of times when my mom was still living in New York, though not as often as they would've if she'd stayed in Manhattan instead of moving to Brooklyn to "claim her own space," making for a really fun commute for me on days I stayed with her. "I wouldn't be shocked to find out she sleeps at the office five nights a week."

"Well, then, that leaves all her shampoo for you *and* plenty of privacy for your new intern boyfriend," Camila says with a grin while I roll my eyes. "Now, go pack your freaking underwear."

Underwear! Right. I knew I was forgetting something.

Chapter Four,

in Which Nat Gets off to a Rocky and Decaffeinated Start

Extremely Melissa Move #1: Scheduling me a flight that lands close to midnight, LA time, so that she won't have to deal with traffic when she comes to pick me up from the airport. Never mind that that makes it almost 3:00 A.M. for me, and I am *exhausted*. I can't sleep on planes to save my life, so I spent the entire flight snacking on Chex Mix and Twizzlers and watching cheesy medical dramas. Now I'm torn between wanting to pass out and feeling like I could perform a halfway decent craniotomy.

Extremely Melissa Move #2: She's twenty minutes late and her car reeks of coffee, something that might be nice first thing in the morning but is just dizzying at this hour. "I thought you might be tired," she says, gesturing at the cup that's apparently for me. There's a gaping space where "Don't worry, I poured in five pounds of sugar" would be if this were my dad, and my brain feels like it's filled with cotton and a single thought: *Why the hell would I want coffee when I could just go to sleep?*

So that's what I say. Minus the hell part.

"Oh. Right." Her lips twitch and now I remember that my mom does not sleep. I don't know how I forgot this about her when I decided to share a house with her for the summer. I used to constantly smell coffee brewing on my way to bed.

How did I forget that?

"We can put it in the fridge when we get"—I stumble over *home* and remember that it isn't, not for me—"back to your house. I'll make it iced coffee in the morning."

She nods and her smile is so stiff and her shoulder-length blond hair is so stiff and we haven't even hugged yet but I know it would be stiff and the thought makes me want to cry. My dad isn't a hugger, but at least I know he's not a hugger. And he has other ways of hugging, like swatting my feet with a rolled-up copy of the *New York Times* when I put them up on the couch. I want to make this better, so I say, "Thanks for thinking of it," and that seems to melt something. But we still don't hug, so I just throw my bag in the trunk and get into the car.

"How was your flight?" she asks, because what else do you ask someone who just got off a flight? It is literally the only question in the world after someone gets off a flight.

"Good. I had a window seat. And a lot of snacks."

"Oh. Good."

Silence, except for the AC and the sound of coffee being

sipped at every red light. I feel like I have to break it, so I say, "I texted Dad when I landed. I didn't think he'd answer, because, you know, middle of the night. But I got a thumbs-up. So. He knows I'm safe."

"Oh, good. That's good."

It *is* good, Mom. Thanks for pointing that out.

I'm out of things to say, and she's focusing on the road, so I let myself rest against the window and close my eyes. When they open again, we're pulling into the driveway of her white stucco house. I've been here before, just a couple of times. The first winter break after she moved, I insisted on staying home with my dad for Christmas so we could be extreme Jewish stereotypes and stuff our faces with Chinese food while watching *Star Wars*. But the next day, I was on a plane, and I spent the rest of the week experiencing the weirdness that is being a Northeasterner in LA during their sorry excuse for a winter. I was so cranky about missing New Year's with my friends that my parents let me come back early, but I'm also pretty sure my mom was tired of me.

So, needless to say, I do not have the best memories of this place, but I do have some memories, at least. When I drag myself inside, I know to go through the kitchen and then through the bathroom to get to "my" room, which does have a few pictures up of me but is otherwise clearly my mom's home office with a daybed in it.

"There are clean towels in the bathroom, and I cleared out the closet, so make yourself at home." I look up to see her standing in the doorway, her hand wrapped around a mug. It takes me a minute to decipher the expression on her face, but then I realize she keeps looking at the desk, and on an ordinary night, she'd be working in here right now.

"I can sleep on the couch in the den," I offer, my stomach sinking with guilt at taking up her space even though this entire arrangement was her idea. "If you want your office."

"It doesn't pull out," she murmurs, and I can't help wondering if that's making all the difference between her taking me up on my offer and not. "No, no." She waves her hand. "You go to sleep. I should go to sleep too." As if that'll be possible with all the caffeine racing through her veins. Or maybe she's immune at this point. And then, of course, "Or, at least, I should get back to work on the Featherston account. But I can do that on my laptop in my room. Do you need anything else?"

I did glance at the sink on my way through the bathroom and confirmed that there is indeed toothpaste. "Nope, I'm good."

"Great." She gives me a weak smile and says good night, and then I'm alone, listening for the quiet sound of her door closing behind her. It's too late to text any of my friends, but after my tiny nap in the car, I'm too wired to go to sleep yet. Instead, I shower the plane ride off me while my phone charges, scroll through stupid videos while I wash up and put some stuff away, and grab the YA thriller I bought in the airport but never actually got to on the plane.

Mistake. Extreme mistake. It turns out to be too good and I don't put it down until I've read it cover to cover and I'm so exhausted I could die, but like the kind of exhausted where you can't sleep because it's too much.

So far, LA is not off to a winning start.

Maybe I should dig up that coffee after all.

* * *

I don't know what time I end up falling asleep, but when I wake up, it's to about a billion messages, most from Camila.

How is it??

Did you land OK?

Why tf aren't you answering me???

Oh, I forgot about the time dif, sry

Are you up yet??

I let out a huge yawn and write back to let her know I'm fine and everything is fine and that I'll call her later. Then I take my time washing up and getting dressed, dreading yet another awkward interaction with my mom. But I shouldn't have worried; it becomes clear with a quick search that she isn't home, confirmed by the empty driveway.

Okay, it's pretty late—jet lag will do that—so she must've gone to work hours ago, but there isn't even a note. There's also no cereal in the cabinet or waffles in the freezer, I have no idea how to work her coffee maker, and last night's offering is nowhere to be found, so I guess I'm going out.

By myself.

In a city I don't know.

Cool, cool. Definitely made the right choice here.

Right now, if I had to guess, Camila's at the park or library with her siblings, Adira's doling out snacks to a bunch of little campers, Lydia's reading her fifth manuscript of the day at her publishing internship, and Isaac's hanging around Leona while she folds shirts at Anthropologie.

I'd kill to have any of them with me.

Truthfully, I hate being alone. I don't know where I got it from, since Lord knows both of my parents are big on sequestering themselves in their offices for some peace and quiet, but I don't even like watching TV by myself; Adira's my designated Real Housewives buddy, and if I'm binging something on Netflix, there's a solid chance I'm texting with Cam, or with Isaac and Leona on our endless "Alphabet Soup" text chain.

But I chose a new city—one where I wouldn't have any friends, wouldn't know a single soul until my internship starts in two days. So it's time to learn new things in a new place. I shed my pajamas for a tank top and shorts, dig through my suitcase for my flip-flops, open up the browser on my phone to look up the nearest coffee shop, and . . . promptly realize I never got the Wi-Fi password from my mom.

Of course.

I can't bring myself to call or text her and have our first real conversation on our first day of me living in her house be about Wi-Fi, so today's gonna be a data situation, I guess. Thankfully, there's a Coffee Bean & Tea Leaf about five blocks away, and while I know LA people supposedly don't walk anywhere, this New Yorker definitely does.

Once I have a vanilla Ice Blended in hand, I take the opportunity to wander around what'll be my new neighborhood for the summer. My mom lives in Beverlywood, which happens to be where she grew up, though her parents moved to Miami as soon as she and my aunts were all grown up and on their own. Now they're spread throughout the country—Aunt Jessica is a dentist in Memphis and Aunt Lauren, the baby of the family, settled with her family and an occupational therapy practice in Boca—but I guess Mom never stopped missing it here.

Dad's refusal to even try a short-term move here was one of the straws that broke the marriage's back—something I learned from one of their many, many hushed yelling fights. Truthfully, it's hard to picture my dad somewhere that doesn't have a winter. But as I walk down Pico and take in all the storefronts, I have to admit to being mildly surprised that he wouldn't try somewhere with this many kosher restaurants. It feels like every other window is advertising pizza, sushi, or falafel—the three great cuisines of kosher restaurants across America. And then there are the Persian restaurants, each and every one of which I photograph so I can remember to go back at some point and try something new.

I also take note of everything I might need—drugstores, nail salons . . . Who knows what my mom plans to show me? If this morning has taught me anything, it's that I better be prepared for the answer to be nothing. After two hours of wandering, photographing, and pausing to post pictures, my "coffee" is long gone and I'm dizzy from everything I've tried to commit to memory. I head back to the house and, with nothing else to do, get changed to go read and sunbathe in the backyard.

I'm pulling on a clean tank top when my phone rings, and I leap for it, assuming it's Camila. Instead, a picture of my Dad refusing to look up from a math book pops up on the screen. It figures that he'd check in before my mom.

"Hey, Papa. How's tricks?"

"I'm so pleased you asked. I've been spending the morning reading Bamberger's new book, and his results in Ramsey theory are—"

"Dad."

"You started it."

"I did. So are you calling to check up on me, or are you still avoiding writing the foreword for that book about making homology theory cool for the young'uns?"

"I'm not *avoiding* it; I'm simply collecting my thoughts. And of course I'm checking up on you. How's LA? How's your mother?"

I take the phone into the den and watch the birds flying past the French doors and floor-to-ceiling windows that bring an unbearable amount of sunlight into the room. "LA is warm. And big. And has coffee that's more like caffeinated milk-shakes. So far, I give it a six out of ten."

"I see you've had a busy day."

"I've been taking in the sights," I say, "by which I mean a vast number of kosher restaurants and also some other build-ings. And palm trees. They really do have palm trees."

"Well, at least your mother's helping you commune with nature."

I decide to sidestep his assumption—if he knows my mom neglected me on day one, it'll just start another pointless fight—and move on. "I also took note of several Persian restaurants. You wanted me to try new things? That is a new thing I will definitely be trying."

"Excellent choice. Go look up which one's the best and treat yourself to some ghormeh sabzi on your emergency card."

"I really like your definition of *emergency* here."

"Have you had really good ghormeh sabzi? Trust me, it's an emergency. Remember my college roommate, Arash? His mother made the absolute best ghormeh sabzi, and tahdig, which I have tried and failed to make properly many times. A PhD in mathematics from Duke and I can't manage a crispy-bottom rice," he mutters, and there he goes, getting lost in his own brain again.

"Noted," I say, before he can dig into all the mathematical reasons he might've screwed it up. I'm not new to my father's ramblings. "Anyway, it's been a decent morning." Let's leave it at that.

"Excellent. And how is knowing no one but your mother working out? Did you meet anyone at the coffee shop?"

"Well, I did have to ask the barista to walk through about half the coffee options for me." It did not make me friends with this one impatient guy on the line who was barking into his phone, but the cute blond girls—freshmen, maybe—giggling behind him as they watched something on their phones didn't seem to mind. The tables were filled by what I'm guessing were aspiring screenwriters, nursing the same cup of coffee or tea for at least an hour before I even got there, who didn't so much as glance in my direction. Everyone else was a blur. As much as I love people-watching, anxiety has a way of taking over when I'm in new spaces. "She was nice."

"Well, good." Of course, neither of us speaks the irony that my father has approximately four friends and would never, *ever* talk to a stranger in a coffee shop unless he was asking them to move out of his way. But he and I are different breeds; if my eyes weren't exact replicas of his thick-lashed blue-gray ones, you would never in a million years even put us in a room together, let alone think we might be related. Sometimes I think he asks questions about my extroversion as a research fascination. "I know you're worried about making friends there."

That I am. But mostly, I just hope the other intern at my mom's office isn't a complete and total douchebag. My hopes aren't high, so maybe my dad's right, at least until I discover a little more of the city. Maybe tomorrow, I at least ask the barista where's good to hang out as a seventeen-year-old with zero guidance or supervision in a new city. After all, there are certainly worse people to befriend than nice ones who sling good coffee, right?

Chapter Five,

in Which Tal "Adventures" in NYC

'm adventuring, I text my dad, adding a picture of the facade of the Nevermore Café, the newest coffee shop to go up against the swarm of UWS Starbucks. Appropriately dark for a spot on 84th Street (aka Edgar Allan Poe Street, where the block in question is between Broadway and Amsterdam), a raven spreads its wings over the Gothic-lettered name, and it's hard to imagine what they serve here other than plain black coffee and maybe amontillado. But I've passed by it curiously enough times, and today I'm making a move. Poe's one of my favorite authors, and I need a job, so I'm taking this as a sign.

Not that there's any advertisement for new help, but I figure if they're a new shop, they're still my best bet. Even if I have zero experience serving coffee to anyone but my dad.

Who takes it plain black.

Actually, maybe that makes me perfect for this place.

I double-check that my folder of résumés is still in the messenger bag slung across my most professional-looking black T-shirt and push open the door, only to stop in my tracks.

The Redhead.

She's here.

Like, *really* here. Like, *working* here. I enter every restaurant and store on the Upper West Side with the hopes I'll bump into her, and at least every couple of weeks, I do. But I've never once seen her behind a counter.

I've never once seen her in a position where I have no choice but to talk to her.

Holy shit.

This is it. This is my opening. But I can't make myself move. I look down at the tips of my blue-polished toes sticking out of my watermelon-print flip-flops and will them to take a step forward, but they just . . . don't.

Until someone slams into me from behind, cursing loudly and making me drop my phone to the black-tiled floor with a clatter. "Move much?" the guy mutters as I bend down to pick it up, wishing I could drown in the curtain of hair that covers my face. At least there's no crack in the screen—my enormous doughnut-patterned case took care of that.

Can I just . . . slink out of the café? Because that's what I'd like to do. Maybe the Redhead didn't see me. Maybe she totally missed this entire embarrassing encounter. Maybe—

Okay, maybe she's looking right at me and clearly trying not to smile, even the tiniest bit, which I would appreciate, except all my thoughts are lasered on how badly I want to melt into the floor.

I tear my eyes away and look up at the menu that hangs on the wall behind the counter. There are approximately five items and a sign that says "We don't do flavors." Now I *really* want to get out of here, except this is the best chance I'll ever get to introduce myself, even if it's also the most embarrassing.

They do have cappuccinos, which can never be bad, so I screw up the courage to get behind my new bestie and studiously avoid eye contact with both him and the Redhead by pulling out my phone and opening my texts to Camila.

> OMFG. New R sighting. Peak
> embarrassment. Meeting her
> in 2.

She answers immediately, which means she must have already dropped her siblings off at day camp. W H A T.

Too many things are in my brain and none of them make it into a text before I hear "Next."

I know her voice, sort of; I've heard her order red velvet cupcakes and ask if some biography or another is in stock yet (always biographies and always of musicians—yes, I do take note) and even once at a Duane Reade heard her ask her mom for some insurance information over the phone (after which I quickly tuned out, because that seemed weirdly invasive). But it's never once been directed at me, except this one time she said "Excuse me" on her way out of Sadie's Stationery while I was getting distracted by macaron-print birthday cards.

Which means I've never gotten the chance to see how her eyes are that rare hazel that seems to have flecks of yellow in it, like a cat. Or maybe a fox. Either Nevermore doesn't require uniforms or the uniform requires black shirts, but even with that blank canvas, the Redhead manages to make everything look vixen-like, all sharp lines and cleverness. It's so exasperatingly hot, especially paired with the rows of rings that line each ear, that I change my order at the last second and order the one cold, fruity thing on the entire menu. "Blood orange iced tea, please," I manage, immediately forgetting basic things like, you know, "Hi." Or "Good morning," even.

The Redhead seems unfazed and gets to work making my drink. She's the only person behind the counter, which bodes well for a potential job opening, but I can't possibly work next to her all summer. I'd drop a mug anytime she glanced in my direction.

So much for the job lead.

"Name?"

It's a question I should know the answer to, but my tongue seems to be stuck to the roof of my mouth, and besides that, I have options. Would she prefer Nat, like my mom, which hints at Natalie? Or Tal, like my dad, which hints at Atalya? Tally, like most of my friends call me? Or should I just offer it all at once, the full Natalya, and then crumble a little inside when she spells it with an *i* or a *u* or just throws in a couple of extra letters for sport? Lord knows I've gotten it all.

At this point, she could just put "The brunette who forgot how to speak in the presence of a hot girl" and the entire café would know that tea is mine.

"Your name?" she asks again, and I blink.

"Natalya Fox," I say, because it's all of me and I want her to have that, even if no human person has ever given their full name in the history of coffee shops.

"Got it," she says, scrawling in black marker on a bloodred cup. "One blood orange tea, coming up."

She doesn't have to go far to make my drink, but it's enough space that I can finally breathe, busy myself with reading the pins on her half apron. The Pride flag pin is there, giving me an ounce of hope, and the rest look like band logos. I recognize Queen and Nirvana, but most are new to me, cementing that she comes from a far cooler realm than I do.

She's back before I can take note of any names, handing me my cold plastic cup. "Natalya Fox," she says, her fingertips brushing mine. "I'd been wondering."

And then she gives me a wink that melts my bones into coffee creamer before turning to the guy in line.

I don't even look at the cup until I have somehow transported out the door, completely forgetting how my own feet work.

Foxy, it says in a jagged scrawl. *Made by Elly Knight.*

Okay, staying in New York was the best call *ever*.

❀ ❀ ❀

Well, maybe not the *best* call ever. Once the high of finally meeting the Redhead—Elly—dies down, I'm forced to face the fact that my best employment lead is now a no-go and none of my favorite bookstores, bakeries, clothing shops, or restaurants are hiring—at least, not people with my minimal experience. I give myself half a day of scouring both the neighborhood and internet for positions before I finally give up and go to the Columbia library to get working on research for my dad.

I don't have strong feelings about math either way, which might be blasphemy from the daughter of Ezra Fox, but I *can* tell you that if you're not that into it (as I am not), spending four straight hours researching and emailing or printing (depending on the length) recent articles on algebraic topology will absolutely melt your brain.

The air's considerably less muggy when I leave the library, so I pick my way back down to 86th Street on foot, phone in hand so I can *finally* tell Camila about meeting Elly this morning. Of course, she's already got her siblings back, so we decide to grab dinner later and rope Lydia and Leona in too. We're not meeting until seven, though, which gives me time to stop in at my favorite bookstore on 104th to look for something for my new two-person mother-daughter book club.

Even though I'm coming from a library, where I've been surrounded by what's probably miles of books, stepping into Pages Upon Pages and seeing all the colorful covers feels like a breath of fresh air. My feet head straight to the crime fiction corner on instinct, but I freeze when I'm a few feet away from the cozy mystery display.

Does my mom even like thrillers and mysteries like I do? Will she think it's incredibly creepy if I pick something with bloody rose petals or shadowy figures on the cover? Was she hoping I'd pick something historical, or maybe women's fiction, or just whatever's the newest celebrity book club pick?

God, how do I know this little about my own mother?

My eye catches on one of those little shelf talker cards underneath a book on the thriller wall, a hardcover with a blurry photograph of a group of friends made to look like it was taken from under water. The effusive bookseller's note is in messy scrawl that I first read as calling it a "SoCal thriller," which seems like a perfect compromise—I love thrillers, and she loves SoCal so much that she abandoned me for it.

Then I look again and realize it says "Social," not "SoCal," but it's already in my hand, so I give it a quick flip-through and decide this is the winner. I am definitely not gonna think too hard about this conversation that may or may not even happen, depending on whether she finds something more important to do. Besides, it looks good.

I take a picture of the book and text it to my mom. **What do you think?**

And because I'm afraid she's already forgotten our conversation and will have no idea what I'm talking about, I add, **For our first book club?**

After three minutes of standing there, looking weird, and staring at my phone like I decided to watch a movie in the middle of the bookstore, she still hasn't responded. I finally decide to just get it, and I'm signing the receipt when I hear, "Hey, Foxy."

I shouldn't be surprised to see Elly Knight at Pages Upon Pages; it's one of the places I've seen her many, many times.

Between her pins and her shirts and her book purchases, I've put together a pretty good idea of her favorite bands, a bunch of which I've listened to in case I ever had an opportunity to talk to her about them, and also just because I was curious. Some of them, I've ended up loving too (the Pretty Reckless, the Decemberists, Foo Fighters). Other ones—mostly metal—I . . . did not.

Today, she's carrying a book of poetry by Halsey, which feels like a good sign.

And yet, all the preparation in the world has not prepared me for the girl of my literal dreams addressing me in this bookstore, looking hotter than a subway car with broken AC in a white Black Sabbath tee and plaid skirt she must've changed into after her shift.

"Elly Knight," I reply, and it requires all the cleverness I possess.

"What do you have there?" She nods at the hardcover in my hands whose name I can no longer remember. I remember nothing at all except—

"It's a SoCal thriller." *No. Wait. Fuck.* "A social thriller, I mean."

"What exactly does that mean?"

"Oh, you know," I say, my free hand waving in the air, grasping at nothing, much like my brain. "It's thrilling. And social."

"I'll bet." The little smirk on her lips kills me a thousand times over.

"It's for a book club." Does that sound nerdy? Yes, that definitely sounds nerdy. "With my mom." No, wait, that is infinitely worse.

"And your mom likes social thrillers?"

"I don't know yet," I say sheepishly, pulling my phone from the pocket of my shorts and showing her the black screen. "Still waiting for her response on that."

And then, as if on cue, my phone lights up with an all-caps text from Isaac in Alphabet Soup that screams I HEARD YOU MET THE REDHEAD!1!!

Judging by the way Elly immediately bites her lip to keep from laughing, she did *not* miss my friend's subtle missive, but I scramble to shove my phone in my pocket anyway, and of course miss completely, made even more obvious by the earth-shattering thud of me dropping my phone on the floor in front of her for the second time that day.

I scramble to pick it up, mumble, "I gotta go," and run out of Pages Upon Pages like a bat out of hell.

It better not be too late to move to California.

Chapter Six,

in Which Nat Becomes a Working Woman

It took me an hour to settle on my outfit this morning, despite having already spent an hour picking it out with Cam and Leona back in New York. But this is it. This is the right one. The white shirt is pristine and shows off the beginnings of my summer tan, the emerald-green skirt swishes dramatically around my knees, my glorious slip shorts keep any and all chub rub fully at bay, the sandals highlight my new pink pedicure, and my favorite dangly earrings bring all the colors together. It's perfect.

More perfect than the pink wrap dress I got on major sale at Anthropologie, I'm pretty sure. And more perfect than the black capris and polka-dot blouse Adira insisted I borrow for the summer. And more perfect than—no. I am not overthinking my outfit anymore. I have two goals for today: get through it, and don't embarrass my mother.

Not that I should really care what she thinks, considering my very first night in LA she worked until nine, calling only long enough to tell me to order myself dinner on her account, and waltzed in to chat about my day over a huge glass of wine (for her, not me) just as I was about to crash. But at least today she's not leaving without me, so there's something.

"Adam Rose started yesterday," she informs me as we get in the car, and the way she says it, I can tell she's keeping some mental (I hope it's only mental, anyway) competition between me and the other intern. "There's only one desk for the two of you to share, so you may need to move some of his things to make space for yourself."

"I hope there are two seats, at least," I joke, because I have no idea what else to say. It's bad enough to feel like I'm infringing on her space at home; now I have to feel like I'm infringing on some other guy's space at a job I haven't even started yet?

She murmurs something in response, and then her phone rings and she picks up the call, a morning debriefing from her assistant, Norman. I'm unsurprised to hear she has meetings and presentations all day, which means I'll be on my own to deal with the mythical Adam Rose.

I've only seen the Cooper Frank office in pictures on the internet, so while the thoroughly modern building looks familiar, I have no idea what to expect when I enter. I'd been picturing something with the same decorating sensibility as my mother's house—lots of neutral colors and open space—but it's the exact opposite, all bright colors and packed with cubicles, posters, and booths lining a wall that's entirely made of whiteboard, which Norman explains is for collaborative conversations.

Even Norman is a surprise—not a skinny white middle-aged nerd but a hot Korean guy with shaggy bleached hair and broad shoulders. In fact, everyone in the office is attractive in one way or another, and I swear that's not me being an Insatiable Bisexual™. I've heard my mom's spiel on how people want to buy things from those who project a certain je ne sais quoi, but as someone who took three years of French, I feel like I can safely say that *je sais* what the *quoi* is now, and it's hotness.

So now, as Norman takes me on a tour of the office while my mom jets off to prepare for her first meeting of the day, I'm questioning my outfit again.

"This is the kitchen," he says, gesturing toward a pristine white room brightened by pops of color from two bowls filled with oranges and a few small plants. "Free drinks are in the fridge, coffee maker's over there, and mugs are in the cabinets." I immediately perk up at the mention of free drinks; I did not know jobs came with free things! I almost say this to Norman, but I can already imagine the look I'd get in response, and anyway, he's moved on and I'm falling behind.

"You already saw reception, obviously, and I assume you met Lucia. When you need to order lunch for meetings, she's the one you'll email your order to, and then she'll place it." Okay, I can remember that. "Down there is the mail room; Hector's the one to contact for any packages you have to handle."

Lucia—reception. Hector—mail room. So far, so good.

"Wendy handles all our printing orders; email her with any requests and *be detailed* with any specifications. She will not guess." I wait for him to tell me what she'll do instead, but it's clearly not forthcoming. Instead, he rattles off the names of which restaurants to use for lunch catering versus breakfast meetings and which printers we use for which kinds of jobs.

I realize too late that I should be writing all of this down, so I pull out my phone and write whatever I can remember in the Notes app, but there's barely any time to write "Lucia" before Norman says, "And here's your desk. Slash his desk. Whatever. I gotta go. Come by if you need anything."

And then Norman's gone and I'm facing a desk that does, in fact, only have one chair. And it's occupied by the douchiest-looking guy I have ever seen in real life. His dark, almost-black hair is gelled into perfect submission. He has those stupid broody-sexy eyes, deep brown and hooded. The jacket draped over the back of his (our!) chair would suggest he literally wore a suit—a *suit*! In LA! In the summer! As an intern!—to work today. And everything about him just drips obnoxiousness and perfection.

And still, he's got more cred than I do, because I'm the nepotism hire.

Wish I could nepotize (?) myself into a shirt that wasn't already wrinkled into looking like yesterday's laundry.

So this is Adam Rose. No wonder my mom already has a mental competition running; he looks like the kind of guy who splits the check down to the penny and can recite back every single time he's ever done anything nice for you. I wish I could take a subtle picture and send it to Camila, because I know she would see exactly what I'm seeing without a single accompanying word.

Meanwhile, Adam hasn't even looked up from his computer since I arrived, as if he has Very Important Work to do when he's only been here a day longer than I have and 75 percent of my briefing was related to ordering food for other people. Norman didn't bother to make the intro, so I guess I'll have to, even if I'd rather stab myself in the thigh with one of his meticulously arranged pens. "You must be Adam."

He looks up, blinks, and smiles pleasantly and cluelessly. "I am."

I wait for a sign of recognition, an acknowledgment that he knows who I am too, but there's nothing. Did they even tell him there was another intern coming? Or did they drop this entire thing into my lap? It would certainly explain why the desk is, as my mom mentioned, completely covered in his crap, with no consideration that someone else might want to put up their own framed photo or phone charger.

"I'm Natalya." Still nothing. "Fox." Still nothing. But okay, maybe he expected me to have the same last name as my mom. "Melissa Farber's daughter."

"Ah, is it Take Your Daughter to Work Day? I never remember these things."

"Is it—No, it's not Take Your Daughter to Work Day," I get out through gritted teeth. "Or maybe it is. But I'm here to work. I'm the other new intern."

"Oh! I heard there was another intern. Good to meet you." He extends a hand. "What was your name again?"

I'm so tempted to ignore that hand and the forearm it's attached to—I hate that I'm such a sucker for forearms on boys—but there's no justifiable way to do that, so I take it. It's a firm shake, warm and dry and confident and maddening. "Natalya."

Here's where I'd normally say, "You can call me Nat," but no, this guy can work for it.

"Cool, cool." There's no follow-up from either of us, and our eyes drop to the desk, which is still covered in his stuff. I wait for him to nudge a little over, apologize for the mess, but it doesn't come. Finally, he says, "So, are you sitting in your mom's office?"

"Uh, no? This is my desk too. So if you could . . ."

He blinks. Apparently, I actually need to end the world's most obvious sentence.

"If you could move your stuff so I can put my things down, that'd be great," I say flatly.

"Oh, yes, of course." His "aw, shucks" voice is annoying as hell, but he does move some stuff. Of course, I don't *have* any things—I didn't think to bring my own mug or any framed pictures or a book to read during lunch, or any of the other crap that Adam has splayed out—but now that I've made my pointed request, I've gotta come up with something.

I dig into my purse. There's a pack of gum, lip gloss, my wallet—ooh, a phone charger. Okay, that's something. I plug it into the power strip beneath the desk, attach my phone so it takes up some space, and search for a chair to pull up to it. I don't get very far before a guy I've never seen before sticks his head over our cubicle wall and says, "Printer needs new toner."

He looks at me. Adam looks at me. I look at Adam, but it's clear he won't be getting up, and given I haven't even sat down yet, I don't have a great excuse for passing it off. So I paste on a smile and say, "Got it."

Not that I have any idea where the printer is.

Or the toner.

Nor do I know how to change the toner.

But I feel good about my ability to figure it out, and frankly, it sounds a lot better than sitting at a desk with Adam Rose.

❀ ❀ ❀

Turns out, there's a lot of menial work to be done at a marketing firm, and I find this out by doing literally all of it while Adam sits at our desk and pretends he has real shit to do because he's been there for two days to my one. Ordinarily, I'd make a bigger fuss about it, but it keeps me away from him and helps the day move faster, so if I have to help with printer jams, book messengers, sign for and pick up packages, proofread presentations, and even make iced coffee runs, fine. Whatever. At least I'm getting some sun.

The preferred coffeehouse of choice near the office isn't a chain, and the barista—a few years older than me, if I had to guess, Latine, spiky lavender hair I immediately covet, and a round face absolutely made for their perfect dimples—cuts me off two coffees into my order. "Cooper Frank?"

"New intern," I confirm, gesturing at the ID sticker on my chest that's standing in until my real one is finished being made. Only the sticker's fallen off somewhere, and now I'm literally just shoving my boob at a cute stranger. "They have a standing order?"

"They do." The barista—Jaime, per their name tag—grins, and, oof, those dimples are truly killer. Guess this job isn't *completely* without its perks, even if Norman did make me listen to a five-minute drink order for what was apparently no reason. "Gimme a few minutes. I'll get you set up."

I move away from the counter and scroll around on my phone while I wait, liking a picture of Adira covered in shaving cream at camp and another of Leona holding her Maltipoo, Matrix, while taking a model-y selfie in a T-shirt that says "The Cis Are At It Again." (Leona is something of a trans fashion icon on the internet, with more followers than I could possibly hope to amass in a lifetime. By the time I like the pic, 43,726 people have gotten there first.)

There are pictures of Emilio and our three other best guy friends—Elijah, Nate, and Isaac—at last night's Yankees game, and an adorable shot of Camila in her volunteer uniform, her little patients' faces covered by emojis for privacy. And then, a picture of Isaac and Leona pointing and cheesing at a poster for *Good Behavior*, the lesbian rom-com coming out next week that the three of us spent months talking about seeing together, not least because it stars the only person in the world I crush on harder than the Redhead: Vanessa Park. The caption, posted by Isaac, reads, "It's not the same without you, @OutFox219 #AlphabetSoup," and I feel a little tug at my heart as I realize that here, I'm entirely on my own for my most anticipated movie in the history of ever.

Jaime returns with a tray full of iced coffees of different sizes, and not to stereotype, but they look like someone who'll definitely be seeing the new Vanessa Park movie. Dare I ask? Is that rude? At home, Isaac, Leona, and I are loud as hell about being gay, trans and pan, and bi, respectively, but who knows what it's like here?

Then again, maybe it's worth the risk to potentially make a friend here, especially a queer friend.

"Thanks for this," I say, pulling the tray over to me. "Do they have a tab here or something?"

"It's all covered, including gratuity." The dimple again.

"Cool, cool. So, um. LA has a lot of movie theaters, right?" Oh, right—I'm not good at this. I totally forgot that part.

They laugh. "Yeah, movies are kind of a big thing here. Guessing you're from out of town. That would explain the way you pronounce *coffee*."

"Oh, you mean the right way? Don't worry, you'll catch on eventually." Another laugh, and this one is not at my expense! High five, self. "So, like, if one were looking for a theater at which to see *Good Behavior* on opening day, my best bet would be . . ."

"It'll be at a bunch of theaters—this is LA—but personally, I'd go with the Sunset in WeHo."

I make a mental note to look that up later. "Cool, thank you. And, uh, if one were looking for someone to *see* said movie with . . ." I give my most winning smile, the one that got Jason Torres to ask me to junior prom even though everyone knew he was planning on asking Lexi Sloan, and flutter my eyelashes for good measure.

They open their mouth to respond, and then a look of understanding dawns. "Oh, this is a little awkward, but, um, I'm straight."

"You're—uh. Oh." There is not a single cishet vibe emanating from the person in front of me, but of course, just because a person's got short pastel hair and a Megan Rapinoe tee on doesn't mean they have to be queer. "Sorry, I—"

Jaime bursts out laughing. "Yeah, no, I just wanted to see if I could pull it off; I'm queer as fuck. Agender, too. But I do have a girlfriend."

"Is that another thing you're trying to see if you can pull off, or . . ."

"No, that's for real." They pull up a picture on their phone of a cute femme blonde in a gray beanie and a polo striped like a referee's shirt. "But she's always down to meet new people. I'm working my other gig at a food truck tonight, and we'll be parked by a bunch of friends' trucks, if you wanna join. Just meet me back here at six."

I don't have time to ask any more questions or even leave my number because the guy behind me is getting impatient and I can see the ice in the drinks is melting, so I just say, "Cool, I'll see you later" and head back upstairs.

Only when I've finished handing out everyone's coffees do I finally sink into my chair and realize I forgot to get something for myself, but I don't even care.

I did it. I sort of made a friend. In LA.

And, like the extremely cool girl I am, I immediately text my dad to let him know.

❋ ❋ ❋

The second five o'clock rolls around, people start packing up to go, which doesn't seem very Melissa Farber–like, but I head over to her office anyway, just in case. As I suspected, she's still firmly seated at her desk, her twenty-third coffee of the day (probably) in one hand, the other hand holding a printout up to the light. She doesn't even notice that I've come in until I give a loud, obnoxious cough.

"Oh, Nat! You scared me." She puts the printout down on the desk. "Did Graziela send you that newsletter template?"

"About six hours ago, Mom. It's five."

"Already?" She glances at her watch without really looking. "Well, I've got to finish up this report by seven. Do you want to order in dinner?"

It's not lost on me that I'm a total afterthought in this, that I'm just expected to sit in the office for two hours twiddling my thumbs. And I would if I hadn't met Jaime earlier, but if I'd been on the fence about going out with a bunch of strangers tonight, this certainly cements my choice to do it. "Actually, the barista at Mocha Rouge invited me to go with them and their girlfriend for dinner tonight, and I think it'd be good for me to meet some other people my own age."

Especially since Adam Rose sucks goes unsaid.

"Oh. Okay, then. Should I be nervous about you going out with strangers?"

"I'll drop a pin when I get there."

"And you'll call me if you need a ride home?"

"Yes, Mom." Even though I'm sure that'll end up with me needing to take an Uber anyway.

"Okay, okay." Her phone rings, cutting off any further conversation. "Sorry, I have to take this," she mouths as she picks it up. And with a "Melissa Farber," I'm dismissed.

I still have half an hour until I'm supposed to meet Jaime, and thankfully Adam disappeared while I was in my mother's office, so I take his seat, pull out my tablet and stylus, and get lost in the drawing of a Poe-inspired haunted house I've been working on since the flight, complete with a bust of Pallas. A minute later, I get nervous that I'm going to lose track of time, so I grab my stuff and head out to the coffee shop early so I can sit and draw there instead.

Jaime gives me a nod when I walk in, but they're busy with a woman holding a wailing toddler against her shoulder and looking slightly overwhelmed. All the customers seem to be taking their drinks to go at this hour, so I snag a little table in the corner, perch on the stool, and get back to perfecting my raven feathers.

I'm finishing up the last little fleur-de-lis atop the iron fence when a flash of lavender hair catches my eye and I look up to see Jaime sit down across from me. "Cooper Frank," they say with a dimple-flashing grin. "You came back."

"I did, but please, God, do not call me that. Natalya," I say. "Nat."

"Okay, Nat. Hey, that's cool. Did you draw that?"

I look down at the sketch, all creepy and Gothic, with a skull window etched into the door and a perched raven over-looking it, and wonder what kind of twisted impression I'm giv-ing this sunny barista. "Yeah, it's just a thing. I was reading a modern retelling of *The Fall of the House of Usher* on my flight over here and I got inspired to draw a haunted house with some details from his other stuff."

"I love that," they say, and they sound like they mean it.

"Cass is waiting outside, but later, I wanna see some more of your stuff. If you're cool with showing me, obviously."

"Yeah, for sure." I stuff my tablet into my bag, my stomach fluttering at all the possibilities here. New friend! New friend who's actually interested in my art! New friend who comes with another friend, maybe! If she likes me! And doesn't think I'm trying to steal her partner! New friends who might be introducing me to my new favorite food! The sky's the limit!

Or at least this is what I'm telling myself as I introduce myself to blond, long-legged Cass and climb into her back seat, wondering if maybe my mother had a point when she questioned me going out tonight with complete strangers.

I should've gotten Cass's license plate number.

My fears are quickly forgotten when Cass switches on the radio and she and Jaime immediately start singing along to Rihanna, both of their voices terrible enough that I have no problem joining in. It feels like we should be in a convertible with the top down, but the AC is desperately necessary, and so all the windows are up, making it an even more terrible echo chamber of tone deafness. We warble through Adele and Ariana Grande and Dua Lipa and it's absolutely awful.

It's my favorite fifteen minutes in LA so far.

And it comes to the most obnoxious halt when we finally get to the food truck—Bros over Tacos—and there, chatting with the guy behind the window, is Adam Rose.

Chapter Seven,

in Which Tal Gets a Job, Sort Of

I wake up on Monday morning to the obnoxious sound of someone alternately ringing our doorbell and banging on the door. I check the time on my phone through sleepy eyes—7:28 A.M.. Given my dad's not roaring about the noise, he's probably sitting on the terrace with a mug of black coffee and the paper, blissfully oblivious, which means I have to get up.

"Chill out! I'm coming!" I call as I stumble my way to the front door, though it emerges out more like a mumble. "Shut up shut up shut up." I scrub a hand over my face and yawn hugely, then peer through the peephole. Adira.

I undo the dead bolt and unlock the door. "Dude, it's, like, dawn. Couldn't you have texted?" Still, I step aside and let her in.

"It's seven thirty, and it's an emergency," she declares, her dark-chocolate curls flying out behind her as she barges inside.

"Well, not an emergency, but important. Becca sprained her ankle and she's gonna be out of commission all week. Are you still looking for a job? Chevi and I desperately need a third, and you've done some babysitting in the building, right?"

"For the Gilmans in 7G, and a couple of times for that family that moved to Stamford. But—" God, I can't think about this while I'm still half asleep. Being a camp counselor was *not* what I had in mind for this summer, but I still don't have any real job prospects, and I promised my dad I'd find something. I can't spend the entire week doing nothing but research for his book and shelving at the library or I'll go out of my mind. Plus, I could definitely use the money, and it's clear Adira could use the help. "I guess I could? What do I need to do?"

"Get dressed. Like, right now. We've gotta be at Grand Central in forty-five minutes."

"You're kidding me." But she's clearly not. She's already dressed in a red-striped T-shirt, navy shorts, socks, and sneakers, which is a good sign I shouldn't wear my flip-flops; probably not the best footwear for chasing after kids. I stumble my way through washing up and getting dressed, stick my head out onto the terrace to let my dad know my plans for the day, and barely remember to grab my bag and sunglasses before following Adira out to the subway.

It isn't until we're on the train going into Westchester—New Rochelle? Scarsdale? I've already forgotten—that I'm finally with it enough to ask Adira what it is I'll be doing at this illustrious backyard camp. "It's been a while since I've done the camp thing for real. I still remember how to play GaGa, but that's about it." I divided last summer among drawing classes, taking

care of my grandparents in Miami when my grandma broke
her ankle, and accompanying my dad to Philly for a math conference. The summer before, I toured the East Coast on this
summer program for Jewish kids, and it wasn't as much ball-
playing and craft-making as it was sightseeing and synagogue-
visiting. "I guess I can draw with them? But I ran out too fast to
get any art supplies."

"We have plenty; Chevi is fully stocked. The only thing
Becca was supposed to bring over was—Oh no."

"What?"

"Snacks," Adira says, her voice dropping to a whisper. "Becca
was taking care of all the food. We have to get food."

Yes, okay, that does seem like a minor emergency. "Text
Chevi. Maybe she can run to get them now."

"She can't leave—a couple of parents are paying extra to
drop their kids off early." Adira drops her face into her hands,
her long brown curls obscuring her entirely. "Crap crap crap."

"We'll have time to run to the store before the first snack," I
assure her, glancing at my phone as if I have any idea what the
schedule is. "What time is that?"

"Ten thirty. But it's not the city, Tal. It's not like you can just
run to the bodega on the corner."

"Well, that's just silly. Every street should have a bodega
on the corner. But okay, so we'll drive. By which I mean you'll
drive, since I am definitely not risking driving a stranger's car
on my five minutes of practice."

"Still better than me—no license at all."

"City kids," we intone together.

"Okay, so Chevi will have to drive," I say with a wave of

my hand. "It'll be fine. And she lives in Westchester, so she's legally required to have a license."

Spoiler: she did not in fact have a license. Apparently going to school in the city is almost as stunting on the driving front as actually living there. "What do we do now?" Chevi whispers as yet another kid climbs out of a massive SUV and receives hugs and kisses through their tears at being left behind in a new place. "We don't even have time for anyone to run out anymore."

"You must have snacks in your actual house." I glance up at Chevi's enormous Mediterranean-style home, which is way too big not to have at least a couple of bags of pretzels in it. "You have a sandbox, a water table, and a swing set. Don't tell me you don't have a package of Oreos."

She sighs. "My brother has Celiac, and if you touch his favorite expensive and hard-to-find snacks, he will find extremely gross ways to get revenge. Ask me how I know." She looks at the kids swarming the yard, quickly forgetting their tears when they spot the swing set and geodesic dome; no question Chevi's yard was made for this. "But yeah, we probably have some random cookies or chips somewhere. I'll go check. We're still expecting two more kids, so one of you should keep an eye on them in the yard while the other stays here to wait. I'll be back with whatever I can find."

Turns out, size of house is not proportional to amount of snacks. Chevi returns with a shopping bag that she opens to reveal three single-serving bags of veggie straws, a couple of granola bars, some potato sticks that are clearly left over from Passover, and a six-pack of juice boxes. "This is it. I mean, there's some fruit in the fridge, but that's really pushing it."

"Hey, is that snack?" Four-year-old Judah, who was the first to arrive and has therefore already been at Chevi's house for an hour, comes running over. "Veggie straws! I call veggie straws!"

"I want veggie straws!" Before you can say *stampede*, that's exactly what happens, a group of toddlers and just-past-toddlers tearing at the bag as if it must contain magic.

"Hey, what—"

"Guys!" I clap my hands. "This is not snack! Drop the food! Snack comes later. First comes . . ." I trail off as I look at everything Chevi's prepared. It's still not quite hot enough for the sprinkler, and lanyard is not gonna be enough to distract them from the promise of sugar and salt. If I do face painting now, they'll get upset when it comes off in the water. Then I spot the box. "Sidewalk chalk! Come on, let's go color in the driveway."

The kids are reluctant to let go of the snack bag and the whole food concept in general, so I draw a massive clown, making it look sillier and sillier with spaghetti hair and shoes that look like blimps until the kids finally come over, giggling, eager to see what I'll do next and to draw their own.

Crisis averted. For now.

❊ ❊ ❊

"I knew you'd be a natural," Adira says as she comes over to watch once all the kids are solidly occupied by rainbows, flowers, and makeshift tic-tac-toe and hopscotch. "Maybe we should just fully replace Becca."

"Oh no, friend. Sorry, but this is definitely a one-week thing." As if to illustrate why, little Shyla Franco suddenly dips out her tongue to taste the pink chalk in her hand, breaking us apart as Adira rushes to stop her. "I was thinking of something a little more . . . having to do with my future."

"And what is that?"

Well, I walked right into that one. "I'm not sure yet. But I do not expect it to involve children or algebraic topology, so I know I haven't found it yet. I've mostly been applying to retail, but I have no experience and I guess no one's desperate enough to hire that."

I wonder what kind of retail experience the Re—*Elly*—has that she got the job at Nevermore. (God, it's weird to realize I can think about her by name now.) My mom once made me watch a movie about a record store, and that place felt exactly like somewhere Elly would work, but I have no idea if they even still exist. Maybe in the East Village. Maybe we could hit one up sometime. Maybe—

Oh, shit, Adira's talking. Of course she is, because we were literally in the middle of a conversation before my libido somehow wandered off. "Sorry, what'd you say?"

"Just that I always thought you'd do something with drawing." She gestures to my clown, which has been joined by a bicycling elephant and an absolutely ridiculous puppy with eyes bigger than most of these kids. "But what do you do with drawing?"

"Million-dollar question," I mutter, because that's exactly the problem. I'm extremely lucky that we've always been financially secure, but we're not "never have to work a real job in my life" financially secure. (And if that doesn't sound like a real level, Lydia and Leona Voegler—daughters of real estate king Herman Voegler—would beg to differ.) My parents are firmly set on me going to college, but it seems like a huge waste of money if I have no idea what I actually wanna *do* there. "You still planning to go premed?"

I know the answer even before she confirms it. I have literally never known Adira Malka Reiss to want to do anything but follow in her mother's footsteps. Well, not her exact footsteps— her mom's a pediatrician, and Adira's leaning toward surgery— but still. It's certainly closer than I want to get to math or whatever marketing is.

"You don't have to do doctor-y stuff over the summer?"

"Nah, not yet. But I figure if one of the kids falls off the geodesic dome, I can always practice my stitching."

I crack up at that, but Shyla, who overheard, does not. Her mouth drops open and Adira rushes to assure her she was kidding, which is quickly interrupted by a frantic series of texts by Chevi.

It's almost ten thirty.

I poured all the veggie straws into 1 bowl.

This is not gonna work.

Adira looks panicked. "I'll go help" I assure her, resting a hand on her arm to calm her. "You stay here and make sure no one needs any medical care." Dusting the chalk off my hands, I slip through the side door.

"Okay," I say, walking up to an even more panicked-looking Chevi, who's surrounded by paper plates and the vast, random contents of the fridge. "What've we got?"

"Baby carrots," she says, holding up a bag in each hand. "Think we can pass that off as snack?"

"Probably have to do a little better than that if we don't want child mutiny." I glance around the room, hoping something will set off an idea, and spy a shelf of cookbooks, one of which claims to be "for kids." "Maybe this will help?"

"We definitely do not have time to cook something," she says, but as I'm flipping through, I see it—a completely "bullshit" recipe that involves using toothpicks to stick stuff together in the shape of a person. It advises either deli meat or cheese cubes, and we have neither, but there's enough string cheese to make it work.

"This," I say, stabbing at the picture. "We can definitely do some gross version of this."

As quickly as we can, we make a bunch of plates of "snack people" out of the cheese, carrots, halved cherry tomatoes, raisins, cream cheese, and, of course, the all-important veggie straws. I take a picture before we send them out to show off my prowess online and, remembering my promise to keep my mom updated on my life, send the picture to her, too, before taking the food outside.

The kids light up immediately when we tell them we come bearing snacks, and Chevi exhales a breath I'm not even sure she realized she was holding. "You are a lifesaver," she says, collapsing into one of the little kiddie chairs as we watch them eat. She gathers up the auburn hair sticking to her perspiration and uses it to fan herself for a few seconds before twisting it into a knot on top of her head. "And hey, if you wanna stay over to-night so you don't have to take the train or wake up super early in the morning, you're more than welcome. Adira is."

The idea of getting an entire extra hour of sleep in the morning sounds heavenly, but I still have to put some shelving time in at the library, even though that's the literal last thing I wanna do right now. "I can't tonight, but I will definitely take you up on that tomorrow night, if that's okay."

"For sure."

The kids have of course shifted into creating chaos by now, so we quickly finish up snack time and corral them into a huge game of Red Light, Green Light. The veggie people idea was definitely a hit, and while I'm not putting that on a résumé anytime soon, it *does* feel nice to be good at something other than drawing.

❋ ❋ ❋

With Adira staying at Chevi's that night, I take the train home alone, which, truthfully, I love doing. The book I bought for "book club" with my mom is still in my bag from when I frantically threw it in upon bumping into Elly, so I settle in for the thirty-five-minute ride with it perched on my knees and thank God Grand Central is the final stop or I absolutely would've missed it.

"Damn, that's good," I mutter as I slip it into my bag, hoping my mom's enjoying it as much as I am. Well, hoping she's reading it to begin with, and *then* hoping that if she is, she's enjoying it as much as I am.

The shuttle from Grand Central to Times Square is too short to pull the book back out, so I put in my earbuds and switch to music instead. It's a little embarrassing how many of my recent favorites have come from looking up the bands on Elly's T-shirts and pins, but what can I say? The girl has good taste. Mother Mother's "Hayloft" is blaring in my ears as I get out on the West Side and make my way toward the 1 train, but I'm quickly stopped short by the sight of a huge semicircle fully blocking out whoever's busking in the coveted Times Square station spot, the surest sign it's someone really good—probably that woman who absolutely crushes all the best diva songs or the hot electric guitarist whose fingers seem to fly at the speed of light.

I silence the song and pull out my earbuds as I make my way to a crack in the crowd, and it turns out to be a string quartet absolutely slaying "Stairway to Heaven." One of the violinists is so into it, his locs are literally whipping him in the face, but he doesn't seem to notice. The sign in front of the cellist reads "Strings Out of Harlem" with a matching social media handle underneath and a note that says "Film and share!"

So I do.

The group is incredible. When they finish "Stairway," they pause to swig from their water bottles while people drop money in the massive open cello case. I wait for some of the crowd to move on, leaving more space for me, and upload my video, adding a quick caption and making sure to tag the group. I don't have a huge following, but I do have a few thousand, mostly people following for my fan art.

And about a minute after I upload the video, as the group

has already started back up with "Bohemian Rhapsody," I get one more.

AKnightCalledFoo has followed you.

Holy shit.

Elly.

Of course I looked her up after finding out her name, but she keeps her account locked, and I felt way too creepy requesting. But here she is, following *me*. Nothing creepy about following her back, right? Or at least requesting to.

So I do.

And she immediately accepts, like maybe she was waiting for it.

I like to think she was waiting for it.

There isn't even time for me to dive into her pictures before a comment pops up on my video of Strings Out of Harlem.

AKnightCalledFoo: I fuckin love these guys. So jealous.

Of course she knows a random subway string quartet. Like, of course she does. I take a deep breath and click over to DMs.

OutFox219: They're still playing. I bet you could catch em if you came down to Times Sq.

It's a ridiculous suggestion. For all I know, they'll pack up as soon as they're done with "Bohemian Rhapsody." But it's not like Elly doesn't know that as well as I do. What she does now is up to her.

AKnightCalledFoo: Kick-ass. Are you sticking around?

To fake chill or not to fake chill? I'd probably toss my life savings into that cello case if it meant Elly'd come down here to listen to them play with me.

OutFox219: Sure, I've got nowhere to be.

AKnightCalledFoo: Awesome, see you soon.

Wait, what the fuck?

This is actually happening?

I am *not* ready for this. Oh God. I dig through my bag and am relieved to find a pack of gum, a piece of which I put into my mouth immediately. There's also lip gloss, which I apply with my phone in selfie mode to make sure that my shaking hands don't make a mess of it. And then I realize I'm doing this in front of the quartet and all the spectators and I quickly put everything away and focus on the music.

And try not to sweat any more than I already am.

Thankfully, Strings stays on past "Bohemian Rhapsody." It takes me a minute to recognize Metallica's "Enter Sandman," and I don't know the next song at all, but I definitely know the one after that, even before a husky voice says, "God, I love when they play 'Sweet Child o' Mine'" in my ear.

"You made it." I only barely glance in her direction, afraid she'll see on my face how deeply I am dying that she's here.

"Wouldn't miss it," she says, and I can see a hint of a smile and how she's recently applied red lipstick. Which, granted, she wears all the time, but it's not lost on me that she put it on to do nothing but come stand in a subway station with me. She even smells good, fresh and a little spicy.

We listen to the rest of the song together, and when they move on to "Hallelujah," Elly whispers to me that it's always their closer. Sure enough, as soon as it's done, they thank everyone for coming, remind people to spread the word, and subtly indicate the open cello case, into which Elly and I each drop a few bucks. And then it's just us, standing in the middle of the Times Square station, a million potential paths laid out before us.

I decide on the sweetest one. "Wanna go get ice cream?"

"Ooh, yes, I do."

We head up to the street, and a half step behind Elly, I allow myself to finally take her in. That gorgeous hair is up in a chaotic topknot, strands escaping all over the place. Too many earrings to count glint in the fluorescent lights of the station, and as usual, her wrists are tangles of chains and leather bracelets. She isn't tall, but her legs look extra long in a pair of super-short jean shorts, which she's wearing with a cropped black top and an open loose red plaid shirt. There's no glaring music fandom on her person tonight, but I already know that when I get home, I'm gonna look up everything there is by Strings Out of Harlem.

The sun's still high enough in the sky that the streets are

absolutely packed with tourists, and Elly and I reach for each other's hands without hesitation to avoid getting swept away by Elmo impersonators or stabbed in the eye by selfie sticks. Her palm is warm and her fingers are less adorned by rings than usual, though I can feel the pressure of a band on her thumb. The polish I'd initially thought was black turns out to be navy blue in the light, chipped enough that it should look like an imperfection, only it doesn't at all.

Since I did the asking, I take the lead, and thankfully, my favorite spot doesn't look too overrun. "Sugarmilk okay with you?"

"Definitely."

We squeeze into the shop and are instantly blasted by a rush of AC that feels amazing on my skin. "God, I love this place." My mouth waters at the sight of all the tubs of brightly colored ice cream—pink bubble gum, lavender honey, golden dulce de leche . . . "I haven't had their rainbow sherbet in forever. Or the s'mores sundae. Oh no, I can't choose."

"Seriously, I'm having the same issue choosing between mint chocolate chip and the red velvet one with the cream cheese ribbon. They're both just so pretty."

We give ourselves another minute, but then fear of losing out on the one empty table gets the better of us and we make our choices. (S'mores for me, red velvet for her.) We each pay for our own, because I'm too chicken to put out there whether this is a date or say anything smooth like "You'll get it next time," and we grab the last free seats just ahead of an obviously tourist couple.

"So, was it just wildly coincidental timing that you followed me tonight as I was watching a band you happen to love?" It's still wild to me that *she* followed *me*, and that part I *do* get to say out loud because it very much unquestionably happened.

"Oh no—I love them so much, I literally get notifications if anyone tags them. That way I'm most likely to catch them. I just didn't expect to see a familiar name among the people doing it tonight." She takes a scoop of ice cream and drags it across her tongue, taking at least fifty of my brain cells with it.

"That big a fan of a group that plays in the subway?"

"Music is pretty much my entire life. Sort of inevitable, given my parents are both in the industry. They tell me I was singing the Beatles before I was even really talking," she says, those red lips curving into a tiny smile. "I actually interviewed the guys from Strings for my school paper and then used it as one of my clips to get a job with this music blog I write for a bunch. So they feel very fundamental to my career, or at least what I hope will be my career."

"Writing about music?"

"Well, it doesn't have to be writing, but music journalism in general, yeah. My best friend, Jaya, and I just started a podcast a couple of months ago that's gotten a nice little following, too."

"That's awesome." *Please, God, do not ask me what I want to do with my life.* "I've, uh, definitely noticed you're a music fan. I can't believe there's not a single pin on your person right now."

She laughs. "I know, I'm such a loser, but I'm a big sucker for merch and all that shit. My parents, despite being chill about everything else on the planet, won't let me get a tattoo until I'm eighteen, so until next month, this is how I wear my love on my sleeve. Literally."

"So where do I find your articles and podcast?" I ask casually, because I *will* Google the shit out of her when I get home, but I'd so much prefer to hear it from her. "I could use some new recommendations."

Her eyes—the warm brown of my dad's favorite whiskey—light up. "What do you listen to now?"

"Depends on my mood," I say, which is true but is also buying me time while I figure out the best answers here. I know what she likes from watching her way too closely, and some of those genuinely *are* my favorites these days. But I don't wanna sound stalker-y sharing so many of her faves, and I don't wanna sound like a geek if she hates the rest. "I was listening to Mother Mother on my way here."

"Yessss, I love them so much. They and the New Pornographers are truly the best things ever to come out of Canada."

"I guess I'll have to try the New Pornographers, then." I pause. "Wait, that *is* a band, right?"

She laughs again, and, God, it feels so good to be the one making her do it. "Yes, it's a band. I know, that name has definitely led to some massively awkward moments, but they're amazing. Start at the beginning with *Mass Romantic*. You'll love it."

I take a bite of my ice cream while I rack my brain to think of favorites that *didn't* come from observing her, but I'm coming up short until I remember the author's playlist for one of my favorite romance novels, which introduced me to a whole bunch of angry girl rock. "I'll give it a shot. And I also really love Halestorm, the Pretty Reckless, Hole . . ."

"Oh, you are speaking my *language*. My parents were *this*

close to naming me Janis, after Janis Joplin, but instead I'm named for 'Eleanor Rigby,' which was the song playing when they met. It was actually a terrible cover of 'Eleanor Rigby' by some godawful punk band in South Jersey, but they like the original, so they went with it."

After that, I have to share my own naming story, and that gets us talking about me being Jewish, which shifts into me talking about working at camp this morning, which of course leads into talking about her job at Nevermore. "Day camp sounds like a much better gig," she says, swirling her spoon around in the dregs of her ice cream. "People are the *worst* before they've had coffee, and I have to wake up at like 6:00 A.M. Which especially sucks because I spend most nights at shows around the city so I can write them up for *NoisyNYC*."

"Is that the blog you write for?"

"Yup. I super occasionally get assignments from other places, but nowhere too big yet. An editor at *New York* magazine followed me on Twitter last week, though, so fingers crossed. I'm just so fucking tired all the time, but I promised my aunt I'd help out."

It takes me a few seconds to process. "Wait, your aunt? Like, your aunt owns Nevermore?"

"Uh-huh. She's an Edgar Allan Poe superfan, in case you couldn't guess. She's dreamed of opening this place up for literally ever. But she was so focused on shit like décor and menu that she didn't actually budget for staff, so she's got me and her son working for tips and free coffee until she can figure that out."

I bark out a laugh without meaning to and immediately

smother it with my hand. "God, I'm so sorry. It's just that—when I came in, I was actually planning to apply for a job, and I guess you saved my ass on that one."

"Oh, yeah, yikes. I mean, the tips are okay, but, uhhh. It's pretty much hell to work a coffee counter with no one but my cousin all day, every day. I really need to start making more cash from writing and get some advertisers on the podcast, because my aunt spent a bunch of years raising me while my parents traveled, and I can't bail on her."

The wheels are working in my brain, but they're not necessarily landing anywhere good. Yes, butting into this messy situation at Nevermore would guarantee me lots more time with Elly—and free coffee—but to work just for tips? With college on the horizon and the price of art supplies what they are? No, Natalya. Do *not* get sucked into this nightmare situation by gorgeous pouty lips and razor-sharp eyebrows. Do *not*.

If Elly's trying to bait me, though, she hides it well. "Speaking of gigs, I have to head down to meet Jaya at one—a folk rock trio from North Carolina they swear could be the next Avett Brothers. Do you wanna join?"

I'm not sure how I feel about folk rock, and I don't know who the Avett Brothers are, and I know I'm going to regret staying out late when I have to get up at seven for camp.

But this is Elly. *The Redhead.* Asking me on what might possibly be a date, following up this thing that might possibly be a date, and it's just so much possibility that I can't help but say, "I'd love to."

Consequences are tomorrow's problem.

Chapter Eight,

in Which Nat Gets a New Perspective

My mom must be able to feel the depth to which I am having Regrets about coming to LA, because at noon she swings by my desk and announces that she's taking me to lunch. Until that point, I'm pretty sure Adam was having doubts about us actually being related, so I toss him a quick smirk as I leave him to his sad little bowl of whatever and follow my mom out of the office.

Okay, so it's probably not a sad little bowl of anything, given that the food truck we went to the night before was run by his brother (and his brother's best friend, an obscenely charming guy named Mateo), and the tacos were the best I've ever had in my entire life. That isn't the point.

We go to a cute café with outdoor seating that's just a block away, so perfect for people-watching that I instantly have a pang of missing Camila. The time difference is only three hours, but between work and babysitting and Emilio and the fact that she's almost never up past eleven, it's been impossible to nail down a window for a video chat. It's weird not to see her face in some capacity every day.

"You're going to love this place," Melissa says with a confidence I don't understand, since she has no idea what I love these days. "Best Caesar salad in LA, and I'm not just saying that because it's conveniently located."

Yeah, if my mom thinks I'm getting salad anywhere, she definitely does not know me. But I don't want to start shit on our first outing alone, so I just pick up the menu and scour it for something that isn't made of leaves. "Is this where you usually eat?"

"Here, or Mocha Rouge, or I just get a smoothie from the cart out front." That a smoothie can be an entire meal for my mother feels like further proof that she and I have absolutely nothing in common. "Speaking of which, how was dinner with your new friend last night?"

I know it isn't a loaded question, but it feels like one. Because here's how dinner went last night:

We rolled up to Bros over Tacos, and "new friend" Jaime—who apparently works at a cupcake truck called Life Is Buttercream a few nights a week—fucking *hugged* Adam Rose. Then Cass did. Then they *introduced* me to the very guy who shares my desk, and I got a *head nod* in response. No smile, no "Fancy meeting you here," no "Hey, bro, come meet the other intern from work"—a Fucking. Head. Nod. With zero acknowledgment that we just spent the entire day in an office together or in fact have ever laid eyes on each other in our entire lives.

I was tempted to head to another truck, but then Adam's brother, Evan, emerged from the truck, and given how nice and friendly he was, I have to assume he was raised by entirely different parents. Three amazing tacos later—two fish, one chicken—I had completely fallen for the elder Rose brother.

The younger one still sucked.

"Good tacos" is all I say, because if I complain about Adam, I'll get a disappointed sigh and a "Just try to get along" and an undercurrent of "Don't embarrass me." The food was the one indisputably good thing (especially when followed up by sea salt caramel cupcakes from Life Is Buttercream), which is more than I can say for this place, given half the menu is quinoa bowls. Maybe I'll be going with a Caesar salad after all.

I don't have anything more to say, and neither does she, so we both scan our menus as if she doesn't already know what she's getting, and I can't decide between kale this and seven-grain that. I finally take my chances with avocado toast, and with my dad and our last Café 84 dinner in mind, I add a lemonade.

God, I wish I were sitting here with him instead of her. Well, no, I wish I were sitting at a burger joint with him instead, even if it meant listening to him talk about his newest revisions to a chapter on homotopy. Or getting pizza with Camila, Lydia, and Leona, listening to everyone fight about whether pineapple as a topping is delicious or grotesque.

And maybe all of that is written across my face, because suddenly there's a hand on mine and Melissa says, "Listen, I'm sorry I've been so busy since you got here. We're in the middle of putting together a huge pitch, and the timing—" She takes a deep breath, which is good, because that wasn't going anywhere successful. "Anyway, I'm sorry. Let's make a plan for hanging out, just us. Beyond lunch."

"Okay." I don't really know what else to say; I've never had to make a "plan" to hang out with my dad before. Not that we have tons in common, but it's enough to sit down to good meals together, to watch the occasional mystery show or just sit in silence in our cozy den, me drawing while he grades papers. But I can't imagine my mother and I passively appreciating each other's company. The air feels too fraught, the pressure for a connection that should be natural but isn't weighing heavily on my shoulders.

"I was thinking—that is, I'd *been* thinking, if you'd stayed in New York, that maybe it would be nice to have a little book club. You know, read the same thing, chat about it. Are you still reading so much, so fast?"

"I am," I assure her, "mostly because I read thrillers that keep me up way too late."

"Ooh, I haven't read a good thriller in a while," she says. "That sounds like fun. Should we try it? Maybe this weekend we can go to a bookstore together and pick something out?"

A free lunch *and* a bookstore trip? Okay, things might be looking up. "That sounds nice," I say, and I mean it.

We're both smiling when we look back down at our menus

just as our server arrives. I open my mouth, but before I can get a word in, Melissa says, "We'll have two Caesar salads."

Well. At least there's the bookstore to look forward to.

❋ ❋ ❋

Okay, I will concede the salad wasn't half bad. In fact, it—or at least the experience of my mother choosing something I liked—was kind of inspiring. When we get back to the office and Melissa immediately rushes off to catch up on the approximately one million emails she missed while we were at lunch, I'm filled (or at least half filled) with a renewed belief in the power of trying to make shit work with other people. So even though the mere sight of Adam Rose sitting at our desk in his stupid button-down, a Very Serious look on his face as he moves some stuff around on a spreadsheet, would've pissed me off two hours ago, I'm now feeling approximately 6 percent more optimistic about the potential of interpersonal relationships with people in my social sphere.

"So," I ask cheerfully, settling down at my portion of the desk, which now contains a printed photo of me, Camila, Lydia, and Leona taped to a pencil cup. "Did you have tacos for lunch?"

He gestures at the empty clamshell container, his eyes never leaving the screen.

"I'll assume that's a yes, despite how there is absolutely no branding on that container, and it could literally be from anywhere. Plus, if I recall the menu from your brother's truck correctly, he doesn't only sell tacos, so even if your point is that it's obviously a container from Bros over Tacos, that doesn't automatically preclude it from being, say, a burrito or a quesadilla."

"Yes, it was a taco," he intones, still not making eye contact. "Three of them, in fact. Two al pastor and one a secret off-menu item that I wouldn't tell you if I were on my deathbed."

Well, now we're getting somewhere. "Is that so? Everyone has their price."

He snorts. That's all I get. I try another tactic.

"Do you cook too?"

He grunts, and I'm sure that'll be the end of the sentence, but I'm shocked when he adds, "I help out sometimes."

"Did you just—did you just give me *four* whole extra words about your life? Why, Adam Jehosephat Rose, I feel like we've just taken a giant leap in our relationship."

Finally, *finally*, he takes his eyes off the screen. They're dark eyes, a hint of mystery in his otherwise corporate-tool demeanor, and they're stony, but for some reason I can't help but wonder what they'd look like with a little heat behind them. "My middle name is not Jehosephat."

"Really? You look like a Jehosephat." It's a lie. He wishes he looked as interesting as a Jehosephat. He could maybe pull off a Nick. "So what do you cook, not-Jehosephat?"

"Adam."

"Adam! I'm Natalya. So good to make your acquaintance."

He gives me a look like I am completely batshit.

"I mean, you seemed last night like maybe you'd forgotten it, or like you never knew it to begin with, so I hope this helps clarify. I'm Natalya Fox. I share this desk with you. I work right across from you from nine to five."

"I know who you are."

"Oh, great!" I flash him a sunny smile. "So it's just a thing where you're too cool to acknowledge the rando girl to your friends. Whew, I'm so glad we got that cleared up. Thanks for making sure I know you're better than me. I was a little confused there for a while, but I'll remember it next time I'm walking right past your brother's food truck."

"Jesus Christ, it is *nothing* like that, Natalya."

"Oh, cool, then what was it?"

Those dark eyes bore into mine, and I wait for something—anything—but all I get is a sigh. "We should get back to work."

In fairness, being a drama queen has exhausted me a little bit, so I just nod, and we do.

Needless to say, it is not a comfortable end-of-day, and we're both out of our chairs the second the clock hits five. I don't know what my mother's timing is, but it's nice out and there's a good bench nearby for sitting and sketching, which sounds like the perfect way to erase the last few hours of ugh. We stay silent for the elevator ride down from the fourth floor and continue on through his unexpectedly holding the front door open for me. But before I can handily make my escape, a friendly voice calls out, "Hey! Jaime's new friend! Talia, was it?"

"Natalya," I say instinctively, before realizing I have no idea who's calling my name. I shield my eyes from the sun and realize that Evan Rose, the Taco Bro himself, is leaning against a car in a Bros over Tacos tee with the arms ripped off, his artfully tattooed biceps suggesting that working in a food truck must be a way better workout than I would've guessed. "Hey, Evan. Thanks again for dinner last night. You make one hell of a taco."

"Eh, I'm okay," he says, and it doesn't sound like he's just being modest, though it doesn't sound like self-pity, either. It's clear he's a man who takes his work seriously, and I'm into it. "Anyway, nothing like I've got planned for tonight."

"Oh?" I probably shouldn't do tacos two nights in a row, but yeah, I'm definitely gonna do tacos two nights in a row. What else is even the point of coming to LA for the summer?

He turns to Adam, then looks up at the building, putting the pieces together that should've been handed to him last night. "Wait. Do you two *work together*?"

"We do!" I say sunnily, flashing a huge smile in Adam's direction. "Oh, did that not come up last night? How incredibly, inexplicably strange."

"Fuckin' A." Evan sighs. "Ad, are you being That Guy?" He turns to me. "Is he doing that thing where he's a ridiculously unfriendly asshole?"

I'm so surprised to see it called out that I don't even hesitate in my reply. "Yes! How'd you guess?"

"Well, for one thing, he's dressed like this," Evan says with a snort, indicating Adam's professional attire. "Let me tell you something about my brother, Natalya. He does not fit in."

I'm not sure what that's supposed to mean, but I'm intrigued. "Go on."

"No, Evan, maybe don't fucking go on," Adam snaps.

"Would you rather she think you're an asshole?" Evan returns, then gives me a charming smile. "My brother does not fit in. Neither of us do. Our parents are hippies. We grew up in a weird-ass commune. We'll be taking our real names to our graves. I continue to be weird, and I am just fine with that. But my dear brother is not fine with that."

"You know this doesn't make either of us sound any *less* weird," Adam mutters, dragging his hands through his dark hair and leaving soft spikes behind.

"The point is, dear Natalya, my brother is trying to fit in. He is *trying* to be a corporate tool. He is *trying* not to let anyone outside of our little circle get to know him, even if that means being an asshole to the pretty girl at work. But this is a stupid plan, because you seem like a cool girl who would probably like my brother for who he is, wouldn't you, Natalya?"

Adam is absolutely on the edge of committing a murder. "Dude, shut the everloving fuck up."

My head is spinning with this information and the sight of Adam's reddening face and that I have just been called pretty and cool. His hands are shoved into his pockets, but if I had to guess, he's dying to take a swing at his brother right now. He won't, though, because if his parents aren't raising him, then Evan is, and you don't take a swing at the guy who's giving you a chance to fit in.

Kind of like how I never fight with the father who let me stay in New York and keep my life.

"I might," I say coolly, pretending to size Adam up. "If he'd give me a little more space at the desk. And tell me what's in the off-menu tacos he had for lunch."

Evan laughs. "I like you. But you are absolutely not finding out what's in the off-menu tacos. You *can*, however, come for the best dinner party of your life tonight. If you're up for it."

I look to Adam to see if this invitation appears to make him want to die, and he hasn't sunk into the pavement yet, so it might actually be up to me. "How can I say no to something like that?"

Evan's face breaks into his widest grin yet, and even Adam seems to relax, just the tiniest bit. "I'm glad you said that. Because I could use an extra sous chef. How are you at husking corn?"

❋ ❋ ❋

"They call it 'Dinner Party,' after the world's most incredibly awkward episode of TV in history," Adam explains to me later, when he's changed out of his work clothes into a T-shirt and shorts and we're standing at the counter of Evan's kitchen, chopping celery leaves and tarragon. (Or at least we would be if Evan didn't keep deciding we were doing it wrong and taking over.) We have a silent agreement not to address Evan's earlier revelations, and in exchange, Adam's being halfway human. "Have you ever watched *The Office*?" I shake my head. "It's brutal. But they think it's hilarious. Anyway, they do this once a month—they all take the same night off, pick a theme, and then do a potluck." He lowers his voice. "But they think *potluck* sounds too lowbrow, so they have to call it something fancier."

"Honestly, if the food is half as good as those tacos, they can call it whatever the hell they want. What's tonight's theme?"

"Two-in-one. Everyone has to make something that's some-how a combination of two different dishes, to be interpreted however they feel like. I don't really know what that means, but trust me, it really will be the best meal you'll have in LA."

"Hey! You two!" Evan calls out from the bedroom of his small apartment, where he apparently keeps a bookcase full of ingredients to compensate for his lack of pantry. "I'm not paying you to chat! Chop faster!"

We've been entrusted with cutting the corn off the cob, which seems impossible to screw up, so we get that done and move on to the onions.

Except, as soon as Evan emerges from his room, inked arms laden down with various jars and spice bottles, he huffs out a sigh at our handiwork and tells us to go set the table instead.

It's hard to stay mad once the scent of Evan's cooking fills the room. The combo of garlic and onions sautéing in butter is too delectable. I consider Evan's comment about how this will be the best dinner party of my life, and I know without a doubt he's speaking the truth.

Not least because I'm pretty sure I've never actually been to a dinner party before.

My phone vibrates in my pocket, and I fish it out to see that my mom has finally responded to the text I sent her a little after five, letting her know my plans for the evening. It's been an hour since then, but I'm willing to bet she's had no idea of the time since we got back from lunch. Have fun is followed by I'll be home late tonight. She doesn't ask how *I'll* be getting home tonight, though I guess it's an obvious assumption that Adam will drive me.

It's still hard to imagine being in close quarters alone, though. He's certainly gotten friendlier since his brother blew his cover, if a little wary, but we haven't yet reached the point of feeling glad for each other's company.

"Hey, working girl!" Evan calls from the kitchen. "I could use some music. My laptop's on that desk in the corner. Go put something on."

"Any specific requests?"

"Nah, I feel like I can trust you." He grins, tosses a spatula in the air, catches it, and gets back to work.

Choosing the music feels like a major test, and it's one I really don't want to fail. He doesn't strike me as a pop or hip-hop guy, and he definitely seems too sunny for grunge. Maybe he's a folk-rock guy. He feels like he could be a folk-rock guy. I mentally go through all my playlists, which are largely built from bands I've seen on the Redhead's T-shirts or pins and tried out myself, but there hasn't been a whole lot of folk rock, and Mumford & Sons feels way too predictable.

"Nat—can I call you Nat?" Evan asks. I nod. "Stop over-thinking it and put something on."

Fine. The Decemberists it is. I cue up *Picaresque*, then wonder if maybe "The Infanta" is not the best cooking music. But Evan immediately grins at the easily recognizable opening crescendo and starts slicing and dicing in time with it. "Man, I haven't listened to this album in years. Petey's gonna love this."

"Petey's the Go Fish guy," Adam explains, referring to the truck that was stationed next to Bros over Tacos last night. "Amazing fish-and-chips. Highly recommend."

"Noted. Thanks for the rec."

We're both quiet then, maybe because this is where normal people who see each other every day and are potentially striking up a friendship would suggest going together some night, but clearly we're still not normal people.

Evan hums as he stirs in the corn, and I realize I don't even know what's on the menu. "What is it you're stirring up over there?" I ask.

"Tonight you will be dining on chilled corn soup with seafood salad," he says, leaving the corn to go pull something—thyme, I see when I crane my neck—from the fridge.

Ah, to mention dietary restrictions or not to mention dietary restrictions? One of the million things that broke up my parents was that my mom was moving further and further into strictly cultural Judaism, whereas my dad had some things that still felt really important to him—eating Shabbat dinner together, going to services on the High Holidays, having a Seder for Passover, and keeping some semblance of kosher among them. It isn't only pork we avoid, but shellfish, too, and I have a feeling seafood salad means just that.

I know that if I don't want to keep kosher while in LA, I don't have to; my mom would probably be thrilled if I didn't. But liking to observe some things that keep me tied to Jewish tradition is yet another way I'm way more like my dad. "So, when you say seafood . . ."

"Lobster, baby." He taps his forearm, where a black-and-red tat of a lobster occupies significant real estate. "Canned," he admits with a sheepish grin. "I'm on a budget. But I promise, it works almost the same."

"Actually, I was just gonna ask if you could leave the salad off mine. I don't eat shellfish."

"Ah, allergy or kosher?"

Something in my chest loosens at the question. "Kosher. I'm not strict, obviously, but no shellfish or pork for me. Or rabbit, if you wanna dig deep. Or bugs. All the explicitly forbidden things."

"You learn something new every day," Adam says, nodding thoughtfully, and I assume he's making fun of me until it becomes clear he isn't, at all.

"Okay, but you can't have the soup without the garnish," Evan says seriously, and I brace myself for one of those annoying-ass comments like "Can't you cheat just this once?" as if I were trying to squeeze into a size zero rather than adhere to religious laws. Instead, he follows up with, "Lemme call Lexi. She works at a kosher Chinese restaurant, and she's always got those mock crab sticks on hand."

"Oh." I don't even know what else to say. This is a lot of unexpected kindness. "Thank you."

He holds up a finger; he's already on the phone. A minute later, he hangs up and says, "Okay, we're good. I'll leave some of the pre-lobster mix on the side."

After that, I only grow more eager to help, so Evan puts me to work cleaning up the place. I'm putting what feels like fifty stray issues of *Cooks Illustrated* into a pile when the doorbell rings.

Little by little, the chefs file in. There's Mateo, Evan's best friend since childhood and partner in Bros over Tacos, who comes bearing enchilada-stuffed shells; Lexi, who brings the promised mock crab sticks along with a turducken, which until now I'd thought was an urban legend; Isaiah, whom I recognize from the Ethiopian food truck last night and who made sausage from scratch, which he then completely encased in homemade everything bagel dough; Liani, whom I *thought* was toting a chicken pot pie, only to learn it was a shepherd's pie covered in homemade puff pastry; Grace (of Life Is Buttercream), who handles dessert—"Oreo"-stuffed chocolate chip cookies, complete with homemade "Oreos"; and the aforementioned Petey, who brings something seafood-based that's so many different shades of unkosher, my brain just tunes out of the actual description.

Everyone wants to put their finishing touches or do their last-minute warming on the spot, so Adam and I are tasked with getting people what they need, whether it's a clean cutting board and knife or a kitchen blowtorch. The small kitchen is so packed with chefs chopping garnish and plating ingredients that they spill out into the living/dining area. It's an amazing thing to behold, especially with so many of the flying arms sporting culinary tattoos, and I absolutely have to sketch it right then and there.

I've just finished a quick close-up of Mateo's enchiladas, much to his delight, when Evan rings an actual dinner bell and announces it's time to sit. One by one, the chefs present their dishes, while others comment on everything from the perfection of the seasoning to the flakiness of the crust to the filthy things they'd do for another bite.

"These need to go on the Bros over Tacos menu," Lexi says with a groan as she puts down her fork after absolutely demolishing Mateo's stuffed shells, which were, in fairness, completely fucking delicious. "Holy shit, that was good."

"I'll tell my mom," he says with what Leona would devilishly call a panty-dropping grin. He's got warm brown skin, a shaved head, and dark-brown eyes that are sort of perpetually crinkled with joy to go with those perfect teeth. I'm glad for Emilio that Camila's not here because she would absolutely lose her mind over him. *Especially* if he's a mama's boy. "You know she'll happily make 'em for you anytime, and better than mine."

I only nibble the dough around Isaiah's "upscale bagel dogs," as he calls them—the warning that I don't eat pork or shellfish yielded his revelation that there's pork fat in his homemade chorizo—but they smell amazing, and everyone else seems to be dying over them. I look over at Adam to see what he thinks and realize he's doing the same thing I am. I know he hasn't gone vegetarian overnight, given he ate all three birds from Lexi's turducken, but before I can ask why he's not touching the sausage, Isaiah beats me to it.

"Yo, you afraid of my food?" Isaiah asks him with a blindingly white smile. "I promise it won't bite you back."

"Ha ha." Adam looks down at where his fingers are tearing the bagel dough apart. "No, I just . . ." His gaze drifts over to me, and I realize that he's not eating it because I can't. Which is both sweet and embarrassing at the same time.

"Please, under no circumstances should you be missing out on any of this for me," I assure him, clasping his wrist on the table before realizing that's a little too intimate but not wanting to yank it away. "Besides, if you don't eat it, how are you going to describe it to me in excruciating detail?"

"Good point," he says with a grin, and he looks obscenely relieved to finally be able to stuff his face with it. Immediately his eyes close in the truest sign of savoring your food, followed by a prompting to get Isaiah to reveal every single spice used.

"There's a great kosher sausage place near the restaurant I work at," Lexi assures me. "The chorizo is *almost* as good as Isaiah's. I'll hook you up." She winks obnoxiously, and I laugh. Lexi has definitely proven to be a good resource.

We move through the courses, and I try whatever I'm comfortable with, eating three cookies to make up for everything I've missed. Adam was absolutely correct that it would be some of the best food I'd ever eaten. If I'd known about this dinner, I would've worn something with an elastic waist to work, but as it is, I'm stuck in cropped olive pants that are now digging deeply into my personal padding. Between that and the heavy scents of cooking and wine in the air, I could use a little breather. Which I guess Adam can tell, because after we do our parts to clean up the dirty dishes while those of legal age help themselves to another round of rioja, he asks if I want to grab drinks and sit on the balcony for a bit.

With the sun finally sinking, that sounds amazing, so we grab cans from Evan's pamplemousse La Croix stash and settle into the two chairs that, together with a small table, take up 95 percent of the terrace.

"This was amazing," I say, wishing I had my sketch pad or tablet so I could capture some of the view. Not that it's a great view—mostly just a busy street and some palm trees—but this was a really good night, and I want to remember it. "Thanks for, well, not inviting me, but I guess not protesting too much when Evan did it."

A little smirk twists Adam's lips, which he quickly covers by taking a drink from his can. "Wouldn't have mattered if I had. In case you haven't noticed, Evan does whatever the fuck Evan wants. Even if that means spilling my business to strangers."

Oh good, so we're not going to pretend that didn't happen. "About that. I mean, I'm not gonna tell anyone."

He waves a hand dismissively. "Whatever. He's right. I can't just be a normal person. I live on my brother's couch. I have no idea what state my parents are even in right now. I graduated high school—barely—and I have no idea what I'm doing after this internship except working the truck."

"What's wrong with working the truck? That's a legit job."

"It's not exactly salaried. Or paid, unless you count free food and getting to stay here." Adam presses his lips together and looks out at the horizon. "I busted my ass to get that internship so I could have some professional experience, but then the boss's daughter slides into the same position and I have to work twice as hard to get them to notice me. Which they don't. And I can't afford college, so." He waves an arm at nothing. "Truck. Forever. Or at least as long as my brother feels like doing it."

"Oh." Well, shit. Maybe he had more than one reason to be a dick to me the first couple of days. "Look, I'm really not trying to steal your thunder at work. They clearly love you; you've gotten way more real work than I have. I'm just . . ." I hadn't planned on talking about this, but clearly I have to. "I've barely seen or talked to my mom in like three years. This is supposed to be us reconnecting. Trust me when I say I'm not any professional competition for you."

"Yeah, well, we'll see." He takes a long drink from his can

and squints into the setting sun. "Three years, huh? That's a long-ass time."

"It is."

"And how's it been since you got here?"

I shrug. "We had lunch today. It was nice, I guess, if a little unimpressive compared to that," I say, gesturing back at the dinner party. "Planning to spend some time together this weekend too. Just taking it day by day."

"You know anyone else in the city? Other than Jaime and Cass?"

"Just you," I say with a sunny smile that makes him grimace. "So I hope you plan to bring me to lots of dinner parties."

Chapter Nine,

in Which Tal Becomes a Career Woman, Sort Of

I'm considerably more prepared for my second day as a camp counselor than I was for my first. Art supplies the kids will love? Check. Confirmation that snacks are taken care of? Check. An overnight bag so I can stay at Chevi's and not have to drag my ass out of bed at dawn to get here on time tomorrow? Check. A brain that absolutely cannot focus on any single task for more than thirty seconds before I drift into memories of being at the show with Elly last night, like the strip of bare skin around her waist seared into my mind from when she took off her flannel, and the music that was somehow simultaneously gruff and dreamy and had her subconsciously moving closer and closer to me all night until I could smell the vodka cranberry procured with her fake ID?

Checkity check check check.

Part of me didn't want to pack a bag for tonight, because all I could think about was what if another opportunity to hang out presented itself and I missed it? She *did* say last night was fun, and *did* comment "Cute" with a winky face on my selfie this morning. (Not reading too much into it, as I do look inarguably cute in these red shorts and nautical-print T-shirt, but still.) But maybe absence will make the heart grow fonder.

Besides, I know exactly where to find her if I want to grab coffee on my way to Grand Central on Thursday morning.

"Tally? Yoo-hoo? Do you have them?"

I blink and realize Adira is surrounded by an impatient crowd of children who are all waiting for me to unload the tempera paint sticks I promised they'd get to use today. "Yes! Sorry!" I flip open my messenger bag and pull out the vivid colors, which the kids eagerly snatch up before running to the cluster of tables where Chevi has set out paper.

They're my favorite drawing implements to use with little kids, because the color saturation is so amazing that they make even toddler messes look like bold endeavors by budding eccentric artists. I'm relieved to see they're as big a hit here as they are with the kids I babysit in my building.

We color for a while, and then the kids get bored and we switch to playing tag so they can get some energy out. When they're finally exhausted, we take a break for snack time. While the kids stuff their faces with sliced apples and pretzel sticks, I sneak a glance at my phone to see if Elly's posted anything new. She hasn't, but Leona's posted a fit check, so I leave a heart-eyes emoji in the comments and then slide my phone back in my pocket.

The sun's starting to beat down for real now, which is our cue to get the kids changed into bathing suits. It's chaos as half of them shamelessly strip down right there in the yard while the other half demands to be taken alone to the bathroom. I supervise the yard kids while Chevi and Adira split up the rest, and when all the kids are suited up and sunscreen-sprayed down, we switch.

It's a beautiful house, no question. The bathroom I'm changing in has gray marble floors and a matching vanity sink, and everything else is pure white except the shiny nickel fixtures. But being in the suburbs this week is teaching me something vital—I am so happy I do not live in the suburbs.

Really, I can't imagine living anywhere other than New York City. It's weird to think that with a different choice, I'd be in Los Angeles right now, getting ready to work with my *mom*. I'd probably be wearing business casual instead of a cherry-print one-piece, dressy sandals instead of my rainbow flip-flops.

Shudder.

The rest of the afternoon passes in a whirlwind of cold sprinkler water, slippery grass, and the best kind of little-kid shrieking. It's exhausting and I can feel my skin burning despite my SPF 30, but it's actually a little disappointing to see that first trickling-in of parents at three o'clock.

The kids groan and complain as we shut off the sprinklers and dry them with towels, some of them hopping right into cars in their bathing suits and some heading back into the house to change. I'm just sending a little boy named Sammy with the absolute cutest curls off with his nanny when a perfectly manicured hand lands on my arm. "Are you Tally?"

"I am." I look up at the woman, then down at the girl wrapping herself around the woman's leg. "Are you Shana's mom?"

"I am!" She has the teeth of someone who sleeps with bleach trays every night. "But you can call me Jen. Shana absolutely adores you. She's been raving about the art projects you do here. And Adira mentioned that you live in her building. We're in the city on weekends and could really use a sitter for a few hours on Saturday. Ordinarily, I'd ask Adira, but—"

"She doesn't work on Shabbat," I fill in. "Sure, I'm free Saturday. My phone number's in the email that went out on Sunday, but I can give it to you again. Just get in touch anytime between now and then."

"Great! Will do. You are a godsend." She ruffles Shana's soft brown curls. "Did you hear that, Shan? Tally's gonna come play with you this weekend!"

Shana looks up at me with huge, bashful brown eyes, and my heart melts a little. I'm really not as big a kid person as this week has made me out to be, so it's pretty amazing to learn that kids have actually connected with me. It makes me feel strangely . . . competent.

I crouch down to her height and give her a big smile. "I am! Is that okay with you?" She gives a shy nod, a hidden little smile. "Great. I'm really looking forward to it. And I'll see you here tomorrow!"

She's practically skipping when she walks off to her mom's car, and not gonna lie, I feel a little like doing the same.

✿ ✿ ✿

From Chevi's enormous Mediterranean villa in Westchester, I find my way to Lydia's and Leona's palatial abode on the Upper West Side. Not that our three-bedroom apartment is shabby, but the Voeglers have the kind of apartment people think only exists in TV shows about bitchy, drug-addicted teenagers. (Only partly true, in their case.) The apartment number literally has ACEFG in it, because those are all the units the previous owner combined to make it before their hedge-fund-manager dad and supermodel stepmom bought it. After a full week of chasing after little kids and coming home covered in paint and glitter, and with a full day of it on the horizon tomorrow, I can't *wait* for a lazy and luxurious girls' night at their place.

I do a quick change out of my day-camp-messy clothes into shorts and a tank, throw a few things into an overnight bag, and give my dad a five-minute rundown of my day and a kiss on the cheek before I practically skip on over, already anticipating the cold mocktails we'll be drinking on their massive terrace overlooking the park.

Leona doesn't make me wait a single moment, greeting me at the elevator in tiny silk shorts and a matching tank top with a pair of air-kisses and a "Fauxmipolitan? Or maybe cosfauxpolitan? I haven't decided yet." Matrix is yapping around her ankles, and I bend down to give him a scratch behind his ears, but Leona has no patience for this. She flips her waist-length butter-blond hair over her shoulder, takes a sip from her own glass, and says, "Whatever, it's delicious. Come on. You're the last one here."

"Yeah, well, I had to come all the way from Westchester, in case you forgot." I trudge after Leona through the apartment with the Maltipoo at my heels, my eyes scanning the walls as they always do, taking in the various expensive wallpaper patterns and priceless art and spotting yet another new portrait of their stepmom, Maryse.

"Hello, yes, I understand the plight of the working woman," she says, leading me onto the terrace where Lydia, Camila, and Dylan Nguyen-Zimmerman—Leona's off-again on-again girlfriend whom I guess is on again—are already reclining on chaises and clutching their own glasses. "Please recall that I have a job in *retail* this summer."

"Ah yes, I forgot you're working class now. What was it, again, that your parents said they'd get you if you held down a real job until your family vacation to Italy?"

She smiles as she reclaims the seat next to Dylan and helps herself to a couple of grapes that rest in a bowl on a table between them while Matrix hops up next to her and rests his head in her lap. "A vespa."

"Yep, we're exactly the same." I make the rounds, exchanging air-kisses with everyone before taking the remaining chaise and sliding on my sunglasses. "And how was everyone else's day?"

"Well, I managed not to misspell any authors' names today, so that was pretty good," says Lydia, passing down a tube of sunscreen. "Though I did almost eviscerate one when she asked me to print out three copies of her manuscript and have them messengered to her home."

"But then you didn't!" Camila says proudly, waving her magazine in the air.

"Look at you! Working on those anger issues!" I rub some of their expensive lotion on my arms, legs, and chest, then hand it to Leona to do my back. "We're all making such strides in our professional lives this summer."

"Oh? Something exciting happen at day camp today?" Camila asks.

"Apparently, I am very in demand." I pull my hair up into a messy knot and lie back with my drink. "I have a babysitting job tomorrow. One of the moms said her kid had been raving about me and my art skills all week."

"And your mom said you couldn't make any money as a professional artist!" Lydia says gleefully.

Okay, I was six when she said it, but it still smarts.

"Speaking of your mom," says Camila, "have you guys been talking at all since you told her you're staying here with your dad?"

"We texted a couple of times this week, but just about work and stuff." So far, our conversations are as stiff as ever, but at least we're keeping to the bargain. I even sent her a picture of a paint stick drawing I did that was supposed to approximate *Starry Night*, which she took me to see at MoMA when I was little. "She wants us to have a book club, and I read most of the book the other night when I was staying at Adira's friend's house, but I haven't heard anything from her about it."

I don't know if it's clear from the look on my face that I want to change the subject, but my unspoken connection with Camila is strong enough that she knows, because she says, "Is that the book you were picking out when you saw the Redhead?"

"*Elly*," Lydia and Leona correct her in a joyful chorus, while Dylan raises a meticulously groomed too-cool eyebrow as she takes a hit off her vape pen before going back to her magazine.

(Dylan, while objectively hot, is not my favorite. She and I used to be best friends at temple preschool, but then her dad made it big with some invention that allowed them to move to a townhouse just off Park, and that was the end of that. She even made sure to tell me that my invitation to her bat mitzvah was parentally mandated. Of course it's just my luck that her parents' house in the Hamptons is next door to the Voeglers.)

"It is," I say, tempted to yank my hair back down into its natural wavy mess so I can hide behind it. Other than a couple of comments on pictures I've posted, I haven't heard anything from Elly since we went to the show together on Monday night. I even dropped by Nevermore for an iced tea on Wednesday night after work, but Elly was definitely not the stoner behind the counter, so I guess her aunt eventually found some other help after all.

Given what a good time I had during our six hours together, I thought for sure it was the start of Something, but it seems to have already fizzled.

Now I'm back to being jobless *and* romanceless.

Suddenly, I feel extra grateful for my friends.

"So why aren't you making out with her instead of hanging out with us losers?" asks Leona, raising her sunglasses so she can fix her laser-green eyes on me.

I take that gratitude back.

"The Redhead remains a pipe dream, I guess." I fish a cube of ice from my glass and crunch it between my teeth, examining the chips in my self-done lilac manicure as an excuse to avoid eye contact. "We had our night. She didn't want another one."

Now it's Camila's turn to jump on my case, though her eyes are considerably softer and more sympathetic. "She told you that?"

"Of course not." My face flames at the mere thought of having a conversation like that with Elly. I still don't even know if I'm . . . on her sexual menu. I mean, *I* think we've been flirting, but that doesn't mean *she* does. "I just haven't heard from her since."

"You mean since she invited you to a show?" Lydia's chewing some intensely grapey gum, and she blows a huge bubble and grins as it pops in her face. "Sounds like it's your turn to do the inviting."

"What? No. I invited her right before that to listen to that band with me in the subway."

"Actually, it sounded to me like she invited herself to that," Camila points out.

"Well, I did invite her to ice cream."

"Right," says Leona, "and then she invited you. So it's your turn. For all you know, she's staring at her phone, waiting for you to text."

"You guys all suck," I mutter, because while they have a point, this is Elly Knight. She isn't sitting around waiting for shit. I met her friends on Monday night—badass Jaya with their half sleeve of tattoos; Hunter, who plays like twelve different instruments; and Nicki, who's a sophomore at NYU and made up her own major studying Black women foundational to rock music. (Yes, I *have* spent the week listening to Sister Rosetta Tharpe and Tina Bell as a result.) I know they're all completely out of my league in terms of coolness.

And yet . . . my friends have a point. She *has* been commenting on my pictures, while I've been too nervous to do it in return for fear of looking like an obsessive creep. (It took everything in me not to enthusiastically click on one showing off a new pair of thigh-high boots.) And yeah, I went to Nevermore to see her, but she doesn't know that. It's ridiculous to think she could possibly have noticed that she's reaching out to me more than I am to her, but.

What if.

I pull out my phone, click into her feed, and open up the pic of the boots to leave a heart-eyes emoji in the comments. In my defense, they don't have an "eyes fully bugging out of my skull emoji," but it still feels a little lukewarm. That doesn't stop her from liking my comment a few seconds later, though, which definitely makes me feel ridiculous things I have no business feeling.

"There," I say, putting my phone aside. "I commented on a post. Now, let's talk about something else."

"Did you comment?" asks Camila. "Or did you leave a stupid emoji?"

"That's it." I pretend to rise from my chair. "I'm going to make new friends."

Lydia snorts. "Good luck with that, darling."

"Well, you're all terrible."

"Thank you," says Leona, one hand over her heart while her other wipes away a tear. "Now, go invite punk girl to whatever it is punk girls do and go get some. Tomorrow night," she adds quickly. "Tonight, you're ours."

I don't point out the hypocrisy of having Dylan at our girls' night, just roll my eyes and finish my drink. But then my phone beeps and I freeze, both hoping and fearing that it's Elly and irritated that everyone is watching those things play out on my face.

We're all quickly disappointed. "It's just Shana's mom confirming plans for tomorrow."

Two seconds later, there's another beep, and everyone's shoulders rise and quickly fall with "It's my dad, asking if I'm sleeping over."

"Damn straight you are," says Leona.

"I'll be sure to respond exactly that," I reply with another roll of my eyes as I tap out a Yup, and then babysitting after breakfast. Post-sleepover breakfasts at the Voeglers always mean iced mochaccinos and cinnamon buns from the amazing café around the corner, which is the best part. Have fun with the Mathmen.

For the most part, my dad and I try really hard to do Shabbat dinner together whenever possible, but every now and again, we each need to play hooky—me, so I can hang out with my high school friends, and my dad, so he can hang out with his group of single-dad mathematicians, whom I love like family and are also the most boring people in existence when they get together.

"Your dad loves me." She tips her glass in my direction and blows a kiss. "Send that from me, too."

My dad does, in fact, love Leona. He thinks she's the most amusing of my friends and also kind of bonkers, both of which are true.

There's another beep, and I assume it'll be my dad, but it's my mom, texting me that she's enjoying the book and asking when I want to chat about it. I honestly hadn't expected to hear from her about it, so I have no answer. Then Camila suggests playing with her new makeup, and Lydia declares that she's getting hungry for dinner, and as I get wrapped up in Fenty lip glosses, online menus, and a heated debate about what movies we're watching tonight, I forget all about it.

Which is whatever. I've waited this long for her to reach out. She can wait a night.

Our movie night keeps us up until 4:00 A.M., and of course I forget to wash off the makeup, so by the time I open my eyes around 11:00, I have less than an hour to get to Shana's apartment and no time to go home and change. Leona's rail thin and about six inches taller than I am, so I yank a casual sundress from Lydia's closet, forgo any cleaning up other than a quick splash of water on my face and teeth-brushing (despite Leona's protests as she chases me with a bottle of micellar water in one hand and a tube of Better than Sex mascara in the other), and bolt out to Marabelle's for a cinnamon bun and iced mocha, because I absolutely refuse to abandon my breakfast dream before a long day of kid watching.

And even though it makes no sense, and even though I have never once in my life seen her here, of course, standing there is Elly Knight.

Crap, crap, crap. I pull out my phone and go into selfie mode to see how bad the makeup damage is, and it is *bad*. Licking my fingers and swiping it away isn't going to do it, but it's all I can manage right now.

"Hey, you."

I'm still mid-lick when Elly notices I've entered the café, and I am so mad at physics that I cannot simply melt into the floor, poorly fitting sundress and all. "Hey. I don't think we've bumped into each other here before."

"There's a first for everything," she says in a voice that sounds scraped just a little bit raw, and how the hell does anyone look that perfect first thing in the morning?

Okay, so it's not *really* first thing, but I'm willing to bet she was up as late as I was last night. Still, her eyeliner is immaculate and the burgundy lace bralette peeking through the wide-open armholes of her loose black sleeveless dress is absolutely destroying me. "I've heard the pastries here are the best, and I'm trying to get Aunt Jaida to expand beyond thirty-seven shades of bitterness."

"Oh God, *please*," I moan without even thinking about it, and Elly laughs.

"Are you trying to say my iced tea wasn't delicious?"

"I'm trying to say that iced tea is not a substitute for coffee, and I absolutely cannot and will not drink coffee that doesn't have a flavor. I bet even Poe liked caramel syrup, occasionally."

"I would bet he was more of a nut guy."

"Well, he was definitely not an iced tea guy. But also, your tip was absolutely correct. The cinnamon buns here are the best thing you will ever eat in your entire life." I sneak a glance at my phone. If I am not out of here in four minutes exactly, I am definitely going to be late. And judging by how many people are ahead of me on line, I'm not making it, even if I skip the iced mocha. "I wish I could stay to watch you enjoy it, but I've gotta run. It was wishful thinking that I'd get a bun in time to make it to 76th and Broadway."

She arches one of her razor-sharp red brows. "Hot date?"

Oh, the temptation to lie and see if it stirs up any hint of anything is so strong. "Very. And she'll be really pissed if I'm late and don't have her favorite crayons." Thank God I happen to have put those in my overnight bag. "I'm babysitting."

"Ah. So I guess you don't want to join me on a mini café tour."

Oh, this is cruel. "Trust me, there is literally nothing I'd rather do, but I promised." I think back on last night, on everyone's commentary about how she's always the one doing the inviting, and I take a deep, shaky breath. "Maybe tonight, though? I mean, probably not a café tour, but . . . something?"

The unexpected warmth in Elly's red-lipped smile makes my knees wobble. "Something sounds good. My friends and I are going to Cliché tonight, down in Chelsea. Do you wanna come?"

Yet again, I'm not sure if it qualifies as a date that I'm coming along on what might be a work assignment for her and will once again involve her cool friends, but who cares? "Sounds like fun. But now I really have to run. DM me details?"

She nods and opens her mouth to respond, but the guy behind the counter calls, "Next!" and I barely get a moment to watch Elly prepare for frosted cinnamon ecstasy before I'm out the door, wrapped in nerves and envy, calling, "Get an iced mocha, too!" over my shoulder.

❄ ❄ ❄

I don't go to clubs often, but Lydia and Leona have put in some time on the scene, so they're in charge of getting me dressed and doing my makeup while Camila does my hair. When Leona does her wolf whistle of approval—the highest level of appreciation—I know I'm good to go, even if this black sequin halter top shows way more skin than I'm used to.

I just have to actually get moving.

"Okay, you look terrified," Leona observes, touching up her own makeup in my bathroom mirror. "I thought you wanted to go."

"I do." I do. It's just . . . I might be a little out of my element. "I will."

Leona huffs out a sigh. "If you want us to come with you, just ask."

"Please come with me."

"Obviously." She walks back into my room and pulls a dress out of her bag that she'd folded up to be impossibly small and a pair of matching underwear. A minute of changing in the bathroom later and she's fully decked out in a clingy, sparkly minidress with a back so low, absolutely no one will be looking at me.

Camila begs off, which is no surprise because her mom and stepdad would ground her for the rest of her life if she went to club with a bunch of strangers, and Lydia agrees to show up, but warns us she'll probably leave early because she hates clubs and music and loud noise and being around other people. Which, fair. We text Isaac to come meet us, and off we go.

In the cab, I'm hoping I'm making the right move bringing friends, even as I'm also hoping that this is a date. When we pull up in front and see Elly standing with Jaya, a white guy I don't recognize with sandy blond hair full of way too much product, and Nicki, who's sporting an amazing new curtain of turquoise braids down to her butt, I'm relieved to have the twins at my side. Elly's the most dressed up I've ever seen her, in a black corset dress that leaves too much of her smooth white skin bare for my sanity, and I don't know how to keep my cool.

"I cannot believe we're finally meeting the Redhead," Lydia says, waggling her eyebrows as we emerge onto the sidewalk. "She's like an urban legend."

"Okay, get that all out of your system," I demand in a hushed whisper, "because if you make a single reference to it, I will Sharpie on every single page of your prized first edition *Alice in Wonderland*."

Lydia tosses her stick-straight blond bob and mimes zipping her lips. Only once she's thrown away the key do I lead her up to Elly and her crew. "I brought along some random stragglers I met on the street. Hope that's cool."

Before Elly can even say a word, Jaya's mouth drops open. "Holy shit. You're @TheL!onQueen," they say to Leona, eyes practically bugging out of their head. "No fucking way."

Oh no. If there's one thing Leona loves more than anything in the world, it's being recognized by a total stranger. "Yes way," she says with a regal pose.

Elly's eyes dart between the three of us. *Who?* she mouths at me. But despite her discretion, Jaya picks up her question anyway. "This girl is my fashion icon. Remember when I got that amazing jumpsuit? That was totally her influence. Please tell me Matrix is somehow hiding in that purse."

God, now I truly will never hear the end of this. Leona's smile could illuminate the entire club at this point, if we ever actually get inside.

"Why, Foxy," Elly says with an impish grin. "You didn't tell me you were friends with royalty." She extends a hand to Leona, then Lydia. "I'm Elly. This open-mouthed fanchild is Jaya. This dork is Beckett, and this fine young woman is Nicki. She's the one who got me the job at *NoisyNYC* and will be taking me under her wing at NYU this fall. Everyone, this is Foxy."

"Natalya," I amend while she smirks. I don't need anyone else calling me that. "My friends call me Tally."

"Not anymore." Leona tugs on the ends of my hair that she coaxed into beachy waves earlier. "Foxy. I like it. She *is* foxy, isn't she?" she says to Elly, waggling her perfect blond, salon-styled eyebrows.

"Very," Elly agrees, and I have to dig my nails into my thighs to stop from turning into goo.

She *cannot* be straight.

Right?

The line to get in is just long enough to give me time to panic that the fake ID Leona procured for me won't work, especially when Isaac shows up with his floppy curls flying everywhere. But it turns out the bouncer knows Jaya's cousin, and he doesn't even look before waving us in.

Inside, the club is only maybe half full, a solid reminder that not everyone is off for the summer. It's easy enough to get a table, which allows Lydia and Isaac to immediately take up the cause of grilling Elly to death. (Thankfully, Leona is distracted by Jaya's approximately one million questions, so glory be to God for small favors on that front.)

"Tally tells me you're a reader," Lydia presses, because there is literally nothing more important to her. "What kind of books do you read?"

"Mostly nonfiction—biographies and memoirs of musicians. I'm not much of a fiction reader," Elly says with a tinge of apology to her voice, clearly having no idea that there are no wrong answers to Lydia's question as long as you read *something*.

"What about movies?" Isaac digs. He's a geek about exactly two things—film and haute couture—and I don't think he'll be bonding with Elly on the latter.

"Do concert documentaries count?"

"Hmm." Isaac strokes his omnipresent five-o'clock shadow. "I suppose an argument could be made. Tally tells us you want to be a rock journalist. I'm guessing—"

"That I've seen *Almost Famous*? Yep. My parents are actually in the crowd of the 'Golden God' scene. Little known fact."

Isaac's eyes widen, and he crosses his ankle over his knee and rests his chin on his hand, the surest sign he's deemed you a person worthy of his interest. *"Fascinating.* Tell me more."

They fall easily into conversation, and I'm about to join when Beckett leans across the table and says, "So you're Elly's newest fangirl, huh?"

Nicki immediately smacks him on the arm. "Shut up, Beck."

"What? I'm just asking a question."

I immediately dislike this guy. So much. And I already had negative feelings based on his hair, so this is just confirmation that I should always trust my instincts. "How do you know Elly again?"

"Oh, we go way back," he says with a grin that makes me wish facial expressions could be punched off.

Until that moment, I hadn't given Elly's romantic and/or sexual history a second thought; past is past, and it's not like I haven't been around several blocks. But if she's been with a guy like *this*, I may have to rethink some things.

"We've all gone to school together forever," Nicki clarifies. "Don't ask me how he also weasels his way into coming out with us."

"You love me."

Nicki rolls her eyes. "I truly do not. But I do love RiRi," she says, pointing up at the speakers, "and I need to dance, so get your ass up."

Beckett blows me a kiss as they go, and I mime catching it and dropping it on the sticky floor.

With them gone, I turn back to my friends in time to hear Lydia say, "Ise and I are going to the bar. Elly? What are you drinking?"

"Screwdriver if they'll serve you, Coke if they won't."

"They will," Lydia says with the smugness of someone who may not party often but always gets her way when she does. Having enough money to buy God will do that to you.

"Shirley Temple, I assume?" Isaac asks with a nod in my direction.

Mmm, best drink. "Make sure they use ginger ale," I remind him, even as he gestures at me that he knows, he knows. "And an extra cherry!"

I wait until they're out of earshot before I turn to Elly with my burning question. "So, that guy Beckett. Is he, like, your ex or something?"

Elly snorts. "Beckett? I mean, we've made out once or twice, but I certainly wouldn't call him an ex. Why?"

I have no desire to cause any shit between Elly and her friends, so I say I was just curious. But I've never been that great a liar, and she squints as she scrutinizes my face. "He said something weird, didn't he. He does that sometimes. I think he thought we would be something someday, like if he just hung on long enough, I might grow interested, but." She shakes her head, red hair flying around the shoulders bared by her strapless dress. "No. Definitely not."

"Good. I had some serious questions about your taste."

"Oh, I'm certain my taste is pretty good," she says, her cherry-red lips slowly curving into a smile that leaves a little less doubt about whether there's something happening here. "I'm glad you came tonight. And your friends seem cool."

"Eh, they're all right," I say, blowing a kiss in response to a stink eye from Leona. "And two out of three ain't bad for you. Where's Hunter tonight? If you've gotta have a cis dude in your crew, he seems like a way superior choice."

"Alas, he's got band practice tonight. He plays electric violin in this trio of kids from my high school, and they've got a show next week. I'll definitely be hitting it up, if you wanna join me. I haven't written about them for the site yet, and Hunter won't shut up about it."

"I wouldn't say that's the *most* compelling invitation I've ever gotten," I lie, because it's an invitation from the Redhead and thus actually might be, "but sure, sounds like fun." It also sounds like a date, but so did this, and I'm not fully convinced.

"How about we go dance? Is that a compelling invitation?"

"Now we're getting somewhere."

Chapter Ten,

in Which Nat Proves Her Worth

You'd think that after two people spent a whole evening together, eating great food and having both light and serious conversation, they might have a lovely time at work together the next day, especially if they share a desk.

You'd think.

But I know Adam Rose better now than I did yesterday. And I'm not simply going to abide this shit. "Dude." I kick his foot under the table.

His gaze flickers up at me, and I'm annoyed that I've seen him in a casual setting now and recognize that he's kind of hot when he's not being the office tool, because it's somehow managing to translate even in the button-down.

I absolutely blame the forearms.

"Yes?"

"Did we or did we not have fun last night?"

"Why don't you say it a little louder so you can give everyone in the office the wrong idea?"

"What's that?" I ask, cupping a hand around my ear. "You're worried the office might think"—I raise my voice—"we hooked up last night?"

A giggle carries over from another cubicle, and Adam buries his face in his hands. "Jesus fucking Christ."

"Oh, no one cares," I say, prying his arm away. "Though, I'm flattered you think the idea of hooking up with me is that miserable."

His eyes narrow into a dark, glittery glare, and I drop his arm as if I'd pulled a hot pan out of the oven. Maybe we haven't reached the next level of almost-friendship after all.

"I already told you," he says through gritted teeth. "This isn't the same for me and you. I don't have the safety that you do as a nepotism hire." The last two words sound like literal filth dropping from his mouth. "And I know you don't take that seriously, but I do. So, please, just do your work and let me do mine."

Well, don't I feel like a jerk. I don't even know what to say, so I just nod and go back to my computer, scrolling through my email without really seeing it. The thing is, they really haven't given me that much work. I don't know if it's because my mom has no faith in my abilities or because they never had enough to spread over two interns, but I spent two hours this morning drafting social media posts and newsletter articles and finding the perfect fonts and clip art for various campaigns, and now I'm just . . . done. Every single project is under review by someone senior to me.

It doesn't help that they've sorely overestimated how long these tasks would take me. I live on artsy websites and social media; finding the right hashtags or taking photographs with the right lighting and cropping or writing up a creative brief on how to effectively use various live features is as natural as breathing for me, and about as interesting.

What *does* look interesting are some of the emails I'm cc'd on, where actual artistic choices are being made, and I'm itching to pull out my tablet to try coming up with my own visual approaches. But the only reason I'm copied on anything is so that I know when there are documents to print or pickups to be made; no one's asking my opinion on a damn thing.

I give it a few more minutes, but when nothing else comes in, I decide to go ahead and do it anyway. I've gathered from emails between my mom and Kyleigh, the account manager for Sunnyflower Tea, that they're really not happy with the package design options the illustrator provided for their upcoming product launch, and now they're in a crunch. Truthfully, yeah, most of them suck, but one of them definitely looks salvageable—it's got a nice font; they just tried too hard to squeeze in a bunch of sunflowers for a garden vibe rather than giving it a focal point that features the product. If they just pull all that out and draw a sunflower right into the flowing curve of the border, that would leave room for . . .

I have no idea how long I spend getting lost in my drawing, trying different variations on the stem as an underline, using the negative space inside various letters to make sunflower shapes, but when I'm interrupted by a very deliberate cough in my ear, I see I completely missed my mom walking up behind me.

Adam sits up super straight at her arrival, but she doesn't so much as glance in his direction, instead stabbing my tablet with a mauve fingernail and asking, "What is that you're drawing?"

"I thought one of those Sunnyflower Tea package designs had potential," I explain sheepishly. "I wanted to see if I could make it work." I slide the tablet back in my bag and try to ignore the fact that Adam is about to see me either get reamed for drawing on the job or *not* get reamed for drawing on the job, and honestly, I'm not sure which one is worse.

She turns her hand palm up. "Let me see."

I pull my tablet slowly out of my bag and hand it over, wishing I didn't have to watch her scrutinize each design, especially in front of Adam. But the end result is a small smile—the first one I've seen from my mom at work, I think. "Not bad, Natalya. A little rough, but there are some good ideas here." She hands back the tablet. "Email me the files."

And then she walks out, her heels barely clacking on the cement floor.

"Oh." I don't know why the word comes out of my mouth, but I suddenly feel a whole mix of things at once, and I'm curious what Adam's thinking and feeling, and I want to know, but I also don't. So I get busy emailing the files, and by the time I'm done, he still hasn't said a word.

A minute of silence is about all I can take. "So what are you working on?" I ask him as cheerfully as I can manage.

"Not a package design," he says wryly. "Just some newsletter stuff for Third and Ten. I don't think I'm hitting the right bro notes, though."

"Third and Ten? They have you working on a sports bar

account? I kind of assumed I hadn't gotten anything for that because they weren't putting minors on it."

"Guessing that me being one of the only two guys in creative overrides my age," he says, gesturing around at the admittedly female-heavy environment. "And Joey is already up to his ass in accounts they, uh, definitely cannot give to minors."

"Seriously?" I pull my chair around the desk and perch myself next to Adam, staring in disbelief at the list of clients he's working on. "Wow. Okay, so this is really the kind of place that thinks 'men—beer' and 'women—makeup.' I can write about plenty of this stuff. Do they think bikes and steakhouses are only for guys?"

"Well then, feel free to help me, because, uh, I'm kinda stuck."

Now, *that* makes me pause and raise an eyebrow. "Oh? So I'm the problematic nepotism hire, but you're somehow superior? How did *you* get this internship, exactly?"

"Fairly," he asserts, turning his monitor aside so I can't see the screen. Except it's a jumbo-ass monitor, so of course I can still see it. "I've done all sorts of marketing stuff for Bros over Tacos, and I've done stuff for some of the other trucks, and I have a great portfolio, thank you very much."

"It's just extremely specific to food trucks," I guess.

"Well, yeah. But I mean, that translates." He frowns. "Well, it should translate."

"You know, you could just stop being pissed at me and overly proud and try working on this stuff together. Despite being a nepotism hire"—I make sure to infuse the words with as much disgust as he does—"I'm actually pretty good at this."

He grunts but turns the monitor back in my direction, so I'll take that as progress.

"Okay," I say, jumping right in and pointing to the newsletter draft open on the screen, "first off, you've got too much here. Readers see a block of text like that and they will absolutely zone out. You have to edit this down and have some sort of callout that catches the eye. Like this?" I point to a list of testimonial quotes. "The design team could've worked these into the background. It'd look way more dynamic *and* take up less space here."

To his credit, he's totally listening, nodding, and taking notes. Together, we work on the text and a list of suggestions for the graphic designers, and then we move on to social media posts, where I learn that Adam Rose has absolutely no idea how to use Twitter.

"Have you seriously been advertising your brother's truck this way?" I ask in horror. "You know that if you start a tweet with your own handle, no one sees it unless they're already following you, right? Especially if you don't use any hashtags?"

"I, uh." He scratches the back of his neck. "I did not know that. That does explain some things."

"You don't even include pictures! How is anyone supposed to know that your brother is a true artist with avocado-jalapeño crema?"

"I wrote about the deliciousness right there in the tweet!"

"Adam. You are continuously missing the key point here. People. Need. Visuals. And it's not like your brother has the most memorable logo, either."

"You don't like the sombrero?"

"I do not like the sombrero."

He spins his chair to face me and puts an ankle up on the opposite knee. "Well, apparently you are a brilliant designer. I'm sure my brother would love to see some options."

"Oh?" I snort. "Who says I can design for free?"

"I'm sure we can work something out." His lips curve in a suggestive smile, and I'm about to ask him exactly what kind of girl he thinks I am when he says, "I suspect there's a certain number of tacos that'll serve as sufficient payment."

"Oh, there is. But it's a high number," I tell him with a flip of my hair. "Now, let's fix your little disaster here, shall we? I don't think anyone wants to go to a sports bar with 'hashtag chicken wangs.'"

"You don't speak for the masses."

I just shake my head, and we get to work.

❀ ❀ ❀

Turns out, we make a great team. Throughout the week, he handles the majority of the data collection and database updates that feel like pulling teeth to me but seem to soothe him, and I teach him the finer points of social media algorithms, responsive design, and posting like an actual human being. On Wednesday, we grab lunch from the coffee shop and eat together while watching a video course on search engine optimization and chatting with Jaime during their break. All in all, not a bad partnership.

At the very least, my mom is certainly pleased. She takes me out to lunch again on Thursday, this time to a Greek restaurant where Melissa once again orders us both salads. Of course, work comes up immediately, but it's hard to mind when the subject at hand is how happy management is with the interns.

"You've been doing some great work this week, Nat. You and Adam both. Elias is really pleased. He had some serious doubts about managing two interns, but it seems like you work really well together."

I do my best to maintain a cool exterior at the praise, but inside, I'm suffused with an embarrassing amount of warmth. Obviously, I'm proud of my work—including the final Sunny-flower Tea package design, which was unquestionably based off one of my own—and proving that even nepotism hires have some value every now and again. And even though we haven't exactly had much mother-daughter bonding since I got to LA, I still like the idea of making my mom proud.

And have I come to enjoy working closely with my co-intern? Maybe. But that's not the point.

The work talk peters out around when my olives do, and Melissa changes the subject. "So what are your plans this weekend? Is there anything you wanted to do?"

"I've actually been thinking about it." I push the lettuce around my bowl, hoping my answer won't piss her off or feel like a pointed pro-Dad dig. I don't know a ton about my mom's upbringing, but I do know that she felt stifled by it enough to drop a lot of the traditions she grew up with. "And I'm, um, kind of missing having Shabbat dinner? I know you're not really into that, but I thought maybe . . ." Well, I don't know what I thought. That I'm her daughter and we've barely spent any time together despite my living in her house *and* working in her office, and maybe she'll do this just because I'm asking, I guess.

Now it's her turn to fiddle, shifting her knife and spoon around on their napkin. "I'm not opposed," she says slowly, "but you have to know I am definitely not qualified to do that cooking. I'm sure we can get some takeout from somewhere. There are a hundred kosher restaurants in the area."

Takeout matzoh ball soup and store-bought kugel never have the same magic to them, but I'm no more capable of cooking a Shabbat dinner than she is; I never ended up getting around to having Adira and her mom teach me before coming to LA. However, I do know *someone* who's a quick study in the kitchen, and I'm willing to bet he's free Friday night and probably wouldn't mind an excuse to get out of the house.

"I think I know someone who can help," I say with a smile, picking my fork back up and taking a bite of feta and red onion.

It takes some convincing to get Adam on board, but I'm 80 percent sure it's just for show. It's not like he has anything else to do—even I know Evan takes Friday nights off from the truck and Jaime has date night plans with Cass that definitely don't include tagalongs. Once I throw in the promise of an early exit from work on Friday, I know I've got him.

As soon as my mom gives us her credit card and the green light to head out at the end of the week, our first stop is a kosher market. I barely know what I'm looking for, but Adam easily guides me to pick out a package of chicken wings to make soup, another package of soup vegetables, a bag each of carrots and celery, and matzoh ball mix.

"You secretly Jewish?" I tease as he hefts a five-pound bag of potatoes into our cart for kugel.

"I did some research," he says sheepishly, examining the onions and selecting a few to put in a bag. "And I've been in LA for a few months. You're not exactly the first Jewish person I've met. But also, please know that I may entirely fuck this up and it might suck. That's not gonna get me, like, smitten by the Lord, right?"

"Oh, it will. It's actually right there in the Torah that if you're a lousy cook, you go straight to hell."

"Well, yikes. I'm not sure I wanna take my chances anymore," he says, but he's already moved on to selecting a London broil. "I know brisket is more traditional or whatever," he explains as he puts it in the cart, "but it seems a little big for just the two of you."

"You're not gonna stay?"

"Am I invited to stay?"

"I mean." I hadn't quite thought out how it would be to have Adam at a dinner with my mom, but it's not like it's a date, right? "You're doing the cooking. Of course you can stay. If you want to. It *is* a Shabbat dinner, so I get if that's weird," I add quickly, even though the weirder part is probably having dinner with your boss and her daughter. Or that I'm having him cook this meal at all.

"Nah, it's not weird." He turns back to the fridge case for a package of chicken, and I see the corner of his mouth turn up in a smile I don't think I was meant to see.

Maybe that's why it sets something fluttering in my stomach.

Or maybe it's because he's sexy-forearm deep in plastic-wrapped chicken thighs, looking for the perfect ones to give me and my mom our first real Shabbos together in years.

Either way, he's getting upsettingly attractive to me, and it's a problem.

I give us both some much-needed space by going to grab salad stuff, grape juice, challah, and a babka for dessert, taking the time to look for the one with the most crumbs on top. What the hell am I thinking, crushing on Adam Rose? Like, okay, he's not the massive pain in the ass he was when I first started the internship, but that doesn't mean I have to suddenly want to jump his bones.

In my defense, it *has* been a while since I've hooked up with anyone. Nate and I made out a little at Lydia and Leona's Sweet Sixteen, and there *was* a girl I met at the LGBTJew Youth Center with Isaac, but otherwise it's been a pretty dry bunch of months. No wonder Adam looks like a steak dinner to me; I've been subsisting on scraps of broccoli, and I am *not* a vegetarian.

First thing Monday morning, I need to swing by Café Rouge and beg Jaime to take me with them somewhere. *Anywhere.* Preferably somewhere with extremely cute queer people, but at this point I'm not even picky.

"There you are!" I nearly jump two feet in the air as Adam pushes the cart up behind me. "I was looking for you. If you've got the challah, I think we're all set."

Ugh, even the way he says *challah*, attempting but not quite making the guttural *ch*, is cute. I'm in so much trouble.

I lift the items in my arms to show him I've gotten the challah and then some, and we make our way to checkout. I'm entirely silent as each item gets scanned, too nervous I'm going to say something stupid, but somehow Adam's the absolute chattiest I've ever seen him.

"I wanted to try stuffed cabbage, but Lexi warned me that it's a lot harder and more time-consuming than I think it's gonna be, so it's going on the to-do list instead. I'm still going traditional—matzoh ball soup, potato kugel, roast chicken with Brussels sprouts, and London broil. It's basic, I know, but—"

"It's perfect." And it is. Too perfect. It's getting harder and harder to talk myself out of a crush on this boy who researched and planned and is now shopping to make me the perfect Shabbos menu. "You are definitely gonna impress the boss."

The second it comes out of my mouth, I regret bringing up my mom and work and that I'm the boss's daughter, but he just grins, and it's clear that food is so deeply his happy place that nothing can bring him down. I pay for the groceries, and we haul them into the trunk of my mom's car and head to her house.

"Who makes your Shabbat dinners when you're home in New York?" he asks as I put the address in navigation, not nearly confident enough in my ability to find my mom's house from here even though it's only five minutes away. Hell, I'm not confident about getting behind the wheel at all, but Adam doesn't need to know that. "Does your dad cook?"

"The Kosher Emporium cooks. Ike's Deli cooks. Havaya cooks, when it's a special occasion." Just thinking about the kosher steakhouse a few blocks from our apartment nearly makes me drool over the memory of their lamb chops. "Ezra Fox does not cook. And unfortunately, neither does his daughter.

Though I really do want to learn." The sophisticated British woman behind the navigation system tells me to make a right, and I do. "My friend Adira lives across the hall from us, and she and her mom were gonna teach me this summer. They have us over all the time. They're Orthodox, so they're serious about doing Shabbat meals every Friday night and Saturday afternoon, plus holidays and stuff. Adira does most of the cooking—her dad taught her when she was younger, since her mom was always working, which is why she makes mostly Ashkenazi food. But her mom could make an amazing t'bit in her sleep, which is like the Iraqi version of cholent."

"I . . . do not know what that is."

It does delight me just a tiny bit to know something that Adam the Food Genius doesn't. "Cholent's a kind of stew a lot of people make in a Crockpot before Shabbos and then eat for lunch on Saturday afternoon. Usually beef, barley, beans, maybe kishka—which I think used to be intestine but isn't anymore?—and some spices and stuff. There are different variations on it, depending on where you're from, and Adira's mom's family is Iraqi, so she makes t'bit, which is more like chicken and rice with eggs on top—like, in their shell. They get hard-boiled and brown and delicious right there in the stuff from cooking overnight—and it's excellent. I tried to replicate it once, but . . ." I shake the memory of half-cooked eggs melting over crunchy basmati out of my head. "It did not go well."

"Guess I've got more to research," he says, and out of the corner of my eye, I see he's literally writing this down in his Notes app. What a dork.

An extremely cute dork, whose nose is tipped with the

beginnings of sunburn and whose hair is growing the tiniest bit too long, but a dork nonetheless.

"What about candles?" he asks. "You light candles on Shabbat, right? Or is it Shabbos?" He stumbles a little over the word. "Sorry, I've heard you use both. I wasn't sure which one was right."

"They both are. Shabbos is Yiddish, so it's used mainly by Ashkenazi Orthodox Jews, and it's what my dad grew up with. Shabbat is Hebrew, so that tends to be more common, especially from Sephardi and non-Orthodox Jews. I tend to switch around to whatever feels right at the moment."

"Ah. So you're not Orthodox?"

"Nope—probably the closest to Conservative, which I always feel the need to make clear means something very different in Judaism than in politics. We try to do Shabbat dinner almost every week, we do a Passover Seder, and we do the extremely stereotypical Jewish Christmas of Chinese food and a movie, so, we're definitely something. And no pork or shellfish, as you know."

"Or rabbit or bugs," he adds with that grin I am coming to like a little too much.

"You learn so fast." British woman—whom I've decided to call Agatha—guides me through another turn, and I finally recognize where we are. Which isn't all that impressive because we're a block from my mom's house, but it's still more than I knew a couple of weeks ago. "And yes, we light candles, make a blessing over grape juice or wine, do a little ritual handwashing, and eat challah. Don't worry, nothing too challenging."

"Your faith in me really warms my heart."

"As it should." I pull into the driveway and let us in through the back door, which goes straight into the kitchen. "You can probably tell this room doesn't get used all that much," I say, gesturing around at the spotless quartz countertops and white white everywhere.

"Well, I look forward to spilling all over it." We get to work unpacking groceries and pulling out pots and pans, and I get water boiling for the soup while Adam gets to work peeling and chopping potatoes and onions for kugel. He looks so much more comfortable with a knife than he ever does with a keyboard, and while I should be peeling carrots or something, I find myself way too distracted by his capable hands.

Thankfully, he doesn't notice, casually asking me to pass him this or that, thinking out loud about proper amounts of dill or paprika. Clearly, working together has turned us into a well-oiled machine, because in what feels like no time at all, there's soup on the stove, chicken and kugel in the oven, and London broil marinating in the fridge.

I've just moved on to chopping vegetables for the salad when my dad calls, and I pick it up on speaker while continuing to shred the lettuce. "Shalom, Abba," I greet him. "You'll never guess what I'm doing."

"Reading the first edition of my book."

"Ha ha. No, I'm cooking Shabbat dinner! And it actually smells good!"

"Your mother is allowing this?" I'm pretty sure I can hear his bushy brows furrowing over the phone. "Have you set anything on fire yet?"

"I have supervision, thank you very much. And what are you doing for dinner tonight?"

"Quiet night in with some articles I had to print all by myself, since I still haven't found an assistant. Glass of Lagavulin. Adira brought over a quart of chicken soup earlier. You should call her. She misses you."

I glance at the clock on the microwave. Shabbos has definitely already started in New York, which means Adira's phone will be off. I'll have to text her another time. "Noted. I'll try her later this weekend. And before you ask, no, I haven't tried ghormeh sabzi yet, but I will. I *have* tried a bunch of other things." I glance up at Adam as I tell my dad all about Dinner Party and see a smile tug at his mouth in recognition.

Okay, yes, Adam's been a part of pretty much every one of my relevant LA experiences. That entitles me to a *little* crush.

"I expect you to replicate this meal when you come home, kiddo. For now, I'll let you go. This chicken soup isn't getting any warmer. Just wanted to wish you a Good Shabbos."

"Good Shabbos, Dad." A pang of missing digs a claw into my chest, and for a moment, all of this feels too bittersweet. I *should* be cooking my first Shabbos meal for the parent who stayed. But I made my choice.

All I can do is shake it off and get this lettuce into a salad spinner.

※ ※ ※

Dinner is so freaking good that I know Adam has permanently surpassed me as my mom's favorite intern.

"Your talents are being wasted," Melissa tells him as she dabs at her mouth with a napkin, surveying the wreckage of half-finished pans and platters. "We've got to find a way to use all this culinary skill at the office."

"Hey, if you can find a way . . ."

It's a nice thought, but we both know neither of us is getting free of spreadsheets and newsletters anytime soon. Instead, we start clearing the table, and Melissa pulls out some plastic containers, insisting Adam take home the leftovers.

While we repackage everything, my mom walks over to get a brown bag off the counter, the scent of fried dough and sweetness wafting in our direction when she returns. "Nat, I know you bought babka, and we are definitely gonna have that with our coffee in the morning, but I wanted to contribute something other than my kitchen." She opens up the bag, and the familiar smell is so strong, I close my eyes against it and inhale. "I remembered how much you like the doughnuts from Sweet Wheels, so I thought that'd be a worthy dessert to our gourmet meal."

She pulls a half dozen from the bag and arranges them on a plate, and despite being absolutely stuffed from dinner, I have to squeeze my hands into fists to stop myself from reaching for one before she sets it down on the table. The three of us take our seats, and she nudges the plate in my direction. "Do you remember the last time we had these?"

I do, but I'm pretty surprised that she does. There's a hint of a question in her eyes, an opening if I want it, but only if I want it. Which, with a quick, nervous glance at Adam, I decide that I do.

"You took me to get them the night I came out to you as bi." I remember that night with acute clarity. Lord knows my mother has disappointed me many times in my life, but that night she was pretty close to perfect, treating it as a celebration, complete with lemon-frosted sugary goodness. It was during a two-week visit the summer before high school, when my dad was at a conference in Europe, and I'd thought about just keeping her in the dark, the way she'd chosen to be about everything else. But in a moment of weakness, knowing it'd be my last chance to tell her in person for God only knew how long, I'd cracked.

Totally worth it.

I sneak another quick peek at Adam to see if he has any reaction to the fact that I'm effectively coming out to him, but he seems more focused on his doughnut than our conversation. I'm itching to know whether he didn't hear me or just wasn't fazed.

"That's right," she says with a soft smile, and I'm not sure whether she's more pleased that I remember or that I'm comfortable mentioning it in front of him. "Remember that rainbow doughnut we had them make for you?"

"Oh, God, I'd forgotten about that part." It was so absurdly covered in frosting and sprinkles, it was almost impossible to tell that there was a doughnut underneath. "It was somehow both delicious and disgusting at the same time."

"Nothing disgusting about these," says Adam, his mouth full of maple bar. "Where has this place been all my life?"

"I know, right?" I can't decide between the strawberries-'n'-cream doughnut and the lemon meringue, so I cut each in half and make a new mega-doughnut. "So good."

We devour our sugar and everyone goes back for seconds

and thirds until the box is completely empty and my mom is lamenting that she didn't get a full dozen. "I think I would literally explode if I had another bite," Adam groans, and I agree. We move on to sipping tea and cleaning up, and then my mom declares that she's going to pass out, and Adam takes it as his cue to call an Uber to head home.

"You're not calling an Uber," Melissa declares, gesturing for him to put his phone away. "Nat, my keys are on the table in the foyer. Take our chef home."

We get in the car, and it takes me a minute to get comfortable again; I don't exactly do a ton of driving in the city (read: none), so twice in one day feels like it's pushing my limit. The only reason I have a license at all is because Camila and I agreed to do it together so she could drive around Puerto Rico, only for her to learn the age for a license there is eighteen. Meanwhile, outside of driver's ed, all my practice has been with Lydia and Leona's car, which is *not* a Nissan Altima, in the Hamptons. I also have no idea where I'm going, so Adam gives me the address, which takes three attempts for me to successfully put in the navigation system.

"Do you want me to drive?" he asks, his voice somewhere between teasing and genuinely nervous.

"Nah, I got it. Besides, I'm gonna have to drive myself back anyway." I move the car into reverse, and after a solid two minutes spent carefully backing out of the driveway, we're on our way, and I'm feeling much more comfortable.

Which of course is when Adam decides to make things weird. And that's not a judgment. He literally asks, "Can I make things weird for a sec?"

"May as well."

"You'll tell me if I'm being totally out of line, right?"

"You're starting to make me worry I'm gonna need to tell you that preemptively."

"Well, it has the factor of being absolutely none of my business."

"But you're gonna ask it anyway." I squint at the navigation, try to figure out where I'm supposed to turn, and immediately make the wrong choice. "Well, we've got some extra time now."

"Okay, so, like, you're at least somewhat religious, right?"

"Feels like that's an accurate depiction of the level, yeah." *Gotcha, you little bastard*, I think as I find the right way back to our original path.

"But you're also . . ." He lets his unspoken question hang in the air, but after the half a minute or so it takes me to get back on my route, I figure it out.

"Bi. Yes. I am that."

"And that's, like, totally cool with your mom?"

"I don't know if you noticed, but that was my mom's first Shabbat dinner in probably five years. She isn't exactly the staunchest observer of the faith." I hit a red then, which gives me a moment to turn to Adam and focus on him, including those dark, inquisitive, genuinely interested eyes. "Even if she were, Conservative Judaism allows for same-sex marriage and even ordination of queer people. But regardless of denomination, I'd still be who I am—Jewish and bisexual and proud as hell of both. I had a bat mitzvah and I fast on Yom Kippur and I made out with Kira Horowitz at an LGBTJew Youth Center's Purim party my sophomore year. I contain multitudes."

He laughs. "That you do. And it's cool that you feel so . . ." He waves a hand around as he searches for the word. "Reconciled with it, I guess. Remember Jaime's girlfriend, Cass? Her family's super Catholic, and she was terrified to come out. Turned out pretty okay, as far as I know, but it clearly still messes with her sometimes."

Cass seems so sunny, I wouldn't have guessed it. But I suppose everyone has their coping mechanisms. "The way I see it, who I'm attracted to doesn't have any bearing on how kind I am to other people or how I pray or how much charity I give or any of the other things that are important in Judaism," I say, smoothing my thumb over the stitching in the leather seat. "And if I marry a woman someday, there's nothing to stop us from hanging mezuzahs in the doorways of our home or lighting Shabbos candles or having kids the same way any other couple who can't conceive naturally would do it. So I don't have hang-ups about how to reconcile those parts of me, because I don't think they clash."

He nods slowly. "That makes a lot of sense. And it sounds like you've thought about this a lot, too."

"Well, someone had to give the preemptively defensive speech to my parents." I see the reflection of the light turning green in his eyes, and set my gaze back on the road. "But I do believe every word."

"And it seems like your mom did too."

"She did. So did my dad. I'm not sure I even really needed the speech. They're both liberal Upper West Side Jews, even if my mom isn't on the Upper West Side anymore. But sometimes people are cool with things in the abstract and not so much when it becomes their reality. I did think they'd probably be okay with it, but I prepped anyway. Which is rare for me— I'm usually the absolute least prepared person on the planet."

He snorts. "Yeah, that was kind of the vibe I got when you came in on the first day and tried to claim space on the desk with the random contents of your bag. But we are definitely opposites in that regard. You kinda have to learn how to get your shit together when you live with parents like mine. Which is obviously part of why I no longer do."

It's the first time Adam's mentioned his parents in a way that suggests he might want to talk more about them, and I'm grateful to see that we're just a minute from his brother's apartment now, because it feels like a big deal and I want to be fully focused. "Are you in touch with them?"

"Barely. Every now and again my mom sends me a picture of something she spotted on the drive that made her think of me. And not once have I actually understood what the connections are, so I think it's more that she sees things and also randomly remembers I exist, and when those two instances collide, I get a picture of a dusty cactus."

I'm already laughing before I realize there's some real sadness to that, but he huffs a little laugh too. Then, a miracle— there's a space right in front of Evan's building. It's not legal for parking, but it'll do for sitting here and talking awhile longer. "Are they traveling anywhere in particular?"

"Not as far as I know. They wanted to experience a true 'nomadic lifestyle,' which was a pretty big surprise to me considering that's what I *thought* my whole childhood had been. But I guess staying in Portland for an entire year so that I could actually finish high school without having my entire life uprooted again was more than they could stand. They were out of there the day of my graduation."

"And you didn't want to join them on their next adventure?"

He snorts, dropping his head back against the seat. "Hell no. But you also assume I was invited, which I was absolutely not."

My jaw has joined the gum wrappers on the floor of the car. "They literally just abandoned you the minute they could?"

"Well, technically, that would've been my eighteenth birthday, so I guess I should be grateful they stuck it out two more months, but, uhhh, yeah, that's the gist. They did give me their car, though, since they didn't wanna be 'weighed down.' I took turns crashing on friends' couches for a bit, but it got weird and exhausting fast, so I just slept in the car. Then one day Evan called and found out I was doing that, and he told me to, and I quote, 'get the fuck down here before I beat your ass.' So I drove down from Portland and ta-da. I am now the handsome and well-adjusted marketing intern you see before you today."

It's so much to process, I can't even fathom it. His parents just disappearing? Living in his car? Somehow getting an internship despite all that? "I still have . . . so many questions."

"Trust me, you are not alone there."

"I don't suppose you're feeling chatty about it."

The smile that curves his lips has me thinking extremely non-co-worker-y thoughts. "*Chatty* is not generally how I would describe myself, no. Especially not when it comes to talking about my parents."

"You're awfully chatty when you talk about food," I point

out. "I couldn't get you to shut up about why arugula is superior to romaine."

"Yeah, well." His voice goes low and playful, edged in gravel. "You've found my one weakness."

Well, that makes us very uneven, I think as my brain turns fuzzy, *because you've found about six of mine tonight alone.*

"I bet I could find more." Unfortunately, my mouth moves faster than my brain does. I blame the two sips of Moscato I drank three hours ago.

"Oh?"

He's fully turned to me now, giving me no choice but to reciprocate. The space inside the car feels both infinite and way too small, and his eyes are so dark, I could absolutely lose myself in their depths. At least that'd be something to do, considering I can't read them at all. If this is a two-way attraction, he's not giving me much of anything to go on.

Maybe I should be playing it safer and more reserved. We *do* have to see each other every day.

"You always forget where to find 'Wrap Text' in Excel," I say coolly. "You're terrible at choosing hashtags on just about every social medium, and you always screw up the group coffee order at least once."

"I've never heard any of them complain."

I snort. "Yeah, because Jaime knows the order better than you do and they fix it every time."

"Oh. Well. Thanks, Jaime." He levels his gaze on me. "Are you done picking apart my flaws now?"

Yes. No. I'm afraid of what I'll say if I stop. "I guess."

A smile plays on his lips. "Good." And then a silence falls

over the car, and the two of us are just sitting there, looking at each other. "You gonna share what you're thinking?" he asks after a minute.

"I'm not thinking a thing," I say innocently, though he can probably hear my heart's overly healthy thump in the empty car. Why didn't I put music on?

Oh yeah, because we were having an extremely personal conversation.

"Natalya."

God, why does the way he says my name make me so . . . *so*. Now I *am* thinking things, and they're not very kosher. "Adam."

"You know, if you're thinking that you're tremendously grateful for tonight's home-cooked dinner, and you'd like to kiss the chef . . ."

Oh God, my cheeks are *flaming* now. "That's pretty presumptuous of you. You think I owe you a kiss because you made me dinner?"

"No, I think you *want* to kiss me, because you're looking at me like you want to kiss me."

"You're the one looking at me like *you* want to kiss *me*," I shoot back.

Another moment of earth-shattering silence, and then, "Yeah." His voice is uncharacteristically quiet, hoarse, but his dark eyes never move from mine. "I am."

Whatever resolve I might've had to keep this crush under control flies out into the jasmine-scented night. I yank Adam to me by his collar over the center console before I even know I'm doing it, kissing him so hard my teeth are probably gonna leave imprints. But then I feel him smile against my lips, and annoyance and aggression turn into melting and wanting, and it doesn't hurt that he smells and tastes of the beautiful dinner he made for me and my mom tonight.

Turns out that not only can Adam (mostly) work a spread-sheet, and not only can he cook a mean dinner, but he can *kiss*. His fingertips slide up my neck and into my hair, and before I know it, I'm climbing over the center console so I can straddle him in the passenger seat. His hands move to hold my hips tight while his mouth moves to my neck, and the sparks are everywhere, tingling under my skin and threatening to burst out of me and ignite the dark night. It occurs to me that we're essentially in public, but then he takes a gentle bite of my lower lip while sliding his hands up to my ribs and back, and I com-pletely give my brain over to this boy, this car, this blessed night of a thousand possibilities.

Chapter Eleven,

in Which Tal Finds a Calling

ecca's back to camp on Monday, which you'd think would leave me unemployed, but no. Apparently, my dad's Mathmen dinner on Friday night revealed that not one but two of his nerd buddies are struggling to find childcare backup on necessary days, and now I'm watching Professor Wilhelm Oppenheimer's four-year-old daughter every other Monday (beginning today) and Associate Professor Yang Zhou's five-year-old twins on Tuesday and Thursday afternoons from three to six.

Thankfully, I'm well rested, having spent a long, lazy day yesterday of sleeping in, tanning and picnicking in Central Park with Camila, and picking myself out a nice new stack of books at the library.

Still, a little caffeine couldn't hurt.

After leaving things in a weirdish "are we dating or aren't we" place with Elly on Saturday night, I was of course too chicken to get in touch with her yesterday. But today I'm worrying that if I don't get in touch with her, she'll forget all about me, which means a compromise of grabbing a quick coffee at Nevermore. (Plus, my very wonderful best friend gifted me a baggie of flavored creamer pods so I can finally admit to myself that I don't like the blood orange tea and get some black coffee instead.) Why figure out something intelligent to say when you can just say "One medium coffee, please"?

There's an inexplicably large line at the café that blocks me from even being able to see Elly's face when I get to the door, but it's still quiet enough with everyone staring at their phones that I can hear her voice and know she's behind the counter. I take advantage of the wait to reapply my lip gloss, fluff my hair, smooth down the front of my handkerchief tank top, fiddle nervously with the frayed edges of my cutoffs, and examine my newly painted nails.

Then finally, *finally*, her bloodred lips, cropped black Bikini Kill tee, and shredded, studded jean shorts appear in my line of vision.

Immediately, my mouth goes dry. It was one thing when she was still a stranger, but how is it that I've now hung out with her repeatedly, exchanged DMs, and even dipped a toe into the topic of her love life, and still she has this effect on me? And it really doesn't help when she sees me and her whole face brightens up. "Foxy!"

The two people in front of me turn to see who she's addressing, and I don't know whether to puff out my chest or melt into the floor. I'm relieved she's happy to see me and not, like, wondering what the hell the awkward girl of the intrusive questions from Saturday night is doing here. I give a little smile and wave, and then scroll through videos on my phone so I don't keep staring.

"Just so you know," Elly says when I shuffle up to the counter, "I gave Beckett some serious shit for being a dick to you. Honestly, I'd be happy to quit hanging out with him entirely, but he supplies the weed to, like, everyone. I would not survive the friendship face-off."

I let out the breath it feels like I've been holding since Saturday night. Not only are we fine, but this feels distinctly like she cares what I think. "I wish I could offer to replace him, but other than the super-occasional drink, the closest I've come to illegal activity is sneaking into an R-rated movie when I was fifteen."

"How very punk rock of you," she says with a grin. "Listen—"

"Sorry, but can you hurry it up?" The guy behind me leans forward impatiently and taps his wrist, which doesn't actually have a watch on it. "Some of us have jobs to get to."

"You are literally at my job," Elly says flatly. "Some of us have already been at work for hours." That shuts the guy up long enough for her to turn back to me and ask my order with a sigh.

"Medium black coffee," I say with a brief smile. "Any blend. Apologies to your aunt and the coffee gods in general, but I genuinely do not know the difference."

"Medium raven, coming up." She goes to pour my coffee but calls over her shoulder, "Are you gonna be around for a bit? I have a break in half an hour."

"I wish," I say, and I mean it with every fiber of my being. "But I've got another babysitting job today." I make sure the "job" part is loud enough for the jerk behind me to hear. "I have to be there in ten minutes."

"You babysit more than anyone I know." She brings over the cup and rings me up. "Since when are you drinking your coffee black?"

"Since I discovered it can be fixed with coconut caramel–flavored creamer and a mountain of sugar," I say, holding up one of the pods Camila gave me. "Miracle fuel." I have to go, and the guy behind me is going to kill me if I take another minute, but I chance it anyway. "I'll DM you from work. Maybe we can hang out later, grab dinner or something?" I don't know if it's clear I'm asking her on a date, but I'm definitely not gonna be more explicit in front of "some of us have jobs to get to" guy.

Luckily, she doesn't need any clarification. "Sounds good to me," she says with a wink, leaving me to float off to my babysitting job on a cloud of caffeine and hope.

❈ ❈ ❈

By noon, Adele Oppenheimer and I have built and knocked down a thousand colorful buildings with magnetic tiles, colored at least seven hundred rainbows, and played restaurant so many times I feel qualified to open one. "Okay!" I say, clapping my hands together as I see her reaching for the purse she loves to wear when it's her turn to play the customer. "It's time for lunch!"

"Noodles!" The purse forgotten, she jumps up and follows

me to the kitchen, where I'm reminded of the note her father left me this morning that begged me to give her anything but noodles for lunch.

"How about chicken nuggets?" I offer, swinging open the freezer to survey the contents. "Or fish sticks?"

"Noodles!" She sounds a little more aggressive this time, and I have a feeling she isn't giving up without a fight.

"I can make you eggs. You want eggs and toast? Or avocado toast?" I do not have an extensive cooking repertoire, which reminds me that I need to talk to Adira about getting some lessons so I can finally make a Shabbos meal for my dad and me. But it's hard to screw up avocado toast.

"Noodles," she says firmly, her blue eyes growing stormy. "No toast. No eggs. No avocado. Just noodles."

This is going well. I'm guessing I'm not going to have any better luck with veggie burgers or tuna, but then my phone rings and buys me another few minutes to think about it.

Melissa lights up the screen.

I'm tempted to ignore it on instinct but remember that we're actually trying to talk these days; plus, she's a mom—maybe she has advice on how to feed a picky eater. (Not that I've ever been one, as far as I know.)

"Hi, Mom." I look down at where Adele is positively glaring at me, tapping her foot on the floor while she twirls a blond curl around her finger. "Any excellent lunch ideas for a four-year-old?"

"Uhhh, kids like noodles, right?"

I sigh. "Never mind."

"Why are you cooking for a four-year-old?"

"Babysitting. I am currently with the lovely Miss Adele Op-penheimer and we are struggling to find something for lunch that is not in the noodle family." I spot a sunny yellow box hid-ing behind a bag of frozen broccoli. "How about waffles?" I offer Adele.

"How about noodles?"

"Sounds like she knows what she wants," Melissa says.

"Yes, which happens to be exactly what her father doesn't want her to have." I give up on the freezer and dig through the cabinets instead, offering various kinds of sandwiches that get similarly rejected.

"Then maybe he should be there to give her lunch," she says in her joking-but-not-really-joking voice.

I decide to leave it at that. "Maybe. So what's up?"

"I wanted to set a date with you for our book club." What-ever she says after that is drowned out by the sound of Adele loudly shaking a box of penne in one ear and cavatappi in the other. For a house that's trying to keep noodles away from her, they sure have plenty. I snatch the penne, sigh heavily, and open the box. She's won this round and there's no use pretend-ing otherwise.

Besides, I wouldn't mind some noodles and cheese myself.

"Sorry, I missed that."

"I asked how Wednesday night was for you. I can do six o'clock, which would be nine for you."

I can practically see her riffling through her calendar, try-ing to find a tiny window. I suspect if pressed, she'd tell me that what she really has is 6:00 to 6:18 exactly. Frankly, if Wednes-day was going to be anything like today, I'd probably say no, because I can already tell my brain will be mush by then. But Wednesday I'm completely free, which means all I'll be doing is a couple of hours of research and admin for my dad's book. So I say yes.

"Okay, great." There's a tinge of surprise in her voice, like she expected a fight, and in fairness, a lot of our conversations do end in them. But she also just sounds exhausted, and given it's only 9:00 A.M. over there, I don't think whatever's bothering her has to do with me.

"Everything okay? You sound . . . not."

"Just work stuff."

"Aren't you supposed to be sharing work stuff with me?" I remind her as I dig out a pot and fill it with water. Satisfied that I'm doing her bidding, Adele's now calmly sitting at the little eat-in table and coloring everything orange in a Mickey Mouse coloring book.

"Touché. It's an issue with the package designs for this company that were just sent over. The illustrator the design firm chose isn't quite hitting it, no one can figure out how to fix it, and I think the client's gonna pull their account with us."

"Can I see it?"

"You're interested in illustrating now?"

I've been interested in illustrating since you were still sleeping across the hall, I think, but I care about seeing the package design more than I care about fighting right now, so I just say, "I am."

She sighs, but a few seconds later, the files come through.

They do, in fact, mostly suck—so overdone and trying so hard to be fancy and flowery that they're fully unreadable. But one of them definitely looks salvageable. It's got a nice font; they just tried too hard to squeeze in a bunch of sunflowers for a garden vibe rather than giving it a focal point. If they just pull all that out and draw a sunflower right into the flowing curve of the Y . . .

"Nat?"

Whoops, my mom's been talking to me, but I've been getting lost in my drawing, trying different variations on the stem as an underline, using the white space inside various letters to make sunflower shapes . . . "I think I'm getting somewhere, Mom. Give me another few minutes, okay? I'll send something over I think is better."

My mom mutters what sounds like "Whatever," but she lets me go, and while Adele eats her noodles, I quickly sketch out some really basic ideas that I'll be able to refine later if she gives me the green light. Despite taking breaks to tend to Adele, I end up with something pretty decent by the time she finishes her second bowl, and I send them over to my mom.

Not that I'm waiting with bated breath for her response, but I kinda am, even though I know her expectations are on the floor. Finally, my phone rings.

"Not bad, Natalya. A little rough, but there are some good ideas here. Well done. I'll let you know what happens."

"Okay," I say, feeling more than a little stunned at her positivity, or at least what passes for it.

"I have to get back to the account manager ASAP, but we'll talk Wednesday, right?"

She hangs up without waiting for a response, but for once, I don't even care. I maybe saved my mom's ass at work today, and even if I didn't, I proved that my passion for art can come in handy occasionally. I am brilliant. I am talented. I am . . . having water slowly trickled down my back.

Adele giggles, jumping away with the cup she'd been pouring out on me for no particular reason, and I quickly chase after her, turning it into a game of tag. Maybe "brilliant" is a slight overstatement, but for now, I'm feeling pretty damn good.

Dr. Oppenheimer returns at five thirty on the dot, right as I'm contemplating giving Adele a noodle dinner just to stop her from asking me if we can play Candyland for the literal twentieth time that afternoon. Part of me wants to go home and crash, but several parts of me want to make good on my earlier conversation with Elly, so I send her a text instead. She tells me she's in Midtown, so we agree to meet in Bryant Park.

It's so gorgeous out that I'm tempted to walk, but I don't want her stuck waiting for me, so I hop on the subway and end up being the one waiting instead. Not that I mind; Bryant Park's the perfect place for sketching.

I manage to snag a table for two and pull out my sketch pad and pencil and pick a bakery kiosk as my subject; I can't resist the racks of pastries peeking through the windows, the climbing vine design on the outside, the cheery sunshine decal above the order window . . . I'm fully lost in my drawing when I hear the chair across from me scrape the pavement, and suddenly, there's Elly, a little bit of beautiful darkness in the sunshine.

"I didn't realize you were crazy talented," she says with a nod toward my drawing, which immediately makes me flush. "I love that."

"I just like to draw," I mumble, closing up the sketch pad and carefully putting it and my pencil back in my messenger bag. "Everyone needs a hobby."

"Yeah, but not everyone's good at theirs," she says with a close-lipped grin. "I used to try to play music and not just write about it, but I sucked. God, I sucked."

"What'd you play?"

"Guitar, of course." Her chipped black fingernails tap on the tabletop in a suggestion she has rhythm that just didn't translate. "I had very Lita Ford–Joan Jett visions, and needless to say I did not come close. So then I tried bass, because D'arcy Wretzky and Melissa Auf der Maur both made it look so hot, and, well, it's bass. I played a couple of shows with my friends and called it a day. Let's just say I was no Kim Deal."

I nod even though Joan Jett is the only one of those names I recognize, but I'm stuck on her talking about women making something look hot and hoping those are queer hints. They sound like queer hints. Or do I just want them to sound like queer hints? I'm like 98 percent sure on the queer thing, but it'd be really nice to get to 100. "I am hereby making it a new goal of my summer to see you play bass onstage."

"Oh?" She raises an eyebrow. "And what are your other goals of summer?"

I realize then that I can't go one more minute without laying it all out there, even though as soon as the words come out of my mouth, I wish I could shovel them back in and swallow them all the way down. But I just need to *know*. "Well, one of them was to finally talk to you, so. I'm doing all right."

She leans forward on the table, her chin resting in her palm, a couple of skinny braids sweeping the tabletop. Her lips are curved in a hard-to-read smile, maybe a little smug but not surprised. "Is that right? And what did you want to talk to me for?"

"Well, you know. I kept bumping into you everywhere. You see a girl who likes books and cupcakes and craft supplies and Sunday matinees and watching the dogs run around in Riverside Park and you get curious." *Especially when that girl is hot enough to drive you out of your fucking mind.* "And in case you forgot our first meeting, it seemed pretty clear you felt the same way."

"I mean. Yeah. Obviously." She plucks one of the black bracelets around her wrist, which turns out to be a skinny hair elastic, and snaps it. "But I didn't think you'd actually be cool."

"Ouch!"

"Oh, I'm kidding." But she isn't, and we both know it. I'm only a little cool, mostly by association with my friends, and you can't really tell by looking at me. But I feel a little cooler these days, broadening my horizons a little bit with her, and it only makes me want to venture out more.

"No, you're not, but it doesn't matter as long as you've decided I'm cool now. So?" I spread out my hands over the table between us. "How am I doing?"

"You get points for recognizing the coolness of Strings Out of Harlem," she says thoughtfully. "And for coming with me to the show. And for having good taste in ice cream shops."

"And you are the one who assigns these points, because you are unquestionably cool."

"Oh no, I'm a fucking nerd," she says, and cracks up laughing. "You get points for coming into Nevermore. It was a good surprise."

"I really was there to apply for a job, carrying around my résumé and everything. I didn't even know you were working there until I was literally in your face, and then I couldn't—" I break off when I realize I have no smooth explanation for why I couldn't try working there because she was. "I just figured it meant they weren't looking," I finish feebly.

"Oh." Now she's the one who looks sheepish, her fingers tracing patterns in the tabletop.

We're both quiet for a few moments, and I know I'm missing something. "What?"

She gives her lip a quick bite, a flash of sharp white on sharp red. "I thought you, like, tracked me down. Not that it matters."

Oh no, it matters. Something that matters is happening right now, in fact, I'm pretty sure. "I would have," I say softly, still afraid I'm not reading things quite right. I put my hands flat on the table, my shamrock-green nails looking overly silly and playful next to her black ones. "I mean. You're just."

"Just what?" she asks, her voice edging into raw.

A million words fill my head, and I open my mouth, unsure which one will fly out.

But none of them do, because while we were obliviously flirting or talking or whatever this was, the sky was turning without either of us noticing. And then, as if the entire sunny day had been a figment of my imagination, it simply opens.

The downpour is fast and furious and suddenly the entirety of Bryant Park is filled with panicked New Yorkers and tourists running for shelter, covering their heads with magazines or newspapers and dashing for the library. Only a few—unquestionably locals—fail to move, well aware that when it comes to summer downpours in New York City, there's no fighting and no salvation.

For the first minute, that's me and Elly, laughing in disbelief, her carefully applied eye makeup taking the worst of it. And then she grabs my hand and we're running, my messenger bag beating against my hip as I follow her lead to I don't know where.

We end up on the B train, pointlessly trying to lend each other our sleeves or bags to dry off where the rain has absolutely soaked us through. In the end, I collapse into a seat while Elly uses her camera in selfie mode to salvage her eyeliner as best she can. I still have no idea where we're headed, but she yanks me off at 72nd Street. I don't ask even as I follow her up and back out into the rain. Because she's still holding my hand, and I don't want to do a single thing that'll make her let go.

Turns out we don't have far to walk from there. She leads me to a building right across the street from the Dakota, and judging by the way the doorman smiles and greets her, we're heading up to her place.

Okay, then.

It's a beautiful prewar building, and I feel that much grubbier trudging through it in my absolutely soaked tank and cutoffs. But the instant Elly lets me into her apartment, all thoughts immediately disintegrate, except one.

This is the coolest fucking place I've ever seen in my entire life.

"I meant it when I said music was my family's everything," she says sheepishly, sitting on a padded bench to yank off her boots. I immediately take the cue and slide off my flip-flops, otherwise standing still so I don't drip on anything. "I know. It's a lot."

"It's *amazing*."

Elly gives a quick smile, like that was the right answer to a question she didn't ask. "I'll go get us some towels."

With her gone, I can gawk unabashedly. The entire foyer is a gallery of portraits, and as I scan the little plaques below each painting engraved with the names and life spans of each subject, I realize they're all musicians gone before their time.

Kurt Cobain. Jimi Hendrix. Janis Joplin. Jim Morrison. Amy Winehouse. Whitney Houston. Michael Jackson. Chris Cornell. Chester Bennington. Prince. Taylor Hawkins. I don't recognize them all, but I recognize enough. And these aren't commercial reproductions; they're all painted in the same style, clearly by someone who deeply felt these losses. My heart twinges in my chest. There's a lot of love and pain in this room.

"They weren't all friends with my parents," says Elly, rejoining me and holding out a towel, which I gratefully take, "but a lot of them were. Most of the 27 Club was before their time, obviously. But my dad got his start trailing Nirvana around when he was still in high school in this small town near Olympia. Like, Aaron Burckhard times. He covered them a bunch while they were still with Sub Pop, and when they blew up, he had one of the first major interviews with the band, which basically cemented his whole career."

"So your dad's a rock journalist?" I ask, squeezing out my hair. "You're aiming to follow in his footsteps?"

"People always think that," she says with a hint of something that stops just short of annoyance, "but it isn't about him. Or I guess it's unavoidable that it is a little bit, but I genuinely love it. I love getting to take these godly experiences and finding a way to share them with people, getting the word out about awesome new artists who don't know how to expand their reach on their own. Plus, you know, it's a great excuse to go to shows.

"Anyway, my dad did it for a while, yeah, but then he got into being a session guitarist, and he started touring like crazy. Writing took a back seat, but he's played with some of the biggest bands in the world, so probably a solid trade-off. Then, when everything went on hiatus during Covid, he started coauthoring some memoirs and biographies, and he's been doing that for the last few years."

"And your mom?"

"Is one of the top music photographers in the world. She did mostly concert photography for a long time—you'll see plenty of it framed in the apartment—but she's also done a bunch of album covers and portraits, and lately she's been working on tour documentaries. And she painted these," she adds with a sweep toward the portraits. "Strikes me as a little morbid, but she insists it's cathartic."

Personally, I couldn't imagine being surrounded by so many ghosts, but I do know that like divorce, grief is personal. "Are your parents here?"

"Dad's on tour and Mom's at a photo shoot. She won't be back 'til late. Come on, I'll give you clothes to change into."

I follow her through another room practically wallpapered in her mom's photography, and it's incredible. There are action shots so close to the performers, you can see the sweat drops fly, and posed shoots with everyone from Madonna to BTS to Lil Nas X. I'm so clearly in the home of legends, I don't even want to speak.

We pass through a library packed with old issues of *Rolling Stone* and *Spin* alongside countless memoirs and biographies—Dave Grohl's *The Storyteller* and Mötley Crüe's *The Dirt* and the autobiography of Chuck Berry are just a few that catch my eye, though my attention is quickly yanked away by the massive display of awards, signed guitars, and photographs. I keep my hands jammed in my pockets so I don't accidentally touch anything. You'd think that after all that time spent at Lydia and Leona's billion-dollar duplex, I'd be immune to this kind of panic, but there's something about this space that feels sacred.

So sacred that I don't process I'm being led to Elly's bedroom until I'm standing right in it.

It's just as wonderfully chaotic as the rest of the apartment. One entire wall is painted in black chalk paint and covered in drawings and signatures; I can pick out Jaya's easily. The rest of the room is covered in posters, article printouts, and magnetic boards littered with ticket stubs. The bookshelves have more memoirs, biographies, and a couple of novels, some of which I distinctly remember seeing her buy, but more than anything, they have candles of every shape, size, and scent. It's all a little dizzying, in the best possible way.

"So this is where the magic happens," she says dryly, pulling open a drawer. I try not to read anything into that comment, but the alternative is focusing on how she's looking for clothing for me, and that's just too awkward for words. Elly is slight all over, whereas I'm hips and boobs and a little padding all around. I can't imagine squeezing into one of her silky black tank tops or leather shorts.

Clearly she can't either, because she tosses me an enormous Bad Religion T-shirt that goes down to my knees and a pair of boxer shorts that I'm praying do not come from a one-time guest. "Bathroom's right there." She points to a door covered with an autographed poster from the Moonlight Overthrow reunion show that Camila would've killed for, and I slip inside and change, tying the shirt up at my waist in an effort to make the whole ensemble look slightly cuter.

When I come back to Elly's bedroom, she's standing by her desk, running her fingers over the spines of the books on the shelf. She's also changed into a white tank top and baggy black pants, her hair split into two braids that drape over her fine-boned shoulders.

"It's so weird how many times we've bumped into each other over the past year and never even did more than smile or nod," she says, sliding a book out and then pushing it back in. "Why do you think that is?"

"I don't know. You've always seemed so . . ." I look anywhere but at her when I say this. "Untouchable."

"Untouchable? Huh." I expect her to sound a little smug about it and am surprised to hear a note of disappointment. "Not exactly what you want to hear from someone you've hoped to, uh, touch someday."

Okay, I can't possibly be misunderstanding *that,* and a look up at her pink-tinged face confirms it. I bounce around on the religious thing, but right now at this very moment I feel absolutely certain there is a God. "Well, if that's the case, why didn't you ever approach me?"

She drops onto the bed and pulls a pillow into her lap, fiddling with the corner of the red plaid case. "I, um. I mean, I was pretty sure on the liking girls thing, but I didn't, like, *know*, you know what I mean? And then this one time I saw you at Barnes & Noble—I think it was the third or fourth time we'd done the same-place-slash-same-time thing—and I sneaked a look at your pile of books, and I could tell they were all fucked-up thrillers and horror, and it was just so unexpected. And besides that, you looked so ridiculously hot in this, like, nothing of a shirt, and I just . . ." She laughs and buries her face in the pillow. "I was not untouchable that day."

The admission comes out so muffled, I almost think I heard her wrong, but if I did not . . . Jesus. "Are you telling me you . . . to me . . . I mean . . ." I cannot believe we are talking about this. I cannot fucking believe we are talking about this.

She picks up her head, the red strands sticking to her forehead, the usually perfect rims of eyeliner smudged just so. "Can we pretend the last two minutes never happened?"

"Um, no fucking way?" I climb onto the bed, simultaneously glad it's big enough to give us space and pissed that she's still so far away. "That is an excellent confession. I love that confession. I will be hearing that confession in my dreams tonight, probably."

"Well, if *you* wanted to make one, too, that might help." She folds her arms over her chest, waiting.

"I can't make the same one, if that's what you're asking," I tell her, yanking my damp hair up into a knot. "When I said you've always felt untouchable, that extended to my mind. But."

"But?" she echoes, tilting her head, the gold rings lining her ear catching the light.

"But I can confess I want to touch you right now, if that counts?"

"That is an excellent confession," she says, her voice full of teasing as she pulls me by the shirt—her shirt, on my body. "I love that confession. I will be hearing that confession in my—"

"Shut up," I say, and then my mouth is on hers, and she does.

Chapter Twelve,

in Which Rules Are Made (to Be Broken?) for Nat

We need to have rules."

I cock my head over my vanilla mocha and give Adam a Look. "What kind of rules?"

After spending Friday night together, we spent the rest of the weekend doing our own things—for me, that meant shopping with my mom, chatting with Camila for an hour, tanning in the backyard, checking in with my dad, drawing fan art for a new dark fantasy series, and hitting up a Pride movie night with Jaime at Cinespia. But now it's Monday morning and we're meeting at Mocha Rouge for what I *thought* was a cute pre-work coffee date but apparently is actually a strategy session.

"The kind of rules that prevent the entire company from knowing the more disposable intern is dating the boss's daughter intern," he says wryly, clutching his tall green tea.

I flutter my lashes. "So we're dating now?"

"Oh, shut up," he mutters, his face reddening as he glances at the counter, I guess to make sure Jaime's not listening.

"I mean, I don't know if taking me back to your place counts as a date," I continue, because obviously I'm going to continue, and I don't really care whether Jaime hears me or not. "Especially since it was really your brother's idea. I think that for us to be dating, you need to take me on an actual date."

"Oh, I do, do I. Why don't you take *me* on a date?"

"You're the one who said we're dating. Besides, I had you at my house and drove you home afterward. That kind of counts as me taking you on a date."

"I cooked for you," he points out. "That should count as me taking *you* on a date."

"Yeah? You cooked for my mom. Were you taking her on a date?"

Adam cocks his head, looking a little bit like he wants to dump his green tea into my lap. "I need to take you on a date."

"That's what I'm saying."

"Okay, let me think about this."

"Stop when it starts to hurt." I take a sip of my drink, which is delicious; Evan may make a mean taco, but Jaime is killing it as my favorite barista in LA. "You know, you could've just paid for this. Then you could've called this a date."

"What part of my sleeping on my brother's couch and working a minimum wage internship suggests to you that I have fancy coffee money, Fox?"

"Fair point. But good news—I'm a cheap date. Please, just

get me to the beach. I can't believe I've been here for an entire week and I still haven't been to the beach."

His dark eyes widen. "Oh wow, that's criminal. But you're in luck. There's a food truck night at Marina del Rey every Thursday night, and I'll be working Bros over Tacos this week. I know it's not the most romantic of dates, but—"

"It gets me to the beach and comes with free tacos? I'm in."

"Hey, I didn't say anything about free—"

"Shh." I put a finger over his lips. "I said I'm in. It's a date."

He rolls his eyes and delicately returns my finger to me before taking another sip from his green tea, but I don't mind, because I have a date. With the beach. And some tacos. And the very cute boy sitting across from me, his foot casually brushing mine like he doesn't even know it's there. (He might not, but I like to think he does.)

I wonder if this is the kind of adventure my dad had in mind. I like to think he'll be proud.

❊ ❊ ❊

Now that Adam and I are working on the same side for real, we're an unstoppable team.

He takes to his social media training quickly and starts handling it for several accounts, though he leaves the hashtagging to me. He also does most of the company database management, which is an absolute snooze but seems to bring him weird joy, while I do more of the presentation preparations. We do mailings together, passing envelopes back and forth for sealing, stamping, and labeling, and check each other's email campaigns for typos.

"We're getting frighteningly good at this," I say when we finish a stack of mailers in record time.

"We really are. Think we have futures in marketing?"

"Is that what you want to do?" I ask, sweeping all the envelopes into neat stacks, then placing them in a box.

"I mean, I'm happy to do it. I'm happy to do anything that's stable. Whatever gives me a future that's the exact opposite of what I grew up with. And now that I'm even better at it than when I came in . . ." He gives me a knowing, grateful smile that crinkles those dark eyes adorably.

"Okay, I definitely get that. But what do you *want* to do? Like, if money and stability were not factors."

"That's a ridiculous 'if.'"

"And yet."

He exhales a huge puff of breath, like he's literally getting something off his chest. "I want to be a chef. Which I *know* sounds like I'm just copying my brother, which is why you are never to tell this to him or his friends, but we have totally different visions for it. I mean, don't get me wrong—Evan works his ass off, and he's a great chef, and Bros over Tacos was totally borne out of his vision, but he got his big break because he happens to be best friends with a guy who had some capital and great family recipes but couldn't cook for shit. He's taken some classes and watched a fuckton of ChefSteps, but he didn't do culinary school like I want to."

"You help your brother out with his food truck, and you

don't think he already knows you want to be a chef? You literally cook for him."

"Yeah, I cook his and Mateo's recipes according to his instructions. That's not the same thing. He'd laugh his ass off if he knew how seriously I wanna do it. Tell me I have no idea how much work it is, how impossible it is to make a living, how much I'll hate it after a whole childhood of never having enough."

"But he's wrong." I mean to phrase it as a question, but Adam looks so firm in his conviction that it takes all the uncertainty out of my tone.

"No, he's completely right—a lot about it would suck. I don't want shitty hours and uncertainty and the statistics of how many restaurants fail in the first year looming over my head."

"Except that you do."

He sighs. "Except that I do. But that's why it's the answer to what I'd do in my wildest dreams where money's not a factor, and not what I'm *going* to do." He gestures at the box of mailers with one hand, the database-covered screen in front of him with the other. "This, or something like it, is the real plan."

"At least you have a plan" slips out of my mouth before I can stop it, and I look away from him and down at the table, where I'm tracing floral patterns on the surface. "I mean, I guess I'm doing something like this too. I don't know. I *do* know it's privileged as hell to feel like there are a million possibilities for me out there and I just need to find the right one. But I also feel like I'm not even eighteen, so why the hell do I need to know already?"

"Why *do* you need to know already? Sounds like you can afford not to."

There's no acid or judgment in his voice, but I feel it in

the question anyway. And I get it, which is why I rarely talk about this particular stress with anyone. But while my parents got their career paths right from early on, I saw what happened when they started something on the hope everything would just work out and make sense someday. Turns out, you can't do that with marriage—or at least they couldn't—and I don't want to try doing it with a huge element of my future and have it blow up equally spectacularly.

But I don't know how to explain that, so I say, "I just do. All my friends know what they wanna do, and I wish I did too. My parents *definitely* wish I did, as they keep reminding me. I mean, they're paying for it, which I know is really lucky," I add quickly, dropping my chin into my hands and wishing I could crawl away. "So."

In the days before his brother unmasked his assholery as a protective front, Adam would've spat something venomous in reply to this, I'm sure. He won't be a dick now, but I know it all sounds like Poor Little Rich Girl shit, and no amount of me acknowledging my privilege is going to make that less frustrating to hear for a guy who's never had the luxury of making his own choices.

"Nat."

"Mmm?"

"Can you please look at me?"

He sounds at least mildly amused, which feels like an okay sign. I look up sheepishly from where I've apparently hidden my entire face in my hands. "What?"

"You're allowed to stress about shit, even if money isn't a factor in the equation."

"No, I know," I lie, wrapping my arm around my midsection instead. "I just—"

"Nat. You're allowed. Even when you're talking to me, okay? I just want to know you."

Well. That is a pretty romantic thing to say, it turns out. "I want you to be able to be a chef" is my brilliant and helpless response.

He laughs, but it's gentle, and he holds out his hand across the table and waits for me to slip mine into it, then squeezes tightly when I do. "I know. I want that too. Maybe someday I'll figure it out. But for now, thanks for giving me an excellent opportunity to practice."

"You're so welcome. I'm really glad I could very selflessly do that for you."

That earns me another squeeze, and then, because this is the closest thing to a path to a professional future either of us has, we get to work.

"I swear, someday we will have a date that isn't at a food truck," Adam says as he licks a bit of guacamole that escaped from his veggie burger off his finger. "Thursdays are just always ridiculously busy."

"Uh, yeah, I think you might have me confused for someone else," I tell him, spearing another noodle from my vegan mac 'n' cheese. "First of all, you got me to the beach, which was my literal one request. Second of all, I do not recall telling you at any point that I want anything more than this. I mean, seriously—have you tried this? How do they do that with cashews? It doesn't make any sense! But it's so good!"

He laughs. "Shockingly good, right? I avoided every vegan truck in this city for months, and then Evan told me I was being an idiot and to try Chirimoya, and, well, you see why I'm there at least once a week. Liani is an absolute wizard."

"I honestly did not know you could make fake bacon this good. This feels like a revelation." I crunch into a piece of the smoked mushroom sprinkled on top of my pasta and close my eyes, inhaling the salt spray of the ocean. "I am definitely not done with food trucks here. Besides, I'm glad you can help out at the truck when Evan needs you. The guy's giving you a place to live; the least you could do is not ditch him for some girl."

Adam smiles and leans over to drop a light kiss on my lips. "I like you."

"Aw, you're also okay."

We dig back into our food, because we both know that any minute now, Evan will—

"Bud! I need you!"

That.

Adam shoves the last two bites of his veggie burger in his mouth and tries to smile apologetically as he jumps up from the curb where we've been sitting and eating, but it just comes out gross and I can't help laughing. While he joins his brother in the truck to help deal with service for a line that's gotten way too long, I pull out my tablet and peruse my newest drawings with one hand while finishing my mac 'n' cheese and the basket of addictive, crispy patacones Adam and I had been sharing with the other.

"What've you got there?" I look up and see Jaime standing over me, holding a clamshell of something that smells really damn good and definitely is not from Life Is Buttercream, where they've been working for the last couple of hours. "I always wonder what you're working on when I see you drawing at the café."

"Usually it's creepy fan art from my favorite books," I admit as they sit down next to me, the scent of what I can now see are thickly sauced wings from the Korean barbecue truck making my mouth water. "But I felt like Bros over Tacos could do so much better than that ridiculous sombrero, so I wanted to see what I could do. Not that I'm expecting Evan and Mateo to use them or anything," I add quickly. "Just giving myself a challenge."

"No, but these are really good, especially this one." They wipe their fingers on a napkin and point to the one that happens to be my favorite, the truck's name curved over a taco bursting with colorful fillings, framed by a corn-studded wreath of jalapeños and garlic. "I would definitely track down that truck and stuff my face. What'd Evan think?"

"Oh, I didn't show them to Evan or anything. Like I said, they were just for fun."

"That looks like a lot of work for just fun. And speaking of fun . . ." The deep dimple alights in their cheek. "Are you gonna tell me what's going on between you and Rosebud? Because outside of food truck central, I've seen him smile about a grand total of three times since he came to LA, and every time I've seen him at the coffee shop this week, including this past Monday, he's been grinning like an idiot."

The observation makes my skin tingle and I fight and fail

to keep the heat out of my cheeks. "I was there on Monday. He was *not* grinning like an idiot."

"He was when you went to the bathroom."

So much tingle, like maybe there was a spicy pepper in my mac 'n' cheese that I just didn't notice. Yes, that must be it.

"We're maybe, sort of . . . something," I mumble, digging my fork through my food as I avoid eye contact. "He's nervous about it getting out at work. But, yeah."

"You know you're the one grinning like an idiot now, right?"

"Oh, shut up."

They laugh, offering me a wing. I shake my head no thanks; it feels like sacrilege to mix vegan with meat, especially when the food's as delicious as Liani's. "He's a good kid. Tough nut to crack, but if you've gotta like a cis boy, he seems like a good one to like."

"He does, doesn't he? Plus, he comes with a good meal plan."

"Ha." They select a wing and pull off a piece of meat. "Cass says the same thing about me. We didn't have the smoothest beginning, but I think it was the free cupcakes that really made her fight for me."

"I thought Grace never gives free food."

"She doesn't. That's how I got started helping on her truck. No pay, just a direct line to the cupcakes that don't sell by the end of the day, which I promptly used to woo my girlfriend."

"Now, that's love," I say with a smile. "How long have you and Cass been together?"

"Coming up on six months. We actually met online. Not on an app or anything. She knits awesome beanies and does these great videos to show them off, and I also knit for fun a little, so I stumbled on her account pretty soon after she started it. Then I realized I was spending every one of my breaks watching those videos over and over, so I started leaving the occasional comment while I got up the nerve to slide into her DMs, and then one day, she slid into mine."

"But she wasn't out yet, right?" I bite my lip as I realize maybe Adam wasn't supposed to have told me, but Jaime just nods.

"Yeah, and she was being pretty squirrely in her message, so I figured it was probably something like that. I already knew from her bio that she lived in LA, so I suggested she swing by the coffee shop—figured that would be less pressure than an actual date—and that's when she told me she was still in the closet and we had to be on the DL for a while." I wait for more detail while Jaime finishes their wing, but it never comes, and I realize we've hit their shield for Cass; protective mode is on, and it warms my heart all the more.

"Anyway," they say as they put the picked-clean bone back in the clamshell, "it's been a journey, but we got there eventually." They nod toward the taco truck, where Adam's hands emerge from the window holding a waiting customer's order. They're good hands, strong and tan and lightly scarred from a hot oil burn, sporting the watch I know now is his one inheritance from his grandparents. "He know you're a Vanessa Park fan?"

"He knows," I confirm, thinking of our conversation in the

car the other night. "Did not have a ton to say about it but has not asked me if he can watch sometimes, so I think he passes."

Jamie laughs. "I knew he was a keeper." They look back at my tablet. "And speaking of keepers . . ."

I nearly drop the forkful of noodles I'm in the process of bringing to my lips when Jaime hollers in my ear.

"Ev! Teo! You gotta see this!"

"Little busy here, Jaim!" Mateo calls from where he's walking down the line of customers, taking order after order until it looks like his hand is gonna fall off. Given he's usually the chillest guy imaginable, seeing him work up a sweat while muttering Spanish profanity under his breath suggests to me it's definitely not a good time to bug him with my little drawings.

It *is* a busy night for sure. Evan must be sweating his ass off in the truck, and Adam is handing tacos, burritos, and nacho platters out at lightning speed. I feel like I should be helping, but I don't think there's anything for me to do, and also someone has to do the important job of watching Adam's food until he can return to it.

There, I'm helping.

"Fine, but come when you can!" Jaime calls back. "You need to see this!"

Finally, things slow down just enough that they send Adam back to finish his dinner. "What'd you guys wanna show Ev and Mateo?"

"It's nothing," I say, feeling sillier at the idea of showing my logo designs to Adam, but Jaime straight-up growls at me and pushes my tablet into my hands, forcing me to unlock it.

"Remember when we talked about me drawing some new logos for Bros over Tacos? I was just showing them to Jaime."

"You really did that? Lemme see."

I huff out a breath and unlock the tablet, shoving it in his hands. It's not often I show people things I've worked on directly, which doesn't feel at all the same as posting online for the world to see. "I was just messing around," I mumble.

"Nat. Wow." Adam zooms in on one, then another, before looking up at me. "These are incredible. I'm torn between these two, but I think this one's my favorite." He points at the same one Jaime and I had picked out, which feels like an excellent sign. "Come on, bring it over. You gotta show them."

"Uh, I'm pretty sure they're a little too swamped to look at my drawings." I gesture at the healthy crowd still gathered in a line at the window, though none of them seem to be burning with impatience.

"This is worth it," he assures me, and the proud way he looks at me makes me think that yeah, okay, maybe it is. So I push myself up from the curb, finish the last dregs of my food, and head over to the truck with Adam and Jaime in tow.

Turns out, Evan and Mateo think it's pretty worth it, too. "Yes, holy shit, *yes*," Evan says, stabbing at the top choice and completely unaware of how hard I'm wincing at the grease spots he's leaving on the screen. (Thank God for Adam, who notices almost immediately and says, "Dude!" while shoving Evan's hand away.) "That's it. That's the one. I want this."

"Whoa whoa whoa, Ev." Mateo claps a hand on his friend's shoulder. "You wanna think about it a little more?"

"What's to think about?" asks a new voice, and I look up to

see that Grace has joined us from Life Is Buttercream, where her sister, Lily, is ably handling the small crowd waiting on their cupcakes. "This is awesome. This"—she points at the hideous sombrero currently staring us all in the face from the side of the truck—"is not."

"Okay, but it's a lot of money to redo the truck. A new wrap is gonna run us at least 3K."

"Still worth it," Grace mutters.

"It *is* worth it," Evan agrees, "but I don't actually have that, is the thing." Now he looks crestfallen, and I feel shitty for ever having brought it up. But as quickly as he hung his head, he picks it back up with a smile. "Eh, we'll figure it out. In the meantime, maybe we can just make a huge decal or something."

"And replace the sombrero on all the social media," Adam suggests.

"Yes," Grace, Jaime, and I say simultaneously.

"Aren't you forgetting something?" Mateo asks Evan, his dark eyes narrowing.

Evan looks at him blankly.

"Dude." Mateo gestures toward me. "You didn't pull that design out of your ass, you know. That ain't free either."

"Oh, right." Evan scratches his head as he smiles at me sheepishly. "Sorry, got a little excited there. What's your, uh, going rate for something like this, I guess?"

I look at Adam, who gives me a goofy, exaggerated grin and taps on the menu. "I was told there'd be all-I-could-eat tacos? Throw in a couple of churros and I'll do your Twitter and Facebook headers, too."

Evan's shoulders relax. "For you, Adam's girl, there are always tacos. Tacos forever."

And just like that, I've sold my first logo.

"You know, a lot of those designs were great," Grace says. "This was a clear winner, but at least three of those were better than what they already had. I know you said at dinner you didn't really know what you wanted to do with your life, but I really hope this is it. You could totally do this for a living. I'd definitely hire you to design some merch for Life Is Buttercream, especially if I can pay you in cupcakes."

"You *should* do this for a living," Evan affirms.

Is that a thing? I'm too embarrassed to ask a question it feels like I should know the answer to, but I already talked myself out of trying to become a professional artist a long time ago. This . . . feels different, though. Like, it's going to be used to sell something. And so was Sunnyflower Tea. And clearly doing *that* was a job, because my mom had someone on hand getting paid to fuck it up and have their work corrected by a seventeen-year-old.

Is it a thing? My mom would know. She'd probably laugh at me for asking and tell me that a few weeks as a marketing intern doesn't qualify me to do something like this professionally and remind me that I have no training and drawing is just a hobby, and . . . what was I saying again?

Guess it's something I'll have to figure out on my own.

Chapter Thirteen,

in Which Tal's Crushing Hard

Okay! Tickets have been purchased, concession stand is confirmed to have Red Vines, and Nicki has texted that she, Jaya, her roommate, and her roommate's girlfriend are no more than five minutes away. Showtime is in fifteen minutes, and we will have our butts in our seats faster than you can say 'gaaaaay.'"

Elly is practically bouncing with this information, which is sort of hilarious to see in her Ramones tee with the sleeves torn off, asymmetrical plaid miniskirt, and combat boots. I thought I would have to beg her to come see a fluff fest like *Good Behavior* with me when Leona and Isaac bailed on our scheduled Alphabet Soup movie outing for other plans (read: making out with Dylan and making out with this cute boy we met at the Pride parade, respectively). But the second I mentioned wanting to see Vanessa Park's first actual queer rom-com, Elly declared she was in.

Somehow, our date turned into a group outing, but I'm not mad about it; it's been fun getting to know new people, and I'll need them when all my friends go on family vacations while my dad stays hunkered down in the city to finish his book draft before fall semester starts.

While we wait, Elly and I stand in front of the theater, an earbud in each of our ears, getting ourselves into max queer mode by listening to Tasha's "Perfect Wife." (It's truly impossible not to shimmy to it, at least a little.) Finally, Jaya's messy lilac undercut comes into view, and then half a head shorter, Nicki's long silver braids. I've never seen either of the girls with them, but I'd know they were a couple even if I didn't know they were a couple—the lightly tanned blonde has her arms wrapped around the biceps of a laughing bronze-skinned girl with thick black waves and a crocheted pink top that reveals inches of enviable abs. They're both gorgeous and happy and make me want to squeeze Elly's hand in a way that tells her I want us to be just like them someday.

But I don't, because we've been together for five seconds, and I don't even know if this is a relationship, and I would like not to get kicked to the curb if she just sees me as, like, a great pair of boobs.

Though I do in fact have great boobs.

"Elly, Nat—this is my roommate, Jasmine." She gestures at Ab Girl, who smiles and lifts her hand in a wave.

Immediately, my eyes are drawn to the necklace that grazes

the top of her shirt. "Hey!" I say, touching my chest in the same place despite not wearing a necklace. "Fellow Red Sea pedestrian! I like the star."

Her expression is puzzled for a second, and then her hand mirrors mine, finding the Jewish star pendant that hangs from her neck with a little Hamsah behind it. "Red Sea pedestrian. That's cute. I've never heard that before." She tilts her head toward the girl hanging on her arm. "This is Lara. Also Jewish," she adds with a grin. "This is why I love New York City. You never bump into random Jews in North Carolina."

"Okay, I've seen this before," Nicki says quickly to Jasmine, "and before you start with who you might each know from summer camp or whatever, I'll remind you that we have a movie to make and popcorn to buy first."

"Jewish Geography is a legal right!" I complain, but I am also here for the gays, so I walk and whine at the same time.

(And of course, as it turns out, I *do* know Jasmine's cousin from summer camp, way back when.)

A few minutes later, we're settled in our seats with all the necessary snacks, and I can't stop looking over at Elly's ring-covered hand. We're on a movie date, right? So I should take it.

Or are we not? Is that why there's a whole group here? I mean, there's another couple here, so it's not like the group isn't romantic at all, but Jaya and Nicki are definitely *not* a couple. Would this be a date if we were out with Camila, Lydia, and Leona? It certainly doesn't seem like Leona and Dylan are on a date when she comes to hang out with us. But that might be because I've known Dylan since we were in Pull-Ups, and no matter how many death glares she shoots at me, I'll always remember her as the girl who cried her ass off at our first and only sleepover.

Huh. Maybe that's why she doesn't like me.

But anyway.

In all the time Elly was the Redhead, I never *really* imagined this part. I imagined a million different meet-cutes—literally bumping into each other at a bakery, or finding her lost phone at the bookstore and needing to track her down—but I didn't imagine them *going* anywhere. I imagined her having a too-cool aura and at best a flirty smile and then stomping off in her combat boots, the chains hanging off her black skinny jeans jangling behind her.

How could I possibly have pictured that she'd be warm and funny and excited about queer rom-coms and shy about her feelings and look incredibly kissable in a pair of sweats and rain-soaked hair, on top of everything else?

Fuck it. I take her hand. And as the opening credits roll, she looks at me, smiles, and squeezes.

❀ ❀ ❀

"Aah, that was so good," Lara gushes as we leave the theater two hours later, bound for a falafel place Jasmine assures us is the best one in the village. "I will officially watch Vanessa Park in anything."

"That was also true before the movie," Jasmine points out wryly, sweeping her long thick hair into a ponytail.

"As it should've been." I offer Lara a high five, and she slaps my hand joyfully before slipping her heart-shaped sunglasses back on. "God, I am gonna draw obscene amounts of fan art."

"Ooh, you draw fan art?" Jasmine digs into her Chloé macramé bag and pulls out her phone, which she immediately hands over. "Show me. I must see it immediately."

"She's so fucking talented, it's disgusting," Elly says as I pull up my FanGallery account and hand Jasmine's phone back.

My face flames at the praise, mingling with my anxiety at having my work checked out in front of my face. I distract myself by chatting with Nicki about her thesis again, getting a new recommendation for Big Joanie. But half a block later, I feel a hand on my shoulder and look up to see Jasmine gawking at me. "Um, these are amazing? I can't believe you have art of *Coven* in here. Do you take commissions? I suddenly have a mighty need."

Jasmine and I chat about drawing and dark fantasy graphic novels and a print she wants for her wall the entire rest of the way to St. Marks, where the glorious scents of herby, garlicky falafel, French fries, and spicy lamb roasting on a spit positively punch me in the face. I'm well aware that consuming a platter will render me fully unkissable for hours, but I don't even care. I have to have whatever it is that smells that damn good.

Between the six of us, we devour a truly absurd amount of falafel, shawarma, fries, and these little cups of mint tea they give out for free to all the customers, despite the summer heat. The sun is sinking in the sky by the time we finish, but no part of me feels done hanging out with these people, so we head over to Washington Square Park to chill in the twilight.

An acoustic guitarist is playing a cover of "Wonderwall" that has the millennial crowd swaying particularly hard, and we settle in to listen while Elly, Jaya, and Nicki argue over the best acoustic covers of all time.

"You can't argue with Johnny Cash's 'Hurt,'" Elly says firmly, her hair glowing like fire in the setting sun. "You just can't. When even Trent Reznor is saying the song isn't his anymore, I mean. Come on."

"Okay, yes, obviously." Nicki rolls her deep-brown eyes and tucks a braid behind her ear, all business. "But tell me *you*, Elly Knight, are not fully discarding the entirety of Nirvana's Unplugged performances *and* Chris Cornell's 'Patience.'"

"Does it always have to be rock with you two? Come on, let's get a little more creative here." Jaya lies back and crosses their ankles, showing off green snakeskin-print oxfords that contrast excellently with their purple pants. "There are some acoustic Bollywood covers that would blow your fucking minds. Hold on a sec, I'm sending you both a playlist."

"Man, if we were still in school, this would make the perfect listening party in our room," Jasmine says wistfully. "I can't believe I am vaguely missing an academic institution."

"What are you doing for the summer?" Jaya asks.

"Heading down to Outer Banks this weekend." Jasmine and Lara's faces light up at the mention, and their hands find each other as naturally as breathing. "My dad has a house there and we go every year. Normally I'd already be there, but I'm taking a two-week photography class in the city first."

My fingers itch to draw this whole group—the easy affection (and, let's be real, glaring horniness) between Lara and

Jasmine; the passion between Elly, Jaya, and Nicki; the various shades of luminous skin, brightly colored clothing, and metallic jewelry glinting in the sunlight . . . It'd make a fabulous fictional girl band or something. I'm not trying to be antisocial, though, so I kick back and join the conversation instead.

The guitarist moves on to an original song that's not bad, followed by a cover of John Mayer's "Your Body Is a Wonderland" that absolutely is, especially because he keeps glancing at Jasmine like he's silently dedicating it to her while she avoids eye contact so hard, I think she might sprain something. Talk quickly turns to him, to creeps we've encountered in the city and beyond, and to our gratitude that we all like girls. "Except Nicki," Jaya says fondly, wrapping an arm around Nicki's shoulders. "Can you imagine being this tragically heterosexual?"

"It's a curse," Nicki says dryly. "I might just become a nun. I go to mass on Christmas, so it's basically the same thing."

I stroke my chin. "I know I'm Jewish, but that doesn't sound right."

"So many great covers out there and this guy chooses Mayer," Elly mutters.

"Could be worse," says Jaya, stretching their long, tattooed arms over their head. "We could've been subjected to yet another 'Hallelujah.'"

Nicki and Elly both groan, and Jasmine cracks up. "God," she says as the others immediately enter a heated debate about which versions actually deserve airtime, "I cannot tell you how many times I have heard Nicki have this argument. Spoiler: they're going to settle on KD Lang as the supreme cover, but laud Pentatonix—which happens to be *my* favorite version, by the way—and then they're going to give John Cale his due as the inspiration for pretty much all the good covers, and trust me, you're going to want to escape before they get into debate number one billion about the best cover songs of all time."

"Duly noted." But I watch them anyway, because this is the most fired up I've seen Elly, and it's a glorious sight to behold, full of flying fiery hair and waving hands.

"How long have you guys been together?" Lara asks, following my eyeline to Elly's bloodred lips.

"Oh." Heat rises into my cheeks, like I've been caught watching porn instead of the girl I'm maybe possibly dating. "We're, um. Just kinda getting to know each other."

She and Jasmine exchange the kind of knowing look that just confirms for me they're couple goals. "Well, you have a smitten look about you," she says, a little smile playing on her pink-glossed lips. "You both do."

I don't really know what to say to that, but I know I like hearing it.

Luckily, Lara's phone rings right then, and she glances at the screen and moves a couple of feet away to take it. The last thing I hear before she disappears is "Hi, Mom," and it reminds me that I have a date with my own tomorrow night.

Jasmine glances at Lara, and when she decides she's far enough away, leans in close. "Okay, so, I do want to commission the art we talked about before and everything, but what I *really* want to commission is art of Lara's characters from this romance novel she just finished writing. She's about to start looking for an agent, and she's really nervous, and I want her to know I believe in her and stuff. I know that's not your usual, but is that something you could do?"

"That is so disgustingly cute, I could die." We exchange information and agree to discuss details later. "So you guys are pretty serious, huh?"

She glances over at where Lara is still on the phone, swaying to the music (currently a cover of "The Sound of Silence") as she talks to her mom. "Yeah." Her voice is a little dreamy in a way that makes my heart flip with the very idea of someone sounding like that about me someday. "I think so."

"Cool," I say, but I'm no longer looking at Lara, or even Jasmine. Because Elly's looking at me, teeth tugging at her slowly smiling lip, and like that, the entirety of Washington Square Park, of Manhattan, of New York City, falls away, and we're just two girls who've kissed before and plan to kiss again.

Ideally as soon as possible.

❊ ❊ ❊

The high of hanging out with Elly and her friends slowly fades throughout my morning of playing dress-up, doctor, tea party, supermarket, and every other game of pretend imaginable with Jenny and Julie Zhou, five-year-old twins who love boas, calling me *ma'am*, and coloring on each other's arms. I don't usually have more than one cup of coffee in a day, but I'm so drained from hours of playing, coloring, and answering questions that while they chow down on the bagels with cream cheese their dad picked up this morning for their lunch, I help myself to his Keurig and a fragrant blueberry-flavored cup. (Tastes better than it sounds, I promise.)

We follow up lunch with an excursion to the playground at Riverside Park, and I sketch the hippo statues as I watch the girls climb all over them, pretending they're pets. Julie keeps "putting out food" for one of them, while Jenny declares she's taking hers for a walk, and I marvel at what it must be like to have a five-year-old brain. At some point, my mom checks in to make sure we're still on for book club tonight, and I confirm that we are.

I consider texting Elly, but I don't.

Instead, I text Adira, ask how the kids at camp are doing and tell her to say hi to them for me. I do miss the little rug rats, even as I have my hands full with new ones. She won't be able to answer me for another few hours, so I switch to camera mode and take some cute pictures of the girls to send to their dad.

I'm decent with kids. I know that. I'm decent at a lot of things. On the days I'm working at the library, I'm decent at organizing and answering questions and whatever other customer service comes up. My grades are decent—math, Spanish, physics, all of it. But there's nothing I love the way Elly loves music, or Lydia loves reading, or Leona loves fashion, or Camila loves babies. Well, nothing other than drawing, which I've been told a million times will lead me absolutely nowhere, career-wise. And every day that I spend babysitting makes me think that my future is going to lie in something that's *fine*. Something at which I'm *decent*.

The thought is just so wildly bleak.

I have to figure out where I'm going from here. Everyone

in my life knows what they plan to do next except for me, and this summer hasn't taken me a single step closer to figuring out what I want beyond to make out with Elly Knight. Maybe staying in New York was a mistake. Maybe LA would've given me the answers to all of my questions.

I guess I'll never know.

But there is one LA experience I'm signed on for, and that's chatting with my mom tonight. I'm weirdly nervous, like what if she thinks everything I have to say about the book is stupid? What if we get on the subject of the future and get into a fight about how mine currently looks like a big gaping void? Or what if we have nothing at all to say and this little experiment in reconnection is over before it even begins?

I shake my head to get the negative thoughts out and refocus on the girls. They're having a contest of who can pump higher on the swings, and it's giving me major flashbacks to doing the same thing with Camila when we were only a little older than they are. How is it possible life is so simple once upon a time, and then it's just . . . not?

The girls are entertaining themselves plenty well, so I sit back on the grass and put in my earbuds as I watch them. A chill day in the park calls for Mumford & Sons, and I wave at the girls and text a bit with Lydia while she takes her lunch break.

We stay at the park for another hour, and then the girls start whining that they're hungry and bored and tired and all the other things they can possibly be, so we go get ice cream and take our time strolling back to their apartment while bright-pink strawberry and muddy chocolate drip down their hands.

As I clean them off and get us set up for a rousing game of Chutes and Ladders, I can't help feeling a little jealous of the twins, born with built-in playmates, while I spent these years drawing alone in my room with the music turned up to keep out the sound of my parents fighting. What a difference it would've made, to have had someone to wear boas and dot paint flowers with. What a difference it would've made to have a second voice begging to go to the park or have a story read, an overpowering that couldn't have been ignored the way a single toddler voice could be.

"Tally," Julie whines. "I want the girl with the barrettes but *she's* taking the girl with the barrettes!"

"I had her first!" Jenny insists.

Okay, so there are perks to having had the toys to myself, but still. While I broker an agreement by promising we'll play two games—one for each of them to have the coveted piece—I think about the weirdness of how ten years after the divorce, and the move, tonight I will have my mother's undivided attention.

Now, when I no longer need it.

Now, when I'm surrounded by people all the time, and even when Camila goes to Puerto Rico and Lydia and Leona go to Italy, I might actually still have plenty of people to hang out with.

And a very tiny, very petty part of me wants to cancel—even better, to say, "Sorry, I have to work tonight." (In fairness, I *do* have those commissions from Jasmine to do.) But I can already hear Camila in my brain telling me it's not the move, that you only get one family.

While I don't agree with her that you have to give people space in your life simply because you share blood, she *is* right that my mom is trying. And so tonight we'll talk books. And work, probably. And whether we talk about anything else, well. I'll keep my expectations on the floor, where they've always been.

❊ ❊ ❊

We planned our call for 6:00 P.M., her time, which gave me a solid window to have Chinese takeout with my dad for dinner, watch an hour of bad reality TV with Adira, and get started on the first piece of art Jasmine requested. Later tonight I'll settle in with the file of Lara's romance novel so I can get the gist of her characters, but for now, in the last twenty minutes leading up to the call with my mom, I'm refreshing myself on the SoCal Thriller, readying myself to share sharp enough insights to make her regret moving across the country.

Or something.

I've been trying to hold off on touching my book club snacks until our call starts, but I made my own snack mix out of peanuts, M&M's, raisins, M&M's, white chocolate chips, and M&M's, and I can't help picking out a few pieces while I wait.

I'm so fixated on picking out the blue M&M's that I somehow manage to be startled out of my seat when my phone rings, despite literally sitting there waiting for it. "Hello?" I answer, as if I don't know who's on the other line, and no, I don't know why I do this.

"Hi, sweetie. You ready for the first official meeting of the mother-daughter book club?"

It sounds like such a sweet event, to hear it from her mouth, as if we're going to an event together at the Y and not piecing something together three thousand miles apart. "I've got my snack and I've got my book—in that order—so I guess so!"

"Great!"

We both fall silent.

Finally, my mother's awkward laugh breaks into the void. "I guess this is new to both of us. Well, I'll start by saying you made a great choice of book. I don't usually read thrillers, but this wasn't what I expected. It was more . . . cerebral."

"It's a social thriller," I say automatically, as if I've always known what that means. As if I'm even completely sure now. But I have to say something or I'll pick at the fact that she just suggested that my favorite genre is stupid.

"Yes, I recall you saying that, but I didn't quite get what it meant until I read it. I thought it was really fascinating, the way institutional racism was woven through the fabric of the plot. It really had me looking at things in different ways, especially affirmative action."

"Same!" A raisin falls out of my mouth at the proclamation, and I quickly scoop it back in, glad this chat is audio only. "That line when Aliyah keeps looking at the different cereal boxes over and over again—"

"Oh, that line absolutely killed me. I was liking the book before that, but as soon as I got to that line, I knew I was going to remember this one for a while. I love that feeling, you know?

When you're still thinking about the characters after the book ends?"

"My absolute favorite feeling," I confirm. "And I couldn't believe how well the author still managed to work a cute romance in. I thought for sure that was gonna blow up in her face, but—"

"So did I! It was almost a twist because it *wasn't* a twist, in a book that was completely twisted." She laughs in a way I swear I don't think I've ever heard from her before. "Clearly, this book got to me."

"Me too," I say, and I realize with only a hint of embarrassment that I'm hugging it as we talk. But she can't see me, and she doesn't need to know that it isn't just the characters but the fact that this is the easiest conversation she and I have had in years that has me feeling some kinda way about it. "I also really loved her sister? Like, I know their relationship was really complicated and messy, but that's what I thought was great about it."

"Oh, she definitely reminded me of Lauren. The whole thing with the Barbie dolls? Lauren did *exactly* that to me when we were younger. I was still finding their hair in my shoes weeks later."

"That's so gross."

"It really was. But when she says she just wanted to be noticed . . . that reminded me of Lauren too. She was always desperate for attention from me and Jessica, wanted to do everything we did. It's part of why I wanted you to be an only child—I liked the idea of you not having to compete."

Yeah, instead you two *did*, I think. Being an only child through the divorce is definitely in my top three grievances in this life, but we're getting along so well, I don't wanna say it, especially since she's never opened up about anything like that to me before. I want to know more, but that also means not pissing her off. "Well, I definitely got my own space," I say instead. "I would not have shared my markers well."

"It was actually your chalk you were most possessive over," she muses. "You had this glitter chalk that one of your preschool friends bought you for your . . . fourth birthday, I think it was? And you were *obsessed* with it. We would take it to the park and you would draw anywhere you could, but if God forbid your father or I reached for one of them, you would scream loud enough to shake the trees. I knew then you were either going to become an artist or a drama queen."

"Por qué no los dos?" I tease, borrowing one of Camila's favorite phrases.

I can almost hear her smiling through the phone. "There's no winning if I answer that, is there."

Finally, she's learning. "Maybe let's just get back to the book."

Chapter Fourteen,

in Which Nat's in for a Surprise

*H*ow's this?" Adam holds out a wooden spoon for me to taste, and either I really like him or LA has just made me stupidly trusting, because I try it even though it's been a solid hour since I've paid any attention to what he's making. After everyone saw my logo for Bros over Tacos, Grace followed up with me about merch designs for her truck, and Lexi asked if I could do one for the catering business she's starting on the side, and suddenly I'm drowning in business.

I mean, it's business that mostly pays in paninis and macarons, but I'm certainly not complaining about that.

Adam, however, has his own preoccupation today: it's the first time ever the group has allowed him to participate on his own at Dinner Party. Turns out he'd told Evan about making

Shabbat dinner, and Evan was so impressed that he'd told the group, and while I'm pretty sure it was mostly to tease him about cooking for his girrrrlfriend, they decided it was time to see what "Rosebud" could do.

Adam has not shut up about it since.

And I know I like him because I can't help but find it cute.

"Okay, I was not expecting that," I admit when the spoon hits my tastebuds, "but that is *really* good. I don't think I've ever had peanut in hot soup form before. Or is that a stew? At what point does a dish go from a soup to a stew?"

"This is indeed a stew," he says, returning to stir it. "Maafe— Senegalese peanut stew. Got the chicken from that kosher supermarket we went to a couple of weeks ago. I was gonna do lamb, but turns out I am not operating on a kosher lamb budget. Or a kosher beef budget."

Okay, but that he went out of his way to get kosher chicken for the stew is weirdly fucking sexy. Which is probably a pretty low bar, but it's one very, very few people clear. If he weren't taking this cooking task so seriously right now, I would suggest we move this into literally anywhere but my mom's kitchen. But I don't want to be the reason his contribution to Dinner Party is a dud. Especially now that I know cooking is a dream for him.

I'll just stare at his ass for a while until he's done.

There's been a lot of making out since that first Friday night. A *lot*. Lips have been chapped, shirts have come off, and butt imprints on both his couch and my bed are starting to look permanent.

When we're not making out, we're either working together

(and probably playing footsie under the desk), eating together (usually at the food trucks while he helps Evan out, but sometimes it's him practicing cooking on me or, in the case of Friday nights, it's Shabbat dinner at my house—something I had no idea if I would keep up for him *or* for my mom, but which has become my favorite time of the week), or hanging out with Jaime, Cass, and a few other people they know. At some point, Adam Rose became the most constant presence in my life, which is terrifying because (a) he's never even met Camila, Lydia, Leona, or Isaac outside of FaceTime and (b) we will not actually be in each other's presences at all after the summer.

We don't talk about it, the fact that I'll be moving back to New York at the end of August and he'll still be here in LA, hanging on to the paid internship for as long as humanly possible. We don't talk about the fact that he's interning in a field whose jobs often require college degrees, while he has no desire to go. We don't talk about the fact that what he really wants is to go to culinary school, but that he has no idea how he'd ever be able to afford it. And only one night, when we were hanging out on the beach and Adam had one too many beers (read: two beers), have we talked about his fear that Evan is going to want his living room back someday, and Adam will be truly fucked when that happens.

It's some awful irony, really, that I have no idea what I want to do, but plenty of space to figure it out, while Adam is dead sure, with no clue how to make it happen.

A guy who can make both amazing matzoh ball soup and amazing peanut stew should be able to go to culinary school, damn it.

I watch as Adam takes one last taste of the maafe and gives a satisfied smile. "That *is* good. Suck it, Petey."

"What'd Petey ever do to you?"

"You don't wanna know. Let's just say—"

"What smells so yummy in here?"

We both jump, our conversation and KROQ on low volume in the background having muffled the sound of my mom letting herself in. For once, I'm relieved we weren't making out. "Adam's cooking," I say, smoothing down my shirt guiltily even though no one's been rumpling it. "Practicing for a fancy potluck dinner with his brother and his friends tomorrow night. You should try this. It's Senegalese peanut stew."

"I didn't realize you were this gourmet a chef." I expect her to turn down the spoon he offers, but she tries it and closes her eyes in appreciation. "Wow, that was delicious. Unexpected. The flavors, I mean—not the fact that it's good," she amends with a wink at me, probably because it's the exact kind of verbal slipup I've called her on a thousand times.

"It's a pretty easy recipe," he admits, "but I'm not going for challenging this time around. I just wanted to make something I've never had before. And it's a theme dinner—everyone has to make two dishes representing a different continent, and I've got Africa. And they can't be northern—since there are eight of us, Lexi got the Middle East and North Africa. I'm still trying to figure out a second dish that's neither Ethiopian nor jollof."

"What's wrong with Ethiopian or jollof?" Melissa asks. "Both of those are great options."

"One of the other chefs is Ethiopian, and I can't embarrass myself in front of him," Adam says with a slight grimace. "As for jollof, I've been warned that I do not want to dip a toe into the battle of which version is best. I thought about attempting smalona, but I don't want to give this one any excuse not to try my food," he says with a nod in my direction. "Pretty sure eel's not kosher, right?"

"Definitely not."

"Some other time, then."

"How long have you been cooking, Adam?" Melissa walks over to the fridge and grabs herself a bottle of Pellegrino before settling into a chair at the breakfast bar. "I have to admit, I hadn't realized it was a hobby that extended beyond our Shabbat dinners."

"It's more than a hobby," I cut in before he can respond. "Adam's really passionate about it, and really talented. I feel like he could do it professionally."

"Nat . . ." There's a trace of warning in his voice, and I shut up, because yeah, it's not like Adam doesn't know what he wants or have any dreams; maybe I'm just pouring salt in a wound.

But if I'm sprinkling it in, my mom has fully opened the spout. "Have you considered culinary school?" she asks innocently, her perfectly manicured hands encircling the green bottle. "With all your experience at your brother's truck and in our kitchen, I'd imagine that's something you might enjoy."

He smiles tightly, making me wish even more that I'd just kept my nose out of it. "I might," he says, "if it weren't so expensive. As it is, I'll have to put in a few more years of work first. Save up."

"That's very responsible of you," she says approvingly, and she's not wrong, but it's clear in the tic of his jaw that Adam is sick and tired of doing the responsible thing. He's never had much of a choice in that. It feels ironic that I spent so much of my childhood wishing I had normal parents who actually liked each other like Camila's, but here I am learning that you can grow up way more stable with one parent who has his shit relatively together than two happily married ones who don't.

The next ten minutes are full of quiet cleanup, followed by an "I should get home." I can't even prolong the evening, because tonight, Adam's got his car and doesn't need a ride. My mom subtly leaves the room, but we exchange a chaste kiss anyway, and then he leaves while I watch him go.

"You found yourself a good kid," Melissa says when I join her in the den, where she's curled up under a faux fur blanket watching a show about tiny homes.

"Well, technically, you found him," I point out, joining her and burying my feet in the ridiculous softness. "So thank you for hand-delivering me an extremely cute and *responsible* boy who cooks."

"And is a good kisser?" she asks, waggling her eyebrows.

"I will absolutely not be answering that question. Just take the W for the intro and let it go."

Her lips twitch and she rests her head on the couch, her straw-colored hair fanning out around her. "You gonna be okay when it's time to say goodbye?"

No. "Trying not to think about it."

"You really like him, huh?"

I turn to look at her, but I've always cried easily; if I open my mouth to answer, now that she's put leaving in my mind, that's exactly what I'll do. So I just nod, clenching my teeth against any tears that might threaten to fall.

A moment later, there's a hand squeezing my ankle, and it rests there through half an hour of loft beds and closets hidden under stairs and bathrooms where the toilet is located in the shower. By the time the episode ends, I don't even notice it anymore, as if it's always been there.

※ ※ ※

With all his work practicing dishes for the next Dinner Party, Shabbat dinner falls to the wayside this week, and despite my offer to handle getting takeout, my mom begs off for some work thing. Adam invites me for pizza at his place instead, and when I get there, I find that Evan and Mateo have decided to stay in and eat with us too. Which is cool, except that they're acting weird as hell the entire time, all shifty-eyes and stolen glances and unsaid words hanging in the air. Mateo keeps fiddling with the gold hoop in his left lobe, which I've only seen him do when he's super stressed out, and Evan's made at least twenty fewer jokes per hour at Adam's expense than usual. Something is definitely up.

When I see Evan and Mateo exchange their fiftieth Look of the evening, followed by a quick peek at Adam, I can't take it anymore. "I need to go outside to get some air," I murmur to Adam as he wipes the grease off his fingers from his third slice. "Come with me?"

He tosses his napkin on the table and gets up, twining his

fingers with mine as we weave around the other chairs and let ourselves onto the small terrace. "Everything okay?" he asks, his brows furrowing with concern.

"I was gonna ask you the same thing," I say as he settles into one of the chairs, then pulls me into his lap. "I figured you were probably feeling anxious with all the silent signals between Evan and Mateo. What's that about, anyway?"

"No idea." He doesn't sound that fussed about it, focusing instead on sliding his fingertips just under the bottom of my shirt to stroke my skin as we watch the last traces of the sun sink below the sky. And not that I want him to stop, especially when he brushes my hair over my shoulder and kisses the back of my neck, but I can't fathom how he has absolutely zero curiosity about what's going on. "They're probably complaining about the pizza. They're both snobs and have been since we were kids," he says affectionately.

"Uhh, I don't think that's it." I peer up at him, admiring his jawline until he looks down at me.

"Then what?" He searches my face, and I'm not sure what he sees there, but his lips twitch with a hint of a smile. "You think they're a thing, don't you. They are *not* a thing."

"I didn't say anything!" I protest, even though yes, that is exactly what I was thinking, and still am. "But, I mean, you see that they're, uh, really close, right?"

"Yeah, they've been best friends since, like, third grade, and now they work together. Of course they're close."

I cough delicately. "That is not the kind of close I mean, Adam."

Adam loosens his grip on my waist, and his eyebrows shoot

all the way up. "I'm aware, but you're still being ridiculous. They would crack up if they heard you."

"You wanna test that theory?"

Now he's starting to look irritated. "Dude, I would know if my brother were gay."

"*Dude*, I'm not saying your brother is gay; I'm saying I think he's head-over-ass in love with exactly one guy, and it's mutual." He starts to speak, but I hold up a hand. "And yes, you obviously know your brother better than I do, but I know the rainbow better than you do. I'm just throwing it out there so you're not caught off guard when I turn out to be totally right."

"Noted," he says with a roll of those dark eyes that makes my stomach twinge.

I'm keeping my voice casual, but the truth is, Adam and I haven't really talked about my being bi since we actually started dating. I'm genuinely curious how he'd feel about Evan, but I'd be lying if I said it wasn't also a selfish question.

"Would you be cool with it? If I turn out to be right?"

He snorts. "Evan is the only reason I'm not living in a ditch somewhere. He could literally start eating steak from a live cow right in front of me and I'd still be in his corner."

"Well, that's . . . graphic."

"You know what I mean. I just don't think you know my brother better than I do. That said . . ." He leans forward to touch his forehead to mine. "I'm not an asshole, and Mateo's practically my family, too. Of course I want them to be happy. Like I'm happy with you."

Welp, he definitely passed that test. I close the barely-a-gap between us and press my lips to his, thrilling in his goodness and the calluses on the hands that cup my cheeks and the way his grip is always the tiniest bit stronger than it needs to be, like he's intent on making sure I don't slip through his fingers.

It's so easy to melt into him, to get lost in the firm safety of his lean muscle and soft hair that's the perfect length for running my fingers through. To feel him shift beneath me to hide just how into our make-out he's getting, then give up and pull me even closer, until I want to drag him inside and kick everyone out so I can have my way with him on the couch.

My brain is so addled with hormones that when the door flies open, I somehow think it was the sheer will of my desire to lay him out on the sofa bed that did it. It takes a solid few interminable seconds for both of us to realize that Evan's come out onto the terrace and now looks as wildly mortified as I feel.

"God, sorry," he says, his face flaming as he covers his eyes. "I just wanted to talk to my brother and figured this would be safe since, you know, you're out in public and everything."

"We just, um, got a little carried away," I manage, starting to climb out of Adam's lap only for him to quickly pull me back. Oh, right. "I'll go," I add quickly. "Just, uh, need a minute."

The embarrassment on Evan's face is replaced by a knowing grin, and not for the first time since seeing the Rose brothers interact, I feel like maybe I got the better end of the deal being an only child. "I'll bet." Then his face goes back to serious, which is so out of character for Evan that it's truly unsettling. "You may as well stay, since Adam's just gonna tell you after anyway."

Adam gives a "yeah, probably" shrug, and I settle in, wishing I was wearing a Pride tee or something so he'd know without a doubt I'm a safe person to come out to. I mean, *if* that's what this is. Who knows. (I know, of course, but for Adam's sake, I'll pretend to be surprised.)

"Are you kicking me out?" he asks before Evan can utter a word, and I immediately want to kick myself for failing to even think of that possibility. He's keeping his voice carefully neutral, but he's gotta be terrified at the answer to that question. Hell, *I'm* terrified at the answer to that question, because if it's yes, the only solution I can think to offer is begging Melissa to invite him to stay with us until he has enough saved up to get his own place. The alternative—tracking down his parents and returning to the lifestyle he hates, putting hundreds of miles between us in the process—is just too awful to think about, if it's even an option.

"Ad, no, of course not." But despite the strength of the words, there's a little falter in Evan's voice. He glances at me. "You know what, actually, Nat, can I have a minute with my brother?"

"Yeah, of course." I start to head back inside, but Adam puts a hand on my arm.

"If this is about you and Mateo, she already knows."

Evan furrows his thick brows. "You do?"

"I mean, I guessed—like knows like," I say, just barely reining in my smugness for a smile at Adam. "I've been out as bi since I was thirteen. I think you guys are really cute together."

"You . . ." Evan bursts out laughing. "No, that is not—Mateo and I are not a couple. I'm not—" He takes a breath, gives one more amused huff, and turns back to Adam. "We have an opportunity to open Bros over Tacos as a taqueria in New York.

Like an actual shop—no more dealing with gas guzzling or parking or maintenance or fifty fucking different permits. Mateo's uncle wants to be a partner, and if it does well, we may be able to do a whole chain. We've been talking about it for a while, making plans, scouting locations and apartments, and now that the lease is coming up on both the truck and this place at the end of August, it's time to make the jump. And we'd love for you to come with us. But you're eighteen, and it's your call; Petey says you can stay with him if you help out on his truck."

It's a lot, and I immediately feel Adam's body stiffen and grow cold at the pronouncement. I slide my hand into his and squeeze, but he doesn't squeeze back. He's not speaking, not moving, and certainly not responding to Evan, and even though Evan has the right to do whatever he wants with his life, in this moment I hate him for uprooting Adam's just when he's finally feeling settled.

And then his actual words sink in. He isn't just moving; he's moving to *New York*. Where I live. Where Adam could live if he wants to. Where we could keep dating, see where this goes, have him finally meet my friends in person rather than through happening to be present for the occasional FaceTime.

So why isn't he responding? Why isn't he squeezing back? What does it mean that this isn't the world's easiest call?

I want not to read into it—it's obviously a big change no matter what—but . . . how can I not?

Finally, Adam smiles weakly and says, "Can I think about it?"

"Of course, man. And listen, if it doesn't work out, I may be back here in a year, dragging my ass to that shitty rental lot and begging. But I wanna give this a shot, and I hope you understand that."

"I do."

They exchange a little fist bump, and I have to look away. No matter what happens here, they'll still have each other.

But what about me?

Chapter Fifteen,

in Which Tal Takes the Next Step

C ome on. You *must* see it."

"Oh, I *must*, must I?" I tweak a strand of Elly's slightly sweaty hair, brushing it against the milky white shoulder bared by her tank top. "I really haven't given much thought as to the shape of my birthmark, let alone exactly which type of drum it's shaped like. You really do always have music on the brain, don't you?"

"Not always," she says with a smile against my lips as she brings her mouth to mine, and we tumble back onto her sheets, where we've been making out for the last two hours to a soundtrack of the Pretty Reckless, Hole, Billie Eilish, and Garbage. I've learned that no one gets Elly in the mood like Shirley Manson, that underneath the long black sleeves lies the world's softest and palest skin, and that the birthmark on my rib cage is apparently shaped exactly like a bass drum. "I promise you I'm very, very focused on something else right now."

"Is that so?" I tease. "Is it this guitar solo?"

"It is not."

"Is it that guy who came into the coffee shop this morning with a bird on his shoulder?"

"Well, *now* it is." I sweep her hair aside to kiss her shoulder, her neck, the little shiver spot behind her ear, and then she whispers, "Squawk."

I absolutely lose it, falling onto my back next to her and laughing into the pillows.

It's our first time at her apartment since the day our date got rained out a couple of weeks ago, and while the plan to meet up here when we were each done with work for the morning was a perfectly innocent way to escape the heat when it was first hatched, we landed back in her bedroom with a serious quickness.

Not that I'm complaining.

"You are such a weirdo, Eleanor."

"I've been trying to tell you." She finds the bass drum birthmark—not exactly difficult, since my shirt hit the floor at least an hour ago—and taps it with her fingertips. "You should run."

I roll over until I'm straddling her hips, soaking in all her gorgeous glory. She is, as always, wearing mascara and eyeliner, but it's faded as we've worked up a bit of a sweat, and her red lipstick is gone. Her hair is splayed out against the pillows, her cheeks flushed pink, and a million things run through my mind, though they're all on the same track.

If it's true that I was her real queer awakening, I might very well be the first girl she's ever been with like this. I don't know what she's comfortable with, and I supremely do not wanna fuck this up. It's not like we've been together for that long. Then again, with how long we've been dancing around this whole mutual-attraction thing, it also kinda feels like forever.

"Should I now?"

While I tossed off my shirt a while ago, she's still wearing a white tank top and a little black bralette I can easily see through it. I'd like to see it up even closer, but I am definitely treading carefully.

"You should. But please don't." Her gaze dips down to my bra, which is considerably more filled out—no bralettes for me, ever—and then lower. "You already feel too far away. Nice view, though."

It shouldn't have such an effect on me to hear those words; they're just flirting, and right in the middle of making out. Of course she's going to say complimentary things. But as a girl who isn't small, currently perched over a girl who is, it's good to get the reassurance sometimes. "You think?"

"I do think." She sits up and wraps her arms around my neck. "You're . . ." She closes her eyes and gives a little embarrassed laugh. "God. Please don't run away when I say this, but I kind of . . . understated my crush on you. Like, a lot. I still can't even process that you're here in my bed, let alone in only a bra and shorts. I have literally dreamed this."

Now it's my turn to laugh, and she shrinks away for two seconds before I scoop her back up. "Elly. My friends fucking call you the Redhead because I spent years talking about you nonstop before I learned your actual name. You are . . ." I wave a hand in the air, unable to put words to it. "I don't even know. It feels impossible sometimes. Like I would've given any single thing to listen to Strings Out of Harlem in the subway with you. And any single thing to go to a concert with you. And any single thing to see a movie with you. And don't even get me started on what I would've given or done to make out with you. And then, I just . . . get you? I get to do all those things *and* keep both my kidneys?"

"That's good, isn't it?"

"So good," I murmur, going in for another kiss. I mean it to be quick, but she pulls me down onto the bed and I can't move away, can't do anything but kiss, taste, touch. I slide my hands down her sides and when they reach the hem of her tank top I slide my fingertips inside, no hesitation this time.

At least not until she pulls away, breathing heavily as she breaks me out of my horny haze. "Sorry," she pants. "I just—"

"Don't apologize," I say quickly, holding up my hands. "Off limits. Got it. You really do not need to explain."

"No, I do. And it's not off limits. Trust me," she says, biting her lip, "I am not looking to stop. It's just that you're gonna see, and you're gonna wanna know, and the answer is yes, I'm okay, and no, I don't do that anymore." She swallows, giving us time to catch our breath. Her fingers start twisting around each other as she meets my gaze full-on.

"I had a hard time with my parents traveling so much. Both of their jobs had them out of the house constantly, and it made everything really rocky for a long time. I took meds for a while, and they helped a lot, and then we all did family therapy and they started making an effort not to be gone at the same time, and things got better, and I stopped. I'm off the meds now, may need them again someday, who knows. So." She sweeps her arm grandly. "That's all of it. I'm sure you're feeling extremely horny now."

Oh. *Oh.* It takes me a few seconds to catch up, to realize exactly what she means, and it makes me want to wrap her up in a hug and just hold her for hours. But it's clear that isn't the response she wants, and I don't exactly need to be convinced to get back to what we were doing.

"I'm sure I can get back there," I say confidently, taking her hand and twining my fingers with hers, tan against pale, clover-green nails against chipped black. "Tell me again about the time you took care of yourself with me in mind?"

"Oh my God." She whacks me on the arm, but she's laughing, and in no time at all we're kissing again, and lying down again, and my fingertips are dancing up her tank top again, pushing the fabric up and over her head, skating over delicate scars as they go. Scars that prove she's a real person, and not this idealistic fantasy I dreamed up in my head, but better. Elly—Eleanor Stevie Knight, in fact—not the Redhead.

She's here and she's real and she's mine, at least a little bit.

"I've never let anyone see them, you know," she says breathlessly as I kiss her collarbone, her throat, the beauty mark situated just so. "It kinda feels good."

"If this only kinda feels good, I clearly need to work harder," I tease, running a thumb over and then under the band of her bralette.

"You are such a—"

I kiss away whatever lovely compliment she was about to bestow upon me, and then there's no more talking except for consents requested and given and directions along the lines of "Oh God, yes, *there*." Frankly, it sounds better than any music ever could, but when she screams out exactly in line with Courtney Love, I have to concede that maybe I've found a new favorite song.

* * *

"Hey, El! We're—*oh*." There's a slam of a door and then silence and then laughter that gets progressively farther away, and my brain swirls around for a solid fifteen seconds before I finally realize that Elly and I dozed off and her parents just walked in on us.

"Oh God." I bury my face in my hands. "Please tell me you have a fire escape right outside your window that I can let myself down so I do not ever have to face your parents."

Elly laughs, and I don't know how she can be laughing at the literal most humiliating thing that has ever happened to me in my entire life, but there she goes. "My parents have spent their entire lives with rock musicians. My mom has literally done a photoshoot of a post-Grammys orgy, not that you'll be able to find those pictures anywhere. I really don't think they're scandalized by seeing us under a blanket, sleeping."

"My bra is on the floor!"

"Foxy." She plants a kiss on my pout. "They truly do not give a fuck. But they will be very pissed if you don't come out and meet them, so get dressed."

"How are *you* being so cool about this?" I demand as I roll off the bed and yank said bra off the floor. "Your first time having sex and your parents caught you afterward?"

She raises an eyebrow as she pulls on her tank top. "I said it was my first time letting someone see me naked, not my first time having sex. I've had extremely mediocre sex with two whole boys, thank you very much. Don't swoon with jealousy or anything." I open my mouth to respond, but before I can, she walks over, places a finger over my lips, and says, "You're going to make a joke about feeling less special now. Do not make that joke. I am not letting you taint this."

I bite her finger instead. I have to do something to break up the five million pounds of feelings sitting on my shoulders. She grins, and then we're back to getting dressed, and soon it's the moment of truth.

Elly's parents are sitting at the kitchen table when we walk in, her dad with a mug of coffee in hand and her mom with a bottle of green tea. They both have full tattoo sleeves, but otherwise they look chill and decidedly more like older parents to a teenager than rock-star adjacent. "Perhaps we should reinstitute the knocking rule," Elly suggests pointedly, leaning against the stainless-steel fridge. "The one I wasn't aware had gone anywhere."

"Perhaps we should make a rule about closing the bedroom door when you have guests over," her mom says, equally pointed and with an emphasis on *guests*, but with a pleasant smile in my direction. "And what's your name, Elly's guest?"

I swallow down the apology threatening to climb out of my throat, which I have a feeling wouldn't be appreciated by anyone here. "Natalya. Fox. I'm, um, Elly and I have been hanging out a lot."

"I see that," her dad says sunnily, taking an elbow to the gut from his wife. "Well, Natalya, I'm Elly's dad, Max, and this is Elly's mom, Ava. But you can call us Mr. and Mrs. Knight."

"Dad."

"He's kidding," Ava says wryly. "Don't you dare. It's nice to meet you, sweetheart. Elly, go get your friend a drink."

"Oh, I'm—"

"Elly will get you a drink," Ava says firmly, pushing out one of the remaining two chairs from the kitchen table with her foot. "Sit."

Oh God. They're about to ask me my intentions toward their daughter, aren't they. Do they think I've taken her virtue and now they want me to marry her? I mean, not that I wouldn't marry her, not that I really want to think about marriage at this age . . . Okay, I'm spiraling. I take a seat, and immediately Max leans forward, tenting his fingers and resting his chin on his hands.

"Top three guitarists of all time. Go."

Oh. Oh no. These are much scarier questions. I look helplessly at Elly, whose eyes widen. She starts to mouth a response, but Ava cuts in sharply and tells her to mind her own business and get a drink.

Deep breath. Okay. I can do this.

Wait, I *can* do this. "Jimi Hendrix," I say immediately. You cannot go wrong with Hendrix. There are only two guitarists you can even potentially argue rival Hendrix, but luckily, they asked for three. "Eric Clapton. Jimmy Page. Not necessarily in that order."

"Not the most innovative list," says Max, "but acceptable. We would have also taken Chuck Berry, David Gilmour—"

"I would've taken not quizzing my 'guest' the moment you meet her," Elly says, putting a bottle of iced tea down in front of me, "but some of us just have to settle."

"I'm good with Natalya, now that everyone here knows my name. Or Tally. Tal. Nat. All good." I unscrew the iced tea and take a long drink, though I'm pretty sure my mouth will be dry for the rest of my life.

"And what are you into, Natalya? Besides our daughter, of course." Ava's voice is so dry, I would think she was being cold if not for a little smirk playing on her lips. It's clear she enjoys giving Elly shit, so at least there's something we have in common.

"Drawing, mostly, and reading. Elly's getting me more into music, but I don't think I'm quite up to Knight-family level yet. Speaking of which"—I gesture toward the gallery—"your paintings are amazing."

"A woman of taste," Ava says approvingly to Elly. "Good choice." She turns back to me. "Are you thinking about art school?"

I can't tell if this is another quiz, and I'm supposed to be more creative with my answer than the expected, or she's genuinely curious. "My parents agree on almost nothing except that neither one would pay for that in a million years" doesn't feel very original. "I'm still trying to figure things out" is what I say instead, which still feels like a failure. "I do love art, and I'd kill to make a living with it, but I don't think doing that as an artist is my future. For now, it's strictly a bunch of drawings on FanGallery."

"Can I see?"

Red alert—I am *definitely* going to fail this—but so it goes. There's a lot more work in my FanGallery account than there was when I showed it to Jasmine a couple of weeks ago. The package design I helped my mom with inspired a floral monogram series that's actually sold a few prints, including an entire set of six to the expectant mom of a girl to be named Kaavya. There's a candid drawing of Elly at a rock show we went to last week, her eyes closed against the music, glowing with sweat and glitter and joy. There are sketches of Central Park and the city skyline, a series of toddler hands at play that I did while babysitting, and of course, some more fan art, including a particularly bloody one from the horror novel I picked up on Elly's and my last bookstore trip.

It's definitely . . . varied.

"These are great," Ava murmurs, paging through. "Your perspective needs some work, and these shadows aren't quite right, but I do like your style. You really don't have any plans to pursue it?"

This time I hesitate before answering. I'm talking to a woman who's living the dream—she's actually made a serious career out of her art *and* managed to keep some of it to herself as a hobby. She makes *something* feel possible; I'm just not sure what my equivalent is yet. "I did help my mom—she's in marketing—with a package design project, and that was cool," I offer, because that's the closest I've come to doing something with my drawing skills professionally. "And I do commissions for authors and stuff sometimes. I just . . . haven't quite figured out how to put it all together in a way that meshes with the corporate world, and I don't think I want to strictly draw for a living even if I miraculously could; I feel like eventually, that'd just suck the fun out of it."

Ava rests her chin in her palm, narrowing her eyes like a bird sighting its prey. "I have a friend who's a brilliant graphic designer. You should sit down with her, have a chat." She taps her fingers on the table; her nails are simple and unpolished, a strong contrast from Elly's perpetual dark colors. "Yes, okay," she continues, as if I've said a single word or even nodded. "I'll send Ainsley a text now, then have Elly pass along her number."

"Um." Is it just me or is everything moving very quickly this afternoon? It's like time moves at a different speed at the Knights'. "I don't actually know what graphic designers *do*, or whether—"

"Yes, dear," says Ava, already typing on her phone with little chicken pecks. "That's why you have the chat."

"Okay." Elly loops her arm through mine and pulls me up. "We have plans, so we're just gonna . . . We'll see you later. *I'll* see you later," she clarifies. "Come on, Tal."

I barely get out a goodbye before she fully drags my ass out the door.

* * *

Elly apologizes the second the elevator doors close behind us. "God, I'm so sorry about that. You'd think my parents would be cool, given everything, but they're just as dorky and invasive as other parents."

"First of all, that means they care, so trust me, it's not the same as other parents." Until this summer and our tentative attempt to reconnect, my mom never would've known a thing about Elly's existence. Elly squeezes my hand, both comfort and concession, before I continue. "Second of all, they're great, and that was actually super helpful. Honestly, I've kinda been floundering with the whole college thing, and maybe it's stupid, but it never really occurred to me there was something I could do with art that wasn't, like, becoming an artist."

"That's not stupid," she insists as the elevator opens and lets us out in the light, airy lobby. "The fact that we're supposed to know what we wanna do at eighteen or risk wasting an absurdly expensive college education is stupid. And it's not like schools are great at telling us all the options. If I didn't wanna do something I already know plenty about because of my parents, I'd have no idea what I was doing either."

"But you do know," I point out. "You know you want to be a rock journalist, and Lydia knows she wants to go into publishing, and Camila knows she wants to be a nurse, and Leona knows she wants to go into fashion and start her own trans-friendly line of lingerie. I mean, she already makes ridiculous money as an influencer. What could I possibly influence people about?"

"Your boobs," Elly says without missing a beat. "I am deeply influenced by them."

"You are deeply influenced by perversion," I reply, but I'm absolutely staring at her lips when I do it, so I do not have tremendous amounts of credibility here. "Now where are we going?"

"Well, it's gorgeous out—wanna get takeout and bring it to the park?"

It's an excellent suggestion, so that's what we do, hitting up Taqueria UWS for nachos, guac, and vegan taquitos to bring to Sheep Meadow. With a quick pang, I miss Camila, who left with her family for Puerto Rico this morning, and Elly takes a picture of me with all the grassy green splendor behind me so I can send it to her.

"So you're really thinking about it?" she asks, dragging a chip through the guacamole before crunching it between her teeth. "A graphic design program?"

"I mean, maybe? I haven't even had time to look into it." I crunch into my own chip, wishing it was more satisfying. Taqueria UWS is never as good as I want it to be, and neither is any other taco place I've been in my neighborhood. I'd kill for a really excellent park-adjacent taco truck.

"Then let's do it." Elly pulls out her phone and immediately looks up the best graphic design programs in New York City.

"I don't *have* to stay in the city," I tell her, though I don't actually have any desire to go anywhere else. Elly will be at NYU, and Isaac's applying early there too. Camila's not sure where she's gonna go yet, but she's definitely planning to stay close to her family. Lydia and Leona plan to be at Columbia and FIT, respectively, and even if they weren't supremely qualified (which they are), Lord knows their dad has given enough money to both to secure their spots. Adira's hoping to go to Barnard, and of course, staying in Manhattan means never being *too* far from my dad. Or from stores open twenty-four hours, more kosher food options than just about anywhere in the country, and the subway, because while I *can* drive, I certainly do not like to. "I mean, I guess it makes sense to look here first."

"That's what I thought," she says smugly. "Okay, let's see."

We bend over her phone as the results load on the screen. Turns out, I really *don't* have to leave the city. "Wow," says Elly, echoing my thoughts exactly. "There are multiple programs that are right near NYU."

"Is that somewhere you'd like me to be?" I flutter my eyelashes prettily, or maybe maniacally. I'm never sure.

"Oh, shut up." She nudges my knee with hers and together we devour the taquitos while reading about School of Visual Arts, Parsons, Pratt, and more. "I would never even have thought of looking at FIT," I say, dipping back into the nachos. "How fun would that be? I could live with Leona. And Matrix, probably."

"You could." She wraps her arms around her knees and looks up at me. "You could live with her in FIT dorms, or you could go to SVA or Parsons and share an apartment, and I'd be right nearby at NYU, either living in a freshman dorm or getting a place with Nicki and Jasmine like we talked about . . . How great would that be?"

"Ridiculously great," I say, and I mean it. Now that the images are in my head, they won't stop, the scenarios playing out like a dream montage from a movie. It's almost too perfect to hope for, and the wildest thing is that there isn't even only one path to perfection. There's just . . . possibility. So much possibility. And for the first time in my life, when I imagine the future, I can see exactly what I'm doing in it.

And yeah, maybe I'm getting ahead of myself. But it's the first time that I want to, and right now, that—and Elly's fingers wrapping themselves in mine—is the best feeling in the world.

Chapter Sixteen,

in Which Nat Can Still Be Surprised

*T*he problem with dating the guy you share a desk with is that when he needs some space from you, you get to be acutely aware of that for every agonizing minute of every day. "It's not you," Adam assures me when I finally call him on his weirdness two days after Evan broke the news about New York. "Or I guess it is you, kind of." Despite us sharing a bench a block from the office, he feels about a million miles away when he says it, especially because he can't make eye contact. "It's just a lot of shit to figure out."

"Okay." It is. I know it is. I just thought maybe he'd come to me to help him talk things through or whatever rather than icing me out. I don't have a ton of relationship experience, but it feels like after a month, we should probably be able to chat about major life decisions. But maybe I've been taking this more seriously than he has. Maybe to him, I'm just a girl to fool around with and practice cooking on. He wouldn't be the first guy to tell me I've got great boobs but he doesn't see this going anywhere. "I guess I'll let you figure that out, then."

I get up from the bench without a real destination in mind—I don't want to go back to work after leaving for the day just to have somewhere to be, but I also don't really feel like being alone with my thoughts. What I really need is to hear Camila's voice, calming me down and reminding me that it doesn't matter if my summer romance falls apart, because LA and the people in it aren't my real life; New York is.

It's what I thought when I came. But it doesn't feel quite so true anymore.

Regardless, I have to move in some direction away from this bench, so I start on the path toward Mocha Rouge, but I only get a few feet before a warm, strong hand encircles my wrist. "Nat."

"What." I keep my voice frosty even though his skin against mine makes me feel anything but.

"Can you look at me, please?"

So I turn, and I do, and fuck, he looks *exhausted*. I mean, he looks a million things, and one of them is sexily disheveled, but it's clear this has been plaguing him and I'm not doing anything to help. Instinctively, I reach up and brush a bit of hair out of his eyes, and he relaxes into a soft smile I haven't seen in far too long.

"It's not that I don't care what you think," he says, his voice coated in gravel, grip on my wrist loosening but not disappearing. "It's that I care too much. I can't make a decision this huge based on the fact that you'll be in New York and I'd be in New York and *fuck* that sounds so good that every time I think about it, I forget all the reasons that moving's a terrible idea. And I can't forget all the reasons. I need to get this right. I literally can't afford not to."

Okay, that's definitely a step up from icing me out. "What if I promise to be objective if you talk it out with me?"

"Do you *feel* objective about it?"

"Hell no, but you clearly need someone to talk to about it." I straighten up and flip my hair over my shoulder. "Try me. What are these reasons that make moving terrible?"

"Well, let's see. I have no job lined up, I'd have to mooch off my brother for housing *again*, and rent out there is astronomical—at best we'd be sharing a studio, which has extreme nightmare potential. At least here I know people, and my nights would be free to get another job. I could couch surf while I save up enough money to get my own place . . ." He trails off into an exhale, and I see now why he's so exhausted.

"Both options sound really hard," I acknowledge softly.

"Yeah, well. Some of us don't have a rich parent on each coast. Or maybe I do—it's not like I know where they are."

Ouch.

"I'm sorry." He scrubs his hands over his face. "Fuck, I'm sorry. I don't mean to take things out on you. Both options *are* really hard, and I don't know how to choose, and it's turning me into an asshole."

All of a sudden, I'm back on the blanket in Central Park with Camila, combing through pros and cons and goals as I choose between New York City and Los Angeles. It's like the fun house mirror version of the same choice I had to make at the beginning of the summer. Now I'm a few weeks from returning to my old life and city and falling way too deeply in like with someone who makes me feel completely unready to do that.

Unless he joins me there, of course.

But I can't think about that when I promised to be unbiased.

But, at the very least, I'm in the "pro" column when it comes to moving to New York.

Aren't I?

"Why don't you come over, we'll get some Chinese food, and we can talk about it for real?" I suggest, silently pleading with him to take me up on it. I hate feeling this needy, but if he's going to make this decision without my input, I want to at least be able to stare at him so I can pointlessly try to decipher which way he's leaning from the set of his jaw or how frequently he fiddles with the cuff of his shirt.

He sighs deeply, and I know immediately there's no lo mein in my future tonight. "I can't." He frowns as he tucks my hair behind my ear, as if it's totally out of his hands, and I feel a flash of irritation and a sudden determination to eat a dozen egg rolls by myself. "I really do have to do this on my own."

"Well, if on your own is how you like it, then I'm sure you'll enjoy both your night and your weekend," I snap, dodging out of his reach. I feel it immediately, not only the loss of his touch, but the knowledge I've just disinvited him from Shabbat dinner, which has become an almost-permanent fixture in our home and my favorite part of the week. But maybe it's just good practice, considering I'll clearly have to get used to doing it without him.

Dammit, I'm really gonna need Adira to teach me how to cook.

"Nat."

"I'll see you at work tomorrow," I spit back without so much as a glance over my shoulder. After all, keeping our eyes on the future is the move of the day, and I'm not going to get stuck looking back at someone who doesn't see me in his.

❋ ❋ ❋

There must be something in the air, because when I find myself a much better date that night in Camila (over FaceTime from San Juan), she tells me that she and Emilio got into a fight, too.

They *never* fight.

"Suddenly, he's nervous about the distance," she tells me, her voice sharp and cutting in a way that doesn't remotely resemble the Camila I know. "We've been together basically our entire lives, we've known all year that we have different plans for after graduation, and suddenly this measly month in PR is making him panic about the distance, even though I come here every summer? Like, what the—" She cuts herself off, and I wonder if her abuela is in the room for this call. "Anyway, it's ridiculous, and we're not talking, and I just need to do something fun tonight, but I'm the only one home with Abuela, so, watch a movie with me?"

"Gimme five minutes to round up snacks."

I'm weirdly excited for a night of hanging out with Camila that's not even in person, but between future stress and this crap with Adam, it's exactly what the doctor ordered. I'm already in my comfiest shorts and a tank top, so I throw a bag of popcorn in the microwave, make my patented snack mix, rummage in the fridge for one of my mom's Diet Cokes, and am back with full arms on the den couch with a minute to spare.

"I narrowed down some options," she declares, crunching on what I know are probably ranch-flavored corn nuts. "Spoiler: three of them star Liam Holloway."

"I'm shocked," I deadpan, though I'm not complaining. We settle on a rom-com about an engaged couple who comes to realize they hate each other, but stay together because neither one wants to lose their group of friends by jilting the other. Of course, they're back in love by the end, but it's still satisfying to see them snipe at each other. In the moods we're in right now, Camila and I take a lot of joy in cheering on the female lead, even as she's going head-to-head with Camila's number one celebrity crush.

"Isn't it amazing how they just forget all that bad blood?" Camila asks, a hint of a yawn creeping into her voice. I was so distracted by the movie, I managed to forget the time difference, but it's well past midnight there. "Like, they were completely awful to each other, and one 'actually, I love you,' and everything is cool again. If only life actually worked like that."

"Oh, come on, there's no way you and Emilio were awful to each other." With parents like mine, believing in love does not come easily, but if anyone in my life could make me do it, it's Camelio. Emilio's the kind of guy who attacks his own hair with scissors to make her feel better when she's crying over a bad haircut, and she's the kind of girl who's so naturally nurturing that she carries around throat drops and tissues when he gets hit by allergy season. They could be their own rom-com, except they've never had enough drama.

Until now, I guess.

"Well, no, not awful, but it wasn't exactly a gentle disagreement, either." She sighs heavily, falling back against her pillows. "Is it so impossible to believe that things can work? Even through distance and having other lives and—" The connection goes out for a second, and on the screen, even in the dimness of her only partially lit room, I can see her face light up. "He's calling. I gotta run, okay? I'll call you tomorrow."

I blow a kiss and let her go, her words still swimming in my brain. *Is* it so impossible to believe Adam and I can be something even if he chooses to stay while I have to go? How much does his choice matter if we want things to work no matter what?

Picking up my phone, I think to follow Emilio's lead and make things right, regardless of the time. Obviously, their fight was keeping him up the same way it was plaguing Camila, and the way I'm admittedly hoping our argument is still taking up space in Adam's brain, too. But just as I'm about to press the button to call him, I think about how the one thing he asked from me was space.

He didn't want to talk this out. He isn't going to answer the phone with his eyes all lit up like Cam did. If he even picks up, he'll be annoyed that I'm trying to butt in where he just needs a clear head. And I can give him that. I should give him that. I *will* give him that, especially if I ever want to play footsie under the desk again, or get another taste of his absolutely perfect mac 'n' cheese or feel his strong, slightly callused hands rub sunscreen on my back on the beach or openly marvel at his dorky, joyful smile when he does a perfect toss of a pan of peppers and onions.

With a heavy sigh, I put my phone away, pick up the remote, and find another cheesy movie to fill the space in my head I can't give to Adam Rose.

❊ ❊ ❊

I wake up dizzy and disoriented, and it takes me a minute to realize two things:

1. I fell asleep on the couch.
2. I woke up to the sound of someone sneaking into the house.

My heartbeat's pace picks up and I yank the blanket around myself like it'll offer any kind of shield, but my gasp dies in my throat when I see that the culprit is none other than Melissa, doing her best to move quietly in a pair of sky-high heels. "Mom, what the fuck?"

Now it's her turn to jump in a panic, and her hand flies to her chest. "I could say the same thing to you, missy. Though I would use more appropriate language," she adds pointedly. "What are you doing out here?"

I point the remote, still clutched in my hand, toward the TV, which has long since shut itself off from disuse. Smart TV indeed. "I was watching a movie with Camila, and then she had to go and I watched another one . . . and I guess I fell asleep." A huge yawn illustrates my point. "And you? Why are you sneaking in at"—I peer at the cable box, but there's no clock, so I check my phone instead—"one thirty in the morning?"

"Would you believe a work thing?"

"Dressed like that?" My eyebrows shoot up into my hairline. In addition to the heels, the dress she's wearing is tighter than anything I could ever pull off and has a seriously daring slit on the side, which is an excellent choice since even I can recognize my mom has the kind of legs that stop people in the street. (I did not inherit them, of course, or anything else other than her original hair color.) Plus, my mom is a firm believer in professional jewelry for work—subtle pearl, diamond, or gold studs in the ears at all times, maximum of one ring and one necklace *or* bracelet—and the gorgeous sapphire earrings dangling from her lobes are definitely not that. "No."

She sighs and tucks her wrap away in the coat closet, puts her purse away on the small table by the door. "Okay. So. I was hoping to avoid this."

"Telling me that you're dating someone?" I ask, fumbling around for the remains of my snack mix. "Why?" My mind dawns with understanding. "Ohh, are you not dating? Was this a booty call? You're awfully fancy for a hookup."

"Natalya!" Melissa tries to look mad, but she ends up cracking up instead, cradling her head in her hands. "God, even though you're right here, I still forget how old you are some-times. And no, it was not a 'booty call,' and yes, I am dating someone. I just didn't know how you'd take it."

"Uh, I hate to break it to you, Mom, but I have no delusions of you and dad getting back together. I'd say that ship sailed a long time ago, but I don't think any of us were ever actually on board."

"Your only reaction to the news of the divorce was to ask for ice cream," she concedes. "And then a week later, you asked if you would get two Chanukahs, because Dylan told you about a friend of hers who got two Christmases when her parents got divorced."

"I stand by feeling shafted that it meant splitting one Cha-nukah rather than getting two."

"It's an eight-day holiday, honey."

"I said what I said." I shift into the corner of the couch and motion for her to sit down. "So, tell me about the guy. Or is it a guy? How much have I missed?"

She laughs. "Yes, it's a guy. His name is Daniel Bloom and he's a doctor."

"Plastic surgeon?"

"Pediatric oncologist."

"*Wow.*"

"I know." She reaches for the bowl of snack mix dregs, and I hand it over, wondering if I've ever actually seen my mother eat chocolate before. I'm pretty sure I haven't. "And you'd think he'd be stressed and sad all the time, but he's like a bundle of sunshine. I don't know how, or why that doesn't make me want to kill him, but he's a good guy."

"How long have you been dating?"

"Not long. We started up a couple of weeks before you got here, which is the other reason I kept my mouth shut. I had no idea if it would go anywhere." She frowns at the candy in her hand. "I still don't, I suppose. But I hope it does."

"Well, that's not nothing." I get up to grab my M&M's stash from the kitchen, not bothering with the rest of the mix, and empty it into the bowl. "And that's a couple of months already. That's significant. Isn't it?"

She smiles knowingly. "Sometimes yes, sometimes no. I think every day feels more significant when you're young, especially when you see each other all the time. Does Adam feel significant? You two look like you feel significant. Having a guy cook for you—and spend Friday nights with you and your mother, who happens to be his boss—is definitely significant."

"Funny you should ask," I mutter, looking down at the chenille blanket in my hands and picking at a loose thread. "I guess I felt like it was. Unclear how he feels. Turns out his brother wants to move to New York with his best-friend-slash-business-partner, and Adam's not sure he wants to go with them."

"And you want him to?"

I look up to meet surprised eyes. "Of course I want him to. Why wouldn't I?"

"Well, not everyone plans for summer romances to continue beyond that, especially when they happen while away. You might feel like he doesn't fit into the world you have back home, or that you don't want a boyfriend for senior year, or a million other things."

"Well, he's already FaceTimed with Camila repeatedly, likes

all the same favorite movies as Isaac, leaves perfect comments on Leona's videos, has heard of almost all of Lydia's favorite authors, and can make Shabbat dinner at least as well as Adira, so I'm not worried about my friends liking him. And Camila manages to have a boyfriend and still have a life, and Leona has like thirty people drooling over her at any given moment, so I feel like there's, you know, room in there to add someone new. Anyway, he'll be working, or in culinary school, or whatever, so it's not like he's gonna have tons of time for me either. I just . . . want him there. Even when I'm not seeing him every day anymore. It's not just that he makes things better; it's that he makes them *good*."

Okay, that might've been a little much, because my mom is giving me that "you are *smitten*" face, and to my horror, I think I might be. I sound like a girl with a massive crush, but . . . well, that's what I am. For as many things as my mother doesn't know about me, that's one I clearly can't hide.

I can't handle the way she's looking at me, and I'm about to tear this blanket to shreds, so it's time to make my exit. "Anyway, he'll choose whatever he chooses, I guess. And I should probably go to bed." I fold up the blanket and clean up the snacks, eager to prove I won't leave a mess of any kind behind. "G'night, Mom. I'm glad you told me about Daniel."

"G'night, Nat. I'm glad I did too."

❋ ❋ ❋

It takes me way too long to fall asleep that night, alternately obsessing over what it would mean for Adam to move and then what it means that I'm way too preoccupied with whether he will. I wake up in the morning annoyed and reminding myself that my life does not hang on some guy's decision, even if I really, really like that guy.

So, today's about me, I decide. I put on my favorite dress—cobalt blue, makes my eyes look amazing—and espadrilles and sit down to an early breakfast with my mom where I am determined to focus on myself and my future. "I have an idea," I tell her as she hands me cup of coffee, both of us surprisingly alert for 6:30 A.M. "Or, I guess it's a thought? I don't know." *Shut up about the semantics and get to it, Natalya.* "I've been thinking about graphic design. As a major, I mean."

My mom cups her pearl pink-tipped nails around her mug, soaking up the warmth. "Just to make sure, you know graphic designers don't generally draw the illustrations themselves, right?"

"They hire illustrators, I know." Lord knows I've spent long enough looking it up. "But I think that's good for me—letting the thing I love to do the most stay a hobby. And I think I'd work *with* the art really well. A lot of the marketing-centric stuff—the data and everything—feels a little too far from what I want to do, but graphic design could be the perfect balance."

"Well, I think that's a great idea, and I certainly agree you have an eye for it. Did you have a specific program in mind?"

My own nails, aquamarine and chipped, tap against the quartz countertop. "I thought maybe we could look at some together. Narrow down some solid options. You definitely have a way better idea of which programs are good than I do."

"I'd love to," she says. "We'll make a date of it. And I'll talk to some of the graphic designers I work with. I'm sure they'd be happy to do informational interviews with you."

"If you ask them to, do they have the option to say no?"

"Not really," she admits before taking a sip of her coffee, "but I'm sure they'll be happy to anyway."

"Speaking of things people would be happy to do—when do I get to meet this Daniel character? Don't I have to make some obnoxious scene where I demand his intentions?"

"Depends," Melissa says calmly. "Do you want me to make a similar scene with Adam?"

"Touché." I add a little more sugar to my coffee, then take a sweet, warming drink. "I really do wanna meet him, though. Why don't you bring him to Shabbat dinner?" Only as the suggestion comes out of my mouth do I realize. "Oh crap, I've been making you ditch him every Friday night without even realizing it. Okay, now you *definitely* have to bring him."

She laughs. "I'm sure he'd love to come. I'm not sure when he last had a home-cooked meal, and dating me has not helped with that."

"Cool." Now I just have to either make up with Adam, re-invite him, and convince him to both cook for an extra person and sit through a double date with my mom, or learn how to cook myself ASAP. But I'll deal with that later. Right now—I catch a glimpse of the time on the microwave—we are running late for work.

Chapter Seventeen,

in Which Tal Saw Elly at Sinai, Sort Of

*T*hat's it?" I look down at the sheet pan covered in chicken and Brussels sprouts, a honey-mustard glaze poured over it, and back up at Adira. "That's all it takes to make roast chicken?"

"That's it," she confirms as we put it in the oven. "This is one way my mom makes it, or sometimes she does it with sliced potatoes, sweet potatoes, and onions, and then a few spices—no glaze. But she likes this one and I haven't made it in a while, so I figured I'd mix it up. Either way, chicken legs plus some vegetables plus some seasoning on a sheet pan and you have like half a Shabbat dinner already done."

"Amazing," I marvel.

"Obviously, there are plenty of other ways to make chicken,

but this is the easiest way to do it and get some vegetables in. Your dad will appreciate it, I think."

"He would." And hopefully he'll appreciate my surprise this week of making Shabbat dinner for us and the Reisses. I decided it was finally time I stop talking about asking Adira to teach me and just straight-up ask. We spent last night after work going shopping at the Kosher Emporium, and now it's Thursday night and time to do the actual cooking.

"It's cool that you wanna learn. None of my friends wanna do this a minute before they have to, but with my mom working all the time, it'd be takeout every week if I didn't, so I thought it was worth a shot. Turns out I love it."

"Huh." I pick up a peeler so we can move on to the next recipe—potato kugel—and get started. "I kind of assumed that was like an Orthodox *thing*—that you all know how to cook Shabbat dinner or whatever."

She laughs. "No, definitely not. I don't think a single one of my friends from school could make gefilte fish if they had to."

"Isn't gefilte fish like the hardest thing? Don't you have to grind stuff and deal with bones?" I shudder at the thought.

"Do you think we're in 'the old country'?" she asks with an even louder laugh than before. "You know how I make gefilte fish? I buy a frozen loaf, take off the paper, put it in a loaf pan, cover it with salsa, and bake it for two hours. Comes out perfect and way easier than boiling it with carrots and onion and whatever. Besides, I've never really liked horseradish."

"I am *fascinated*. I've only had the jar kind, like at random events at temple."

"The jar kind is an abomination unto the Lord," Adira informs me, peeling potatoes at twice the speed I am. "We can make one, if you wanna try. It's really eaten at lunch on Saturday, not Friday night, but—"

The ringing of my phone cuts her off, and I glance over to see Elly—tongue hanging out and hands in devil horns—lighting up the screen. It was meant to be a joke, but when Adira looks at the picture on my ringing phone, I can't help wondering what she thinks. "Who's Elly?" she asks.

I bite my lip, buying a second before I reply. Adira knows I'm bi—I very awkwardly slipped it into a conversation one time, not quite knowing how to tell her—but we never talk about it, and I certainly don't mention hooking up with or dating girls to her. She's cool, obviously, and in my experience young Modern Orthodox Jews are absolutely chill with queer people, but I worry sometimes that she's cool with it more conceptually than practically.

Or maybe I'm just fixated on a couple of ugly stories I've heard at the LGBTJew Youth Center I attend on occasion.

But then I remember how much more good there's been than bad, how many parents specifically brought their kids to the center for events, and how positively joyful and spiritual my cousin's gay and very Jewish wedding was. And I bite the bullet. "My girlfriend. Well, I think I can call her my girlfriend? I feel like it's been long enough that I can call her my girlfriend."

"Now I'm dying to know how she'd answer that question," Adira says with a grin, picking up another potato, and my shoulders relax. "Maybe you should invite her to dinner tomorrow."

"Oh, yeah, ha ha."

"I'm serious! I'd like to meet her, and you know my mom's always happy to have more guests. Has she met your dad yet?" I shake my head. "Well, what better time? Go pick up the phone and invite her before you miss her call entirely."

I cannot in a million years picture punk-ass Elly, with her ears full of piercings and random ink perpetually drawn on her skin in preparation for when she turns eighteen and can get the real thing, sitting down at a Shabbat table with my dad, Adira, and Dr. Reiss. But the very mental picture of it *does* make me smile. I may as well invite her. It's not like she's gonna say yes. She probably has a show to go to anyway. It's a freaking Friday night. She'll wanna do something cool, not chat about the high and low points of our respective weeks over slices of challah and bowls of chicken soup.

Stepping out of the kitchen, I answer the phone with a "Hey, you," and receive a "Hey, yourself" in response. "Where are you?"

"I'm at Adira's—my friend who lives across the hall from me. She's teaching me how to make Shabbat dinner."

"That's your friend who watches *Real Housewives of Bumblefuck* with you so I don't have to, right? She's my favorite."

"Ha ha."

"Anyway, I guess that's more important than meeting me for cupcakes, especially since it was going to be quick—I'm way behind on a deadline. How's the lesson going?"

"Good! The chicken soup is on the stove and I wish you could smell it because it is literally divine. Chicken with Brussels sprouts is in the oven, we're making potato kugel now, and next up is something called deli roll that apparently involves nothing but cold cuts, mustard, and puff pastry. Adira assures me she's teaching me the full Upper West Side Ashkenazi experience."

"Yum. You two are doing God's work."

"Was that a pun?"

"Kind of? Is that unholy?"

"Do I seem like someone who gets to make that determination?"

I don't know why I'm nervous to extend this invitation, but oh, wait, yes, I do. It means Elly meeting my dad. It means Elly coming into this part of my world she hasn't touched yet. She knows there are things I won't eat and that meeting her at shows on Friday nights has to wait until after dinner with my dad—which has resulted in us doing some of these dinners before sundown, since he doesn't want me heading out for the night after dark—but things like sitting through kiddush and hand-washing, hearing the Hebrew and seeing all the rituals . . . It makes me feel weird. Or rather, it makes me worry she'll think *I'm* weird. Maybe *too* weird. And suddenly I understand why each of my parents was super intent on marrying another Jew.

"Did you invite her yet?" Adira calls from the kitchen, so loudly that Elly asks what she said, and I just laugh helplessly, because what else can I do now?

"She wants me to invite you to Shabbat dinner. She was yelling at me for not having done it yet. But you really do not have to come. I know you've probably got a show to go to or—"

"Tally." I shut up immediately. She never calls me Tally. "Do *you* want to invite me to Shabbat dinner?"

"I mean, I always like to see you, obviously. I just don't want—"

"Tal."

"Yes."

"Okay." I can hear the smile in her voice, slow and creeping but definitely present. "I'll be there."

I stare at my phone in disbelief for a full minute after we hang up.

❋ ❋ ❋

"It was a chicken bone! Who does that with a chicken bone?"

The rest of us crack up laughing, Dr. Reiss's face still the picture of absolute bewilderment, even though she's sharing a story from her residency twenty years ago. I've never heard her be even the slightest bit graphic—she's always so proper—but both she and my dad, who thinks bathroom humor "is for the absolute dregs of society"—are absolutely roaring.

Elly's cracking up too. So far, it's been scarily good. She showed up right on time, bearing a bottle of kosher wine and wearing a shockingly appropriate outfit of a clingy black crushed velvet dress with lace-edged bell sleeves and platform black patent leather Mary Janes, which looks so insanely good, I choked on my gum when she walked in. Her makeup is toned down but still looks like her—rimmed eyeliner a little thinner than she'd otherwise wear it but still present and accompanied by a bright-red lip. I wouldn't say she blends in, exactly, but she looks like she made an effort, and that's gotta be the hottest thing of all.

No, wait, it's still her mouth. But the effort is at least top three, along with her legs in those shoes.

My dad isn't the most conversational of men; no one chooses to spend all that time with numbers if they're all that fond of people. But he was very impressed when I told him I was bringing a date, and he's only quizzed her with math problems twice. Turns out, on top of everything else, my girlfriend (yes, I did confirm I could introduce her that way at dinner, and yes, she laughed her ass off before she said yes) is pretty damn good at math. So, between that and the fact that she's been willing to at least try everything on the table (except for the London broil, since she doesn't eat red meat), my dad is pleased.

"I can't believe you helped cook all this," Elly says quietly as Dr. Reiss launches into another story, squeezing my knee under the table. "I'm so impressed."

"She did great," Adira agrees, the concept of a private moment totally lost on her, which is pretty par for the course. "She basically did the entire kugel by herself, minus some potato peeling."

"And minus when you had to rescue me from forgetting to put that thing in the food processor."

She grins. "I was trying to make you look good." Then she turns to Elly. "Do you cook?"

"Literally not one thing," Elly admits. "We're a very deeply takeout family. But my dad would love this. He actually converted to Judaism in the nineties after a few months on tour with Lenny Kravitz." She fumbles in her bag for a few seconds while I process this wild and completely new-to-me fact and pulls out her phone, then searches for something on it while I try not to cringe. Dr. Reiss and Adira are strictly Shomer Shabbos—they don't use phones for the entire twenty-five hours (unless it's a work call emergency for Dr. Reiss, but that's strictly an exemption for doctors) or TVs or computers—and while my dad and I aren't, we never bring our phones to the Shabbat table.

Then, it manages to get worse. "See?" she says, showing the phone around the table so we can all see the picture of her dad, shirtless, sporting a Hebrew tattoo on his well-defined pec. There's a hint of confusion on her face when everyone just nods or says "cool" without touching the phone, and since we all *also* abide by the biblical commandment against getting tattoos, I'm feeling awkward-upon-awkward. "I forget what it says, but that's his Hebrew name."

Adira takes a closer look, still being careful not to touch, and I love her for it. "Akiva."

"Right, right." Thankfully, Elly puts the phone away. "He never really practiced, but he definitely still takes pride in it. Whenever he tells me a story about touring that he thinks is particularly awesome, he tells me to make sure I share that one at his shiva."

For whatever reason, my dad decides that's the funniest thing he's ever heard, and he laughs for a solid minute, stopping only to tell me he's sorry that the best I'll have when it's my turn to sit shiva for him is the time he accidentally submitted a paper to a math journal with his own name spelled wrong. It's definitely not unusual for us to joke about death—we're Jews—but I've never seen my dad laugh his butt off like this.

Elly's goofy grin at the sight just completes the best thing I have ever seen.

"In your defense," I say to my dad when his laughter finally dies down, "it's really hard to keep up with the coolness level of a guy who's toured with Lenny Kravitz. And interviewed Mick Jagger. And"—I know this one will impress my dad the most—"played with Bob Dylan."

"No." My dad's hand bangs down on the table, his eyes widening. I realize then that my dad has definitely consumed multiple glasses of wine, and it's pretty fantastic. A quick glance at the bottle on the table—the one Elly brought—shows that it's almost empty. This is new; there's never wine at the table when it's just the four of us. Maybe it should become a regular thing. "Your dad has played with the master?"

"You're a Dylan fan?" Elly immediately lights up, and I can't believe I didn't think to nudge the conversation into her wheelhouse earlier. She's been holding her own so well all night, I didn't have to. "What's your favorite album?"

"*Blood on the Tracks*," I answer at the exact same time he does, because I have heard that album played in our apartment at least once a week for my entire life. "I saw Dylan on tour in '88 and it changed my life," he adds, tipping his wineglass toward me. "When Tally's mother and I were talking names, I wanted to go with Johanna after 'Visions of Johanna,' but Melissa said she didn't want to name her after any songs because she didn't want them getting in her head all the time."

"Which is ironic from someone named Melissa," Elly says, picking up her glass to take a sip of water.

My dad stares at her in disbelief. "You know, somehow, I never once made that connection."

"You're joking. She's probably had people singing that song to her her entire life." Elly looks to me, but I had no idea there was even a song named "Melissa," which clearly shows on my face. "You don't know it? The Allman Brothers?" She sings a couple of lines.

"Wait, okay, I thought I knew it when you mentioned the Allman Brothers, but I thought it had no words."

My dad, Elly, and even Dr. Reiss look at me like I've lightly injured a small animal. "That's 'Jessica,'" they all say simultaneously, like a Greek "well, actually" chorus.

"Okay, well, I don't know this song either," Adira says, backing me up.

Out of the corner of my eye, I see Elly reaching for her bag, and I realize she's about to play it for us on her phone. This time, I cover her hand with mine and tell Adira, "We'll have to listen to it after Shabbos. Maybe it's just someone's extremely off-key singing that's ruining it."

"Hey! I am not off-key!" Elly protests, and she isn't, but I know after a moment that she's put together the "no phones on Shabbos" thing, and she squeezes my thigh briefly under the table.

"Maybe this is our cue that it's time for dessert," Dr. Reiss says with a wink, and Adira, Elly, and I immediately jump up to help clear the table while she gets together a bowl of fruit and the brownies Adira and I made that afternoon. It's not the most impressive display of baking skills, but the only other cake Adira knows how to make is banana, and my dad will not touch anything that's been within fifty feet of a banana. "Elly, I'll pack up some food for you to bring home to your dad."

"Oh, wow, I'd say you don't have to do that—and of course you don't—but he would *love* that, thank you," she calls into the kitchen. Of course, Dr. Reiss comes out with so much food, Elly has to take a cab back to her apartment to carry it all, but both of them seem delighted at this arrangement, so who am I to step in?

A few brownies and many handfuls of berries later, the night winds down, and Elly thanks us all profusely for dinner. I help her bring the packages downstairs and wait with her while cars whiz by on Broadway, my heart so ridiculously full I know that if I speak, I might say something incredibly stupid.

"That really was fun," she says with a grin, clearly every bit as surprised as I am. "Thank you for having me."

"Thank you for wanting to be had. I truly did not think you were gonna wanna sit through that."

"I'll sit through damn near anything for you," she says suavely, and I'm supposed to laugh, but all I can think about is how badly I wish we were alone and not standing on the busiest street in one of the busiest cities in the world. "Did you really think I wouldn't come? This is important to you—I know that. And you come to stuff that's important to me all the time."

"Yeah, but." But what? But her stuff is cooler? But I don't get to make requests? But I don't get to think about what I want? "But this involved meeting my dad."

"You met mine first. And got quizzed."

"You got quizzed too," I point out.

"Yeah, and I aced it." She gives her rich copper hair a toss and those red, red lips twist into a smirk, and I have no choice but to shake my head and laugh.

"I am really fucking crazy about you." I don't mean it to come out, but it does, and I want to shove it back in, except that her face goes all soft, and she leans in to kiss me, and she tastes like Diet Coke and chocolate, and the entire fucking island of Manhattan can watch for all I care.

An obnoxious honk and catcall ruin the moment only a few seconds later, but Elly says "Yeah" all slow and dreamy-like and nothing else in the world matters.

A cab pulls up way too soon, and we squeeze hands once, quickly, before she gets inside and shuts the door, and I don't know how I'm ever going to pull myself back upstairs in one piece.

❋ ❋ ❋

I know realistically that no one upstairs could've seen me and Elly kissing on the street, but my cheeks feel warm when I return to the Reisses' apartment anyway. "I'm sorry about the phone thing," I apologize immediately as I join in cleaning up the table. "I should've told her not to bring it. And I didn't know—"

"Tally," Dr. Reiss says lightly but firmly. "She seems lovely. And our rules aren't her rules. Besides, she was very respectful."

She was, and I wasn't expecting her to be, which makes me feel like a rat, but that's a me problem that I don't need to whine about to Dr. Reiss. That Elly constantly manages to exceed my expectations is surreal, but it probably also says something about me that my expectations are what they are to begin with. "I'm glad you liked her," I say instead, glancing at my dad to see if I can read anything in his expression.

But the corner of my dad's mouth simply lifts in a small smile, and he says, "I am too."

A few minutes later, the table is clear, the leftovers are away, and my dad and I say good night and head back to our apartment across the hall. It's already pretty late—Shabbos didn't start until after eight—but lying on the couch and reading quietly together is part of our weekly ritual, so we both head straight to the living room after changing into pajamas.

My newest book club book is sitting on the end table waiting for me, but when my dad sits upright on his usual couch rather than kicking back with a hefty book on mathematics in ancient Babylonia, I realize I'm in for a Talk.

"Did you not like her?" I ask, sinking onto the perpendicular couch, both of us in our usual spaces but nothing feeling at all usual about this. "It really seemed like you did. Were those just starry eyes about the Bob Dylan thing?"

"Tally," he says, shaking his head with his eyes closed, like he truly does not understand where his progeny came from. "I do in fact like her. I was just curious to hear a little more about how things with you two are going, away from the Reisses. Much as I've tried to avoid knowing anything about your romantic life," he adds wryly, "I know you've been interested in her for some time. And despite how much we *want* things to work out, they don't always. Although I will say you really do seem to enjoy each other."

I'm so relieved that he isn't sitting me down for a critique session (which, yes, he has done in the past—Gavin Unterson absolutely did not pass the Ezra Fox test) that I don't even feel my skin crawl at his unintentionally smutty phrasing. "For what it's worth, I had the same fear. I still do, sometimes. Like, this was just supposed to be an obsessive crush for all times that I would look back on when I was your age and be like, 'Wow, remember that girl?' It feels like actually getting her wasn't supposed to be possible, let alone this good." I cannot believe I am spewing these thoughts to my dad of all people, but I need to get them out, and Camila's early to bed and early to rise, especially when she's in PR. "It's so good, Dad," I finish in a near-whisper, feeling silly and superstitious about saying it out loud.

"That makes me really glad to hear, Tal." He sounds like he means it, and it's weird to hear my dad take on any sort of romantic sentimentality. (At least about things that aren't brilliant new theorems.) "The only thing your mother and I have ever agreed on—other than the divorce—is that we don't want you getting soured on the idea of love just because we didn't work out."

"When did you get so soft?" I ask him, drawing my knees up to my chest. Even though staying here for the summer should've meant zero change between us, I feel like he's become a bit of a mush ball ever since I decided not to go to LA.

"Since I realized that after next year, I'm officially going to be an empty nester," he says with a rueful nod that's more to himself than to me. "First a serious girlfriend, then college—it's getting harder to ignore the fact that you're growing up."

"But you'll still try."

"Of course I will. I'm your father. That's what we do." He scratches his beard, which is still way more pepper than salt. "But speaking of college, have you made any progress on that front? Application time is going to be here before you know it, and last we spoke, you didn't have much of a list."

Now it's my turn to get shifty, and I flex my fingers, hoping this isn't going to land with a dull thud. "So, I actually had a conversation with Elly's mom about maybe looking into graphic design? And she said she had a friend who'd talk to me about it? And Elly and I looked into programs, and there are a lot of great ones close by?" I don't know why I'm saying every fucking sentence like it's a question, especially since it's one of my dad's biggest pet peeves in life. To his credit, he's keeping his wincing to a minimum, but I can't tell if that's a reaction to my upspeak or the plan itself.

"Try again with statements, Natalya. Not questions."

Well, hopefully that means it's the former. "I'm interested in graphic design," I amend. "I have someone to discuss it with, I've looked into programs, I'll do some school visits in the fall, and I'd really like to see what it's about and if it's right for me. The combination of art and business does feel like a potentially good fit, though, doesn't it?" I frown. "That was a legitimate question. I'm allowed to ask that as a question, right? I mean, I am allowed to ask that as a question. Period."

"Good. And yes, it does sound like it could be a good fit. I'm proud of you, Tal. But you know who you should really talk about this with? Your mother. Working with graphic designers is a big part of her job. She'll know much more about this than I do. If you're sure you don't want to major in math."

"I am extremely sure of that."

He sighs deeply. "It's like my genes were skipped completely."

"Dad. Look at my face. Your genes were most certainly not skipped. Meanwhile, no one looking at us can even tell Mom and I are related. And stop smirking at that."

He stops. And starts again, but tells me, "I mean it. Talk to your mother. This conversation was made for her."

And then he lies down on the couch, puts on his reading glasses, and moves on to the Babylonians.

My own book is still calling to me from the end table, but I finally have the beginnings of answers about my future, so I pull myself up and pad over to my room to get my phone.

> Hey. Do you think maybe we could have a non-book-club conversation in the morning?

Just some college stuff, I add quickly, because observant or not, semi-estranged or not, she's still a Jewish mother, prone to assuming the worst.

I don't expect to hear from her for a while—at this hour in LA, she's probably still in the office—but the three dots show up immediately.

> I'd like that.

* * *

Despite the time difference, my phone rings at nine on the dot, which would normally bug me except that it means Melissa was being genuine about wanting to chat. That's enough to drag my lazy ass out of bed. (Metaphorically, of course. I am absolutely still lying in bed for this conversation. It's only 9:00 A.M. On a Saturday.)

I fill her in on everything up to that point, and I swear I can feel her kvelling through the phone. "Oh, that's so great, Nat. I love this idea. Graphic design is perfect for you, though now it's really a shame you didn't take the internship here; that would've looked really nice on a résumé for a graphic design program."

"Mom."

"I'm just saying—"

"Please don't. I didn't take it. I can't take it now. Everything's still working out fine." I hope. Of course, now it'll haunt me that I could've had relevant work experience on my résumé and don't, and if I don't get in anywhere, I'll know exactly why. "Can we just move forward?"

"Yes, of course," she says hastily. "I work with a ton of graphic designers I'm sure would be happy to do informational interviews. At least one of them went to Pratt, and I *think* another one went to SVA." She takes a deep breath, which means she's about to ask me something she thinks will make me mad. One thing about having a relationship almost entirely by phone—you sure do learn a lot from how people breathe into the speaker. "Would you consider leaving New York?"

"I . . . would rather not," I reply carefully, knowing I'm shutting down the idea of living anywhere near her for the second time that summer. "There are a lot of great programs here, and Dad's here, and most of my friends are planning to be here. . . ." I know none of this is softening the blow, but I can think of one thing that might. "And *not* that I would ever stay for a girl, but . . . there's also a girl."

As I suspected, that works immediately, and the low-grade hum of disappointment disappears. She's constantly asking me if I'm "seeing anyone," which I did not think was a phrase people used in this century, so this is kinda the news she's been waiting for. (Once Gavin Unterson failed the Ezra Fox test, I didn't bother putting him through the Melissa Farber version.) "Oh? And this girl is staying in New York?"

"She's starting at NYU in the fall, studying rock journalism and music business. Her name's Elly. She actually came to Shabbat dinner at the Reisses last night."

I know this last bit will sting—not only that my father's met her, but that it was at a Shabbat dinner, which is one of the many things my mom left in her rearview even before my parents split. Though she hated that my dad and I were continuing to bond without her on Friday nights, she hated the expectation of a religious family dinner on a traditional date night even more. But they're still meaningful to me, and if she wants to know me better, that's another thing she needs to understand.

Even if it's not something we'll ever do together again.

"That's so nice. How'd you two meet?"

"She works the counter at a new coffee shop on 84th. It's called Nevermore, and it's all Poe-themed. You'd like it." I'm not sure why I say that; Gothic lit is way more my thing than hers. But she agrees that it sounds cool, and then there's that breath again.

I wait for the question, but it never comes, so it's my turn. "Did you want to say something?" I ask, bracing myself for some sort of judgment—I'm not sure of what yet, only that it's coming.

"Well, in the interest of candor about our dating lives, I should tell you that I'm seeing someone as well."

"Oh?" Now, *that's* interesting. I'm sure my mother's dated plenty over the years—or at least I assume she has, but she's pretty married to her job, so who knows. Either way, she's certainly never mentioned a guy to me before. "And how'd you meet?"

"Friends introduced us," she says dismissively, which I take to mean they probably met through a Jewish dating app. "His name's Daniel and he's a doctor—pediatric oncologist. It's only been a couple of months, but I think I like him very much."

"You think?"

She laughs. "I do. It's been a while. And he does admittedly remind me a bit too much of your father sometimes, but in fairness, they're both Jewish men in STEM. Is Elly Jewish?"

"Well, I learned last night that her dad converted when he was on tour with Lenny Kravitz, so . . ."

"Okay, I'm going to need a *lot* about that sentence explained to me immediately."

"I know, right?" I settle in against the pillows and tell my mom about everything from meeting Max and Ava to the portrait gallery to dad's shock and awe over Bob Dylan, and she tells me all the dating stories I've never heard, and for the hours we talk, there isn't a single one of those breaths. It's after eleven by the time we hang up, and she promises to get back in touch about the informational interviews, and of course to talk on Wednesday night for book club.

As soon as we say goodbye, I text Elly.

Good morning, sunshine 🖤

I think I'm finally ready to move forward on this graphic design stuff

> Do you think you could ask your
> mom to set up that call w/her
> friend?

I wash up while I wait for Elly to text back, then consider whether it's worth getting dressed or if I just wanna hang around the house watching TV. I'm leaning toward TV when my phone beeps with a series of reply texts.

> Of course.

> I'm at Nevermore, btw.

> Any chance you wanna come down
> and say hi?

> I think I can probably sneak
> you a free ☕

Aaaand TV can wait.

❀ ❀ ❀

Nevermore's relatively quiet when I show up fifteen minutes later, so I walk right up to the counter and sneak a quick kiss. "I think this is the emptiest I've ever seen this place," I muse, looking around at the vacant tables. "Is this normal?"

"Just wait; there'll be a lunchtime crowd beginning in about half an hour, but I wouldn't say it's a particularly popular brunch spot. Might be because the one and only breakfast item we have is the Duke De L'Omelette, which is literally just a scorched French omelet. Do not recommend."

"Then what do people get for lunch?"

"Usually the Black Cat, which is blackened catfish—that's actually pretty good—or the Fall of the House of Mushrooms, which is pasta with—you guessed it—a crapton of mushrooms. We also pull out the salad bar, the Purloined Lettuce. It's . . . really more about the puns than a cohesive menu."

"Understandable, and I respect it. I think I'll have a coffee for now—take advantage of all these empty tables to finish up that commission for Jasmine—and then I'll have the mushroom thing when lunchtime hits."

"I would also recommend a Tell-Tale Tart. It's more blood orange but way more delicious than the tea. My aunt's not stingy with the butter."

"Sold."

I put my stuff down while Elly makes the coffee, but when I pull out my wallet to pay, she covers my hand. "Okay, you can totally say no to this, but I'm kind of desperate for another set of eyes on this article, and the coffee's on me if you provide them."

"So if I refuse to read your work, I pay for my own coffee."

"Correct. Welcome to capitalism."

"I don't think that's—I mean, yeah, sure, of course I'll read it. I've never gotten to read one of your articles early before. I feel extremely fancy and celebrity-like."

"You are," she assures me as she emails the article over. "You absolutely are. And you are also my absolute favorite for reading it, thank you. I just feel like it sounds really clunky for some reason, and I've read it way too many times. But also, when you read it, please remember that I am a better writer than this."

"Eleanor, I've read like five thousand of your articles. I know you are an excellent writer." I pick up the coffee cup and tip it slightly in her direction. "But I will definitely take you up on the free coffee."

I head to my seat when a "Wait!" calls me back.

"El, seriously, I'm not gonna judge your writing by this piece," I promise.

"No, not that—totally unrelated thing I meant to ask you earlier, until I got a deadline reminder and panicked. What are you doing next Saturday night?"

"Ummm, something with you?" I guess.

"That *is* the correct answer, but not just anything. My friends are throwing me a birthday party at Harlow and I really want you to come. I know it's short notice, but it was supposed to be a surprise, and then they fucked that up, and whatever, not important—can you make it? It was gonna be Friday, but I made them move it."

I would've gone anyway, obviously, but knowing that she specifically bumped her birthday party a day so that it wouldn't conflict with Shabbat dinner definitely seals it. "I'll be there. Now, let me drink my coffee and eviscerate your article."

She sticks out her tongue and I blow her a kiss, taking a seat with my drink and her piece as a small group approaches the counter seeking Tell-Tale Tarts.

Having read just about everything she's ever published, I

see immediately why she's less than thrilled with the quality of her article; she clearly hated the band and is bending over backward to find ways to say it that aren't vicious. She's told me before that *NoisyNYC* always makes sure to include at least one positive, and judging by this article, she hasn't been able to find one.

"Hey, Tal. I thought that was you. Can I sit?"

I look up to see Jaya standing over me with a fragrant tea in hand, their undercut freshly shaven and ice blue. "Of course." I nudge the other chair out with my foot, and they take a seat.

"What are you reading?" They glance over my shoulder. "Is that an Elly Knight original?"

"Sure is! Just giving it a quick edit before she submits it. Did you go to this show with her? It sounds awful."

"Nah, I was warned they sucked, so I made her go by herself. Feels like I made a good life choice there." They sip slowly from the cup, short purple nails tapping on the surface as they do. "But hey, wow, she's letting you read something early? She must *really* like you. I tried to read an article early once and she nearly gave me another piercing."

"Pretty sure it's just that she desperately needs help."

Jaya rolls their dark-brown eyes and pulls out their phone. "Yeah, I'm sure that's it."

I look back down at the article, a slow smile spreading across my lips faster than I can stop it.

Chapter Eighteen,

in Which Nat Cautiously Hopes

The smell of warm vanilla hits me a second before the cup containing a latte hits the table in front of me first thing Monday morning. "Can we talk?" asks the voice presumably attached to the cup, the voice I've been waiting to hear say those words for what feels like a million years. Now that I hear it, though, it has the effect of filling my stomach with lead. If I'd eaten anything for breakfast, it'd be rising in my throat right about now.

Still, I say, "Sure," and gesture across the desk, which is just silly dramatics at this point because it's already his seat.

I focus on the coffee while he sits, letting the sweet aroma calm me and get my head on straight. It's only when he leans across the table, clearly bidding for my attention, that I finally meet those unfairly pretty dark eyes.

"I'm still thinking about things, and I don't have any answers, but I really don't want to fight with you. It feels shitty and I miss you even when you're sitting right across from me and I just want to enjoy the time we definitely have together. Can we do that? And just . . . agree that a conversation about the future is off the table for now?"

It's not even close to what I was hoping for, but I do like the part about not fighting. And he definitely makes a good point about spending our time together better, given who knows how much of it we've got left. (Though, I mean, maybe he does! And only I don't! That is the whole point! But!)

My hesitation must be showing on my face, because he pulls out the big guns. "I didn't wanna have to do this, but I went to Grace's truck last night, and . . ." He plants a biodegradable cardboard clamshell in front of me, and I know he's won this round.

"Is this what I think it is?"

"Depends. Do you think it's a banana-caramel cinnamon bun?"

"I am hoping with every last breath in my body." I flip the lid, and there sits the most delicious pastry known to man, which means I can no longer be mad about anything for at least an hour. "Okay, fine. Conversation tabled. All good. Now hush so I can consume this glorious breakfast in peace."

A satisfied smile creeps over his face, and he sits back proudly in his chair. "Does this mean I'm invited for Shabbat dinner?"

"I suppose I can make some room. I should warn you, though—this one's gonna be a double date. Turns out my mom has a boy toy."

His dark eyes narrow. "Please tell me you actually mean an adult boyfriend and you're just being a jerk about it."

"If you insist on not letting me have any fun, then yes, that is what I mean."

"Wow. So your mom has a boyfriend. How do you feel about that?"

"Fine, I guess?" I pull off a piece of bun and lick the caramel glaze before eating the whole bite. "Weird that she's apparently been hiding it all summer and I guess lying about where she's been, but then, it's not like I've been asking. I'm just hoping he's not a total d-bag. So, are you still in? Wanna meet the pediatric oncologist who's banging my mom?"

"I hoped you'd never ask," he says dreamily, and I just smile and drink my latte.

❋ ❋ ❋

Daniel Bloom is pretty much the epitome of a nice Jewish doctor—smart and polite and awkward and sometimes funny but not always on purpose. He's incredibly impressed that his dinner has been prepared by children, which is not the word he uses but is clearly the word he thinks. (I would hold this against him harder, but in fairness, he's in pediatrics and I am, in fact, of the age that would be among his patients.)

At points, he reminds me exactly of my dad—a thinner version with a little more hair and a lot more patience for people—and at points he could not be more different. Like when the conversation turns to how Adam wants to go to culinary school, and instead of, "I think that sounds like an excellent idea, for after he gets a four-year education at a solid university," Daniel says, "That sounds very cool," and compliments the food again.

He's a man of a lot of questions—how we're liking our internships, how Melissa's day was, what's in each dish, what I've been reading lately, if I've drawn anything new that he can see, what I've done in LA so far, et cetera et cetera et cetera, and it occurs to me as I watch my mom watching him during dinner that this is what she likes about him. My dad will remember to ask how your day was approximately once a week. Despite how close we are, almost all our text exchanges are either me showing him the new foods I'm eating (he was thrilled to hear that Adam, Jaime, Cass, and I went to a Persian restaurant for ghormeh sabzi) or him saying, "Still doing okay over there?"

If there's one thing I've learned from their many loud fights, it's that my mom often worried he didn't find her and her work interesting. And if there's one thing I can guess about my dad, it's that she was right.

But here Daniel is, pediatric oncologist and all, asking about a hard seltzer account like we're, well, curing cancer.

Makes sense she'd be into it.

"So, Nat, do you do Shabbat dinner regularly?"

I glance at my mom, knowing this conversation is gonna take us into Dad territory, but her face is blank. "Pretty regularly," I say. "My dad and I try to do it every week—"

"Except when he's meeting with the Mathmen," Melissa cuts in dryly, as if there's something wrong with him having friends.

"The Mathmen?" Adam eyes me quizzically while cutting into his (perfectly cooked) brisket.

"His friends," I clarify, "and yes, sometimes he hangs out with his friends and I hang out with mine. But usually we do Friday nights together, either alone or with our neighbors, the Reisses."

My mom gives a little twinge that isn't quite a shudder, and I claw my thigh to stop myself from saying something. She didn't have a problem with Adira as far as I know, but she hated adhering to their rules whenever we ate with them, especially since it meant a few hours of cutting her off from her work phone, which is basically her lifeline. I definitely do not miss her impatient asides at those dinners, and I'm sure I'd be on the receiving end of them here if she wasn't allowed to have her phone with her like an external but vital organ.

"I'm impressed that you've gotten your mother to pick them back up," he says with a smile. "I distinctly remember her telling me on our first date that Shabbat observance was off the table."

I'm surprised to hear that, only because it's terrible first-date conversation, but knowing my mother's history with her strict religious parents, it's not unexpected. "So I guess this isn't a typical Friday night for you either."

"I'm usually working on Friday nights, to be honest. The other pediatric oncology attending at the hospital is Orthodox and prefers to be home with her family. In return, she makes sure I'm free for good golf days." He reaches out and takes Melissa's hand, and she softens into his touch. "And for seeing your mother as often as possible."

"I guess I haven't been dramatically responsible for keeping her from you on Friday nights, then," I say awkwardly, pushing my salad around on my plate. "If you're working anyway."

They exchange a look I can't read, and my fork makes a horrible screech as it scrapes the plate in exactly the wrong spot. I put it down and look to Adam for help, and he immediately launches into a whole thing about how much he loves cooking in this kitchen, and soon we turn the conversation to the dinner parties, and the weirdness is mostly forgotten.

We're finishing up dessert when Dr. Daniel's phone rings, and with an apologetic smile, he says, "It's the hospital. I have to go in. But it was so great to finally meet you both." He clasps Adam's hand in a shake, then hesitates as to what to do with me. I cut him a break and extend my hand, and he shakes it, gives my mom a kiss, and heads out.

"So?" she asks as soon as he drives off. "What'd you think?"

"He's very nice," Adam says, and I nod.

"I like him," I add, and I hadn't even realized that my mother's shoulders were kissing her ears until I see them relax.

"Good," she says, and then she repeats it as if talking to herself. "Good. Since you two made dinner, I'll go ahead and clean up. Thank you again for another delicious meal, Adam."

"Thank you again for financing it and providing the kitchen," he replies with a grin.

"Speaking of which." Melissa gestures to us to sit back down at the table, and she does the same. "I did want to mention something to you. I was able to talk to a few colleagues of mine, and long story short, if you're interested, I might have a work-study opportunity for you in Manhattan that'll help cover some of the costs of culinary school." He opens his mouth to respond, but she holds up a hand. "I also have a friend who runs a group that gives out small financial grants for trade school education, and I convinced him that culinary school should fit in there. There's an application to fill out, and it isn't a hundred percent guaranteed, but, well, this is definitely a friend who owes me a favor.

"I know you haven't made up your mind yet about going, but I figured you should have all the information," she says with a brief smile. "That's it."

It's a lot, and neither Adam nor I know how to react to it, especially since it's clear my mother's trying to give him space. Given I'm supposed to be doing the same, we opt to help clean up so we can extend the silence a little more. Still, I hope my mom can feel my gratitude from across the room.

When the leftovers are packed away and the dishwasher's full, I'm still not ready to call it a night, and I'm hoping Adam's not either. If we were at my dad's house, all screens would stay off tonight in favor of reading together on the living room couch, but since we're not, I offer, "Wanna stick around and watch a movie?"

He shrugs. "Sure." Then, like the polite young man he is (or maybe because she's his boss—I keep forgetting that part, or at least trying to), he turns to my mom and asks if she wants to join us.

My mom shoots me a look, and I plaster a smile on my face. "Yes, Mom, please join us."

"Thank you both for what I'm sure was a very sincere invitation to have your mother-slash-boss join you, but I'm exhausted. Time for me to treat myself to a glass of wine, a bath, and an early night. But you kids have fun."

We say good night and she goes off to her room while we

head to the den, closing the door behind us, and then it's just me and Adam, the elephant returning to the room in all its massive gray glory. But while I'm still bursting at the seams to talk about the future and Adam's plans and at least see what he's thinking about my mom's suggestions, he's avoiding eye contact so hard I'm half worried snakes just grew out of my skull.

If there's one thing I definitely *don't* wanna do tonight, it's fight, so I swallow down the million questions threatening to fly out of my mouth and click through the different streaming options instead. "What are you in the mood for?"

"Are you actually going to watch the movie if I choose one?" he asks, his eyes still on the TV, "or are you going to continue to stare at me in the hopes I'll crack and talk about the thing I absolutely do not want to talk about?"

"Hey, I'm not talking about it. You can't force me not to think about it. I didn't promise that."

"Okay, well." He finally turns to me, a hint of playful warmth in his eyes that tells me he's not terribly pissed. "What if I say I'll do anything to take your mind off it?"

"Why, Adam Rose." I flutter my lashes. "That is mighty slutty of you."

A sound like a duck being strangled emerges from his throat. "I meant that you can pick the movie, or we can make cupcakes or something."

Whoops. "Oh."

"But, uh, I'm definitely not opposed to slutty."

Oh. "Oh."

We both glance at the door at the same time, as if to confirm it's really closed, and then his mouth is on mine or my mouth is on his and our tongues really do not seem to give a damn who's on who.

His hands palm my cheeks and slide down my throat, his thumbs putting the slightest pressure on my collarbone, and I quickly grab the remote and put on absolutely anything to keep up the pretense of us being in here for a movie. He smiles against my lips, his hands inching down, and I arch into his hands as he moves to kiss my neck.

It's a lot, and it's so good, almost too good, and I fall back onto the couch, where we continue to make out without missing a beat.

"I really like you slutty," I breathe as he pushes the loose neckline of my dress aside and presses kisses to each newly revealed inch of me. "More slutty Adam. Please. Always."

His low laughter leaves little gusts of heat on my skin, and then his hand is gone, only to resurface at the hem of my dress. "More, did you say?"

Even if I could think in that moment, I wouldn't need to. "Yes, more. I did say that."

And now, just teasing, in his voice and slowly up my thigh. "More?"

"Adam. I will make you leave and finish the job myself."

The threat works, even as his laughter skates over my lips, and then he's kissing me again, doing his damnedest to swallow all the unholy sounds I can't hold back while I rock into his hand like I've been possessed by a demon king. Finally, I grab a throw pillow to stuff into my mouth because while I've mostly forgotten my own name, I have definitely not forgotten where I am or who else is home.

This was supposed to make me forget about the future, but it doesn't do that either; if anything, it's made it worse. All I can think while I come down from the high of it is how many times do we have left to do this? (Well, that and how soon can we do it again?)

But I don't want to think about that. I don't want to think about anything other than how good I feel and how good I want to make *him* feel. So I kiss him, and I reach for his belt, and I remind myself that all the time left can be time that feels like this, if we let it.

Chapter Nineteen,

in Which Tal Sees Her Future (and Likes It)

I'll say one thing for Elly and her friends—they sure as hell know how to throw a party. Harlow isn't a huge club to begin with, but tonight its gilded and glamorous interior is absolutely flooded with people who know Elly from school, from *NoisyNYC*, from Nicki and Jaya, and from random shows around the city. It's daunting to see how big a world she has, and I'm trying really hard not to worry that maybe I'm a much tinier piece of it than I thought.

It helps when she returns from talking to some guy I've never seen before and wraps her arm around my waist. "You having a decent time?"

"A great time," I half lie, thinking about how I *could* be having a great time if I didn't keep feeling so damn insecure at things like this. She looks like a Gothic goddess in a black lace romper with bell sleeves that nearly cover her glittery black fingertips and a deep V neckline I plan to trace with whatever she'll let me as soon as we're in private. Her lips are a glossy black cherry, daggers that nearly graze her shoulders hang from her earlobes, and I am still so confused as to how, of all the people in this room, I'm the one she's chosen.

In the back of my mind, I hear Beckett asking whether I'm Elly's "newest fangirl," and even though I know he was just being a bitter dickhead, it won't let me go.

I'm scary close to falling for her completely. I know that. But when it's like this and she feels larger than life, I can't help getting in my own way.

"I'm sorry I keep disappearing to talk to people. I swear," she says, leaning in, "I forgot half of them even existed. I have no idea where Jaya and Nicki dug up this guest list. Promise me I'll get to celebrate alone with you later."

"Happy birthday to me," I tease, gently tugging her hair. She laughs into the crook of my neck, and God, I wish the rest of these people would disappear. "Come on. Let's dance."

The pop-punk band onstage is wild with infectious energy, not that much older than we are and mixing up their original stuff with covers of Fall Out Boy, Machine Gun Kelly, and, per Elly, Avril Lavigne. It's impossible not to bounce and flail like a dork. But we're all dancing like dorks, and it's fun and amazing and I am so damn happy to be with this girl.

They wind down their set, and I open my mouth to suggest to Elly that we get drinks, but the cute lead singer doesn't step away from the mic. Instead, she pulls it close and declares, "Y'all, we've got a birthday girl in the house tonight!"

Everyone cheers, including me, and Elly sinks into my shoulder while her friends laugh. "And I hear this birthday girl has got some talent with a bass!"

I look at Elly in shock. "Are you going to play? Was this planned? *Please* tell me you're going up to play."

She gives me a wink and heads up to the stage, and I watch as someone hands her a bass and she somehow becomes even hotter, something I did not previously think was even a possibility that existed in nature. She looks so comfortable with it in her hands, and in that moment I send up a silent prayer that this isn't the last time I get to see her onstage.

I recognize the bassline for Pixies' "Debaser" as soon as Elly kicks them off; she's told me more than once that it's her favorite song to play. As she strums next to the lead singer, she leans into the mic and, her eyes finding mine, declares, "This one's for my girl."

The crowd erupts, and the guitar kicks in, followed by the drums, and I'm standing frozen to the ground, feeling my heart pound out of my chest in time with the bass as I watch Elly onstage, my birthday-girl rock star. I can feel dozens of eyes on me, all taking in that I'm the girl, *her* girl, and I've never felt such a point of pride in my entire life.

And it's not just pride. It's pride and awe and affection and attraction and a million things I can't even put a name to that make me want to do everything with her from dance in a club while dressed to kill to roll around in her bed while dressed in nothing, and all the stuff in between. I love to talk to her, walk with her, eat with her, drink with her, watch movies with her, draw her, listen to music with her . . .

I love . . . her, maybe.

It's a terrifying thought, and one I have to push away for a while, because it's too much, and I don't have any space to think here, or to do anything else except watch and listen to the girl I am falling for.

So that's what I do.

❃ ❃ ❃

When Elly stays up there for a second song, I head over to the bar and get myself a water. I'm sipping and watching when I hear a voice in my ear. "Well, that was something."

I look up to see Jasmine Killary standing there in leather shorts and a loose French-tucked white button-up, opened low enough to reveal a fountain of gold charm necklaces hanging over cleavage that rivals mine. In another life, one where we weren't both obsessed with other people, I'd be putting on some very shameless moves right now; instead, I take another sip. "She is something indeed."

"As are you." She folds her arms over the small round-top table and looks at me with laser focus. "That drawing you did of Lara's characters was *amazing*. I know I told you already, but I had to tell you again in person. Like, that was some of the best work I've seen in a while, and I read graphic novels like other people read the backs of cereal boxes. You have some serious talent."

I'm not *great* at receiving praise, so with heat rising in my cheeks, I change the subject away from me. "Did Lara like it?"

"So, *so* much," she says with a slow smile that suggests she was abundantly thanked. "She made it the wallpaper on her phone."

"Aw, I love that."

"So does she. And speaking of which, I've been thinking about it, and I don't know if this is something that interests you at all, or if you even have time, but I have a little business I started a couple of years ago kinda by accident, and, well, it's taken off and I really need a partner in it. It's a stock photo website, plus some templates, stuff like that, but I've been dying to expand into illustration and I just do not have any talent in that area at all.

"Is there any chance that's something you might be interested in partnering on? I already have the site established, social media accounts, et cetera, so it'd just be the art. Although, I wouldn't say no if you wanted to freshen up the site design a little."

The question, especially in this venue, is so wholly unexpected, I don't even know how to respond. And then I do. "Yes. Yes, I am definitely interested in talking about this. Maybe not here, considering I'm about to cough up a lung from half screaming this conversation over the music, but let's have lunch or something before you go back to Outer Banks."

"Awesome. I think it could be really cool. And Elly tells me you're planning to go to school around here, so that's convenient."

"I mean, I hope." I press the sides of the empty top half of my water bottle in with my thumb for the satisfying crackling sound. "I've gotta get in somewhere first. Must be nice to have that stage over and done with, and for it to have worked out nicely with your girlfriend, too."

"We make it work. It's not always easy," she says, fiddling with a link on one of her chains. "I mean, it's pretty sweet for me—Lara stays with me just about every weekend—but she has to get on a train every weekend to do it."

"She doesn't go to school in the city?" For some reason I assumed they must've been together as close to 24/7 as possible.

"Nope—she's living at home and going to community college while she works at a bookstore, hoping to transfer after saving up for a couple of years and lifting her GPA. And even when she transfers, it isn't gonna be a school that costs a royal fuckton of money like NYU, so."

"But it works?"

She tilts her chin slightly to where Lara's dancing with Nicki and Jaya across the club, blissfully happy as her blond waves swish around her sharp jawline. Her jade-green minidress glitters in the shifting lights, and when she catches Jasmine looking at her, she blows a kiss without missing a beat. "Oh yeah, I'd say it works."

I let my own gaze travel to Elly, who's still jamming her fucking adorable little heart out, bell sleeves flying. That could be us this year. It *will* be. She'll be in the Village, I'll be on the Upper West Side; she can come uptown for Friday-night dinners and I can go downtown to shows with her and we can meet in the middle for everything in between. And most importantly, she'll have a parentless place for us to stay . . .

A girlfriend, a business partnership, a college list, a planned major—even things with my mom have improved by a thousand. I don't know how the hell this became my life this summer, but I do know one thing: I am so, so happy I chose to stay in New York.

Chapter Twenty,

in Which Nat Sees Her Future (and Likes It)

dam and I manage to go the whole week without having another Real Conversation about New York, but that's not as much of a feat as it sounds, considering just about all his focus seems to be going toward Dinner Party. He decided to go ahead with the Senegalese peanut stew, and after agonizing over approximately twelve million different recipes, chose South African bunny chow for the second dish. Which meant making his own bread for the bread bowls. Which meant obsessive taste testing of both different white bread recipes and curry seasonings, which hasn't left a whole lot of time for talking.

When Dinner Party day finally arrives, Adam is full of nervous energy, moving around my mom's kitchen like a lightning storm (with Evan doing his cooking in their kitchen, he needed somewhere to go) and then transporting his food back to the apartment as if he were handling newborn babies. He's usually so chill, it's wild to see the way his focus and intensity change when it comes to food. No matter how the bunny chow comes out, I know he's still going to stress about whether he crushed the cardamom pods the exact right amount, or if dried curry leaves would've been better than fresh.

The surest sign I like him is that I think it's kind of adorable instead of absolutely fucking maddening.

"Whatcha got there?" Evan asks, peering over at the huge tray of bread I'm carrying inside from where he's standing by a wok at the stove. "Did you *bake*?"

"Did he bake." I pick up the towel covering the loaves of bread we're about to scoop into bowls. "Please. Smell that."

"Hot damn. Impressive, Bud. Make yourself some space on the counter. Everyone's gonna be coming in the next twenty minutes."

I get to work setting out and scooping the bread bowls while Adam gets the soup and curry heating on the stove. A heady mix of spices quickly fills the apartment, and combined with the scents of Evan's cooking—he had Asia, from the delicious garlicky, gingery smell of it—it gets overwhelming fast. I crack open a window, and not a moment too soon, because Petey and Grace arrive, followed shortly after by Lexi, Isaiah, Liani, and Mateo, and start prepping their food too.

No one was allowed to be assigned their continent of origin, so Ethiopian Isaiah gets to work on forming his arepas, while Peruvian Liani gets right to chopping some parsley for a dish in red sauce I think may be—

"Is that octopus?" Mateo asks, peering over her shoulder.

"Damn straight. Greek style." She sprinkles the parsley on top, then neatly and expertly dices a tomato. "I thought about doing lutefisk, but I wanted to be invited back."

I don't know what lutefisk is, but judging by the way everyone laughs, I have a feeling I don't wanna know. Anyway, octopus is off limits for kashrut reasons, so I have an excuse not to be *too* brave tonight.

Circling the room, I peer over more shoulders, taking in scents and sounds as everyone gets hyperfocused on the task at hand. The only talking happening is about appliances and utensils, and while I set the table, the chefs take turns on the various burners—including an electric one Evan pulls out of a cabinet—and negotiate oven times. Only Mateo, who assigned himself Antarctica, is relatively calm. I half hoped, half dreaded that he was gonna try to cook penguin or something, but it turns out he just made some basic stuff out of ice. (In case I wasn't sure before that he's 100 percent invited to Dinner Party because of Evan . . .)

It's total chaos in a space that barely fits everyone, but they do it at Evan's because both his pantry and his appliance collection are unparalleled. I've seen him provide everything from a kitchen blowtorch to a bamboo steamer to a whipped cream siphon, and I honestly don't understand where he stores it all. At one point, Lexi calls out, "Time to discuss menu order!" and they immediately start spitting out whether they made appetizers, entrées, or desserts while she frantically organizes it.

Beautiful, beautiful butter-scented chaos.

It's determined that Evan's tom kha gai is more of a soup

than Adam's maafe, so he opens up the evening, ladling out bowl after bowl of the creamy spicy-sweet dish. "No pork or shellfish," he tells me, handing me a bowl once I've helped pass out the rest of them, "just chicken. So eat up."

"Mmm, thank you." I dig in with everyone else, and as I absolutely devour it, it strikes me that whether Adam moves to New York or not, Evan's coming no matter what. Somewhere along the way, he started feeling a little bit like my big brother, too, and I'm glad to know I'll have him even if I don't have the Rose I most care about moving.

"Mate, *why* is this one of the best tom kha gais I've ever had?" Petey demands, spooning the lemony, coconutty soup into his mouth even as he's asking the question. "This is ridiculous. I can't believe you finally learned how to cook and that's when you decide you're leaving."

Evan gives him the finger before launching into a joyful exposition of the ingredients he secured at his favorite Asian market, and everyone reacts enthusiastically to how you can really taste the curry paste and the freshness of the lime juice. Well, everyone but Adam. He's eating quietly, his eyes on the table, and I don't know if it's nerves about his dishes or what, but his knuckles and jaw are both so tight, I think he might explode.

I rest a hand on his thigh, which is bouncing up and down in time with his foot. "Hey, are you okay?"

He freezes, and then, as if he can't control the words coming out of his mouth, he declares, "I'm coming. To New York, I mean. I'm moving."

The entire room goes silent, and I'm praying I just heard what I think I heard.

He turns to me, his voice quieter, though you wouldn't know it by the way it's carrying in the room. "I'm—I meant to tell you that privately, but later, or I didn't know when, and I just." He exhales sharply. "Is that okay?"

"Is that—is that *okay*?" At some point I've dropped my spoon, but food is the last thing on my mind, and apparently on everyone else's, because they're all staring at us, tom kha gai forgotten. Well, except Petey. He's still going to town on his bowl. "*Yes*, that's okay."

I'm dying to kiss him, to fling my entire body at him, and obviously it shows because Evan sighs and says, "Please finish this conversation in my room with the door closed."

We do not need to be told twice.

The second the door closes behind us I positively body-slam him onto the bed and fuse my lips to his. His arms circle my back, and we kiss like the world is ending, except that it isn't, it's beginning, and I cannot believe how happy I am right at this moment.

When we finally part, he looks me in the eye and says, "So you really are totally cool with it. I didn't just, like, kill your plans for ditching your summer fling."

"That is literally the most ridiculous thing I've ever heard in my entire life, Adam, and I've watched seven different franchises of Real Housewives." I sit up and cross my legs, sweeping my mussed hair behind my ear. "And to give you an idea of how on board with it I am, I can finally admit that I took a cue from my mom and did some yenta-ing, just in case."

His left eyebrow shoots skyward. "Oh?"

"I talked to a bunch of friends and worked out some potential housing options, in case you couldn't stay with Evan; Isaac's brother's going off to college in Wisconsin, so they have an extra room. Leona also said if you're up for doing some dog walking, you've definitely got a job with them, and I assure you, the Voeglers pay *well*. I also checked with Adira, and if you're up for it, she says the roster from her summer camp would definitely be into doing a weekly or monthly cooking-class kind of thing after school." I bite my lip as I take in his widening eyes. "I know, it's a lot, and you don't have to follow up on any of it. I just wanted you to feel like you had some options."

"No, I—" He coughs, shakes his head. "Thank you. This is amazing. Thank you," he says again, softer, a prelude to a kiss, and then another. "I can't believe I get to do this. I owe so much to you and your mom, and—"

"You don't owe us anything. I don't ever want you feeling like you owe me anything," I say, squeezing his hand. "Obviously, I wanted you to come to New York so we could stay together, but more than anything I just wanted you to get to live your dream for once. And I get the distinct sense that working in marketing isn't it."

"That obvious, huh?"

"Amazingly so."

He smiles and reaches out to smooth my hair. "It's too early to say a thing, so I'm not gonna say it. But I'm gonna think it really hard."

Before I can even formulate a response, there's a banging on the door. "Rosebud!" Mateo calls. "Let's go! You're on! Time to dazzle us!"

We sheepishly get ourselves together and head back into

the kitchen, pointedly ignoring everyone's annoying catcalls and whispers. They only shut up when they actually taste the maafe, and you can practically hear the drool hit the floor and the spoons scraping the bowls.

The rest of the dinner is similarly delectable. Petey (who got North America by virtue of being a Brit) did a bang-up job with a Three Sisters casserole and cedar-plank salmon, Evan managed to find mutton to make Mongolian buuz, Lexi made good on her promise to make sure I got to try kosher sausage by making her own merguez for a couscous dish, and Adam's bunny chow came out absolutely perfect. There's a lot of food I can't eat, including Isaiah's pork-filled feijoada and Liani's octopus, but I make up for it with extra dessert. There's definitely no shortage of that, from Grace's coconut-dusted lamingtons to Liani's sweet, raisin-studded ástarpungar (which she insists on calling "love sacks"). Even Adam has a surprise to add to the mix.

"Rosebud, you seriously outdid yourself here. Where do you get off showing us all up with a delicious snack on top of your dishes?" Lexi holds up a perfectly crackling golden pillow of Adam's freshly fried chin chin. "This is amazing."

Adam flushes with pride, only the fingers worrying at his pockets betraying how ridiculously nervous he was about this dinner. "They're good, right? Kwame Onwuachi's recipe. I wasn't sure if I was a big nutmeg guy, but I'm into it."

"I can't believe we just discovered your culinary talents and now you're taking them with you," Grace says sadly. "Evan and Mateo can fuck off, but you should definitely reconsider staying."

"Hey!" Evan barks.

"Look, she's found the superior Rose," Adam says coolly. "It's just a fact. But"—he wraps an arm around my shoulders—"I'm gonna stick with the move. Though I'm assuming you're all gonna come visit."

While everyone relaxes, cracking open beers and making plans, I melt into Adam's arm, my head on his shoulder for the rest of the night.

A boyfriend, the start of a business, a college list, a planned major—even things with my mom have improved by a thousand. I don't know how the hell this became my life this summer, but I do know one thing: I am so, so happy I chose to come to LA.

Chapter Twenty-One,

in Which Tal Says Goodbye . . . for Now

S o we're agreed," Melissa says as we've officially talked our newest book club pick to death. "We are not the target audience for generational epics."

"We are in agreement on that, yes." I can't help but laugh after listening to Melissa absolutely go off on every single character in the book except the contemporary lead. Now that I've met Daniel and we've cracked open her childhood with the Shabbos discussion, various truths and memories just keep on coming. If there's one theme I've taken from her experience with her own life, it's that digging into your roots isn't the healthiest move for everyone. "Next time, maybe we just go with a bloody slasher novel."

"That sounds wonderful." There's a genuine smile in her

voice, and it's truly amazing to me how far we've come in this summer we didn't even spend together.

Judging by her next statement, she's thinking the same thing. "You know, if you'd come for the summer, now is when you'd probably be leaving me. I wonder if you'd be happy or sad about that, if you'd been here."

"I wonder that too," I say honestly. "But I think this was good for us. Being together in person is not our norm, you know? And it's not going to be, as long as you stay out there. And you should stay out there!" I amend quickly. "I get that it feels right for you, that you never really felt at home in New York. But it's good that we learned how to sustain something long-distance, because this is what it is."

"That certain you're not coming to school in LA, huh?"

I'm trying to formulate a tactful response when she spares me from having to with an "I'm just teasing. I heard you loud and clear, Nat."

"I'd still like to see you more," I say, and I mean it. "I was thinking maybe winter break I could come out there?"

"I'd love that," she says, and it sounds like she means it, too. "You're always welcome here, Nat. I hope you know that. If you want to come spring break, come then, too. Hell, if you're still with Elly by then, I'd love to meet her."

Something warm and fizzy that feels like possibility bubbles inside me, and while I can't quite imagine hopping on a plane with Elly to go to LA and stay at my mom's house, I say okay to that too, because maybe someday soon that'll also change.

"And of course I'll be at your graduation. I can't wait to see you walk on that stage. I really am so proud of you."

Truthfully I didn't expect her to come, so hearing that showing up is already a foregone conclusion in her mind makes me feel some type of way. And as long as I don't worry too much about what it'll be like to have her and my dad in the same room again, the feelings are good. "Thanks, Mom. I'm excited to see you then too."

In happy genetic news, we're both really bad at Feelings, so she immediately changes the subject. "What's on tap for the rest of the day?"

Now, *that's* something I'm happy to discuss. "Huge end-of-summer party on the twins' parents' boat. It's going to be absolutely ridiculous and I can't wait. Isaac and I went shopping yesterday and I got the cutest dress for it. Plus, Camila just got back from visiting her grandparents in PR yesterday and I haven't even seen her yet. It's gonna be her first time meeting Elly—most of my friends' first times, actually—which feels big."

"I'm sure it'll go wonderfully, honey. She sounds like a lovely girl."

"She is, and Camila's already planning double dates, so I'm cautiously optimistic. It's hard to imagine two people who have less in common than Camila and Elly, but I figure if they just talk about Olivia Rodriguez, they'll do perfectly."

"Wow, you've got everything all figured out."

It's pretty surreal to hear someone say that after how long I've felt like the only person who absolutely does not have her shit together. But at this moment in time, my mom is absolutely right—I do have everything all figured out. And it feels damn good.

❀ ❀ ❀

Every time I think Lydia and Leona cannot possibly outdo themselves, they prove me wrong.

The theme of the party is Prohibition (Leona originally tried to do a *Gatsby* theme and was treated to a twenty-minute rant from Lydia on how absolutely absurd and fundamentally misunderstanding of the text *Gatsby* parties are), and everything is as lavish, gilded, and Art Deco–styled as humanly possible. There are feathered streamers and centerpieces, servers fully decked out in their 1920s best walking around with canapes and mocktails, and a gorgeous blonde with an incredible growl in her voice is in the corner with a three-piece band singing jazzy covers of modern songs.

"I cannot *believe* your friends got them for this party," Elly says in awe, her kohl-ringed eyes widening at the sight of the band who's clearly more famous than I realized. "Though, seeing this boat, I guess there's really nothing they can't afford, is there."

"Nope," I reply with a pop to my *P*. "But I have greatly enjoyed reaping the benefits of their wealth."

I squeeze the arm looped in mine, which is covered by black lace elbow gloves to match her black flapper dress and heels, all of which look stunning on her. It's definitely not her usual style, but she looks incredibly sexy and glamorous, and that she's clearly trying to make a good impression on my friends doesn't hurt.

"Well, tonight I guess I am too." She points at a passing tray of glasses holding mesmerizingly green drinks, the one *Gatsby* nod Lydia allowed. "I think I will reap the benefits of whatever that is."

In true Prohibition fashion, the drinks being served are alcohol-free but flasks are "hidden" all over the place. "This is absolutely ridiculous," I tell Lydia fondly when Elly and I go over to say hi with our Green Lights in hand. "I'm surprised you didn't have the servers pouring alcohol into each individual drink."

"Leona tried," Lydia says wryly. "They wouldn't do it for a party where the guest list was primarily minors. But believe me when I tell you my sister did try."

Elly snorts. "I've only met her twice and I absolutely believe you."

Isaac sweeps over then, doffing his cap in our direction. "Ladies. This party is the cat's pajamas, Lyds. And you," he says to Elly with a cheesy grin, "look marvelous."

"Charmed, I'm sure," she replies, holding out her hand to be kissed. Then she furrows a brow. "I'm not getting the right decade, am I. Or phrasing."

"I think you're just being British," Isaac says thoughtfully, but he kisses her hand anyway. "And Tals, you are absolutely slaying in that dress. I knew I had a great eye, but this seals it. Doesn't she look stunning?" he asks Elly.

"That I'm not staring at her right at this moment is a testament to my tremendous inner strength." She squeezes my arm again while Isaac laughs, and then of course he brings up Sailor Moon so they can be nerds together while Lydia and I roll our eyes over their heads.

Suddenly, Lydia breaks into a huge smile. "Morales alert!"

I whip around so hard I nearly yank Elly away with me, and I quickly disentangle myself so Lydia and I can run over to wrap Camila in a huge welcome hug.

"You're here! You're here!" I cheer, practically shoving a laughing Emilio out of the way as we bounce with her. Then I step back and take a good look. "My God, your tan is amazing. I cannot believe how well you are pulling off a white dress right now."

"I know, right?" Cam does a slow turn, complete with jazz hands, allowing us to appreciate her to the fullest. "Now, take me to the girl!"

I pull Camila toward Elly, who's still talking to Isaac and has also been joined by Leona and Dylan.

"God, I am so excited to *finally* meet you," Cam fawns, and it would make me want to die except that instead of cringing, Elly's cheeks pinken with what looks a little like . . . joy? "Can you imagine if Tal had gone to LA? You guys would probably be bumping into each other tomorrow at Sephora or Tally's third time seeing *Good Behavior* and going your separate ways again."

"You mean if I'd listened to *you* and gone off to see distant lands?" I snort, twining my fingers with Elly's. "If I'd gone to LA, it would've been your influence. And missing out on this would've been entirely your fault."

"I see you haven't gotten any less dramatic while I was away."

"Not even a little bit," Elly confirms, and I do not appreciate the conspiratorial glance they exchange at *all*. "How was your trip?"

"Oh, it was all the things." I've missed the way Camila's hands fly as she talks, her dagger-sharp nails slicing through the air as she talks about long days of playing Rummy and Dominoes with her grandmother alternated with all matters of sporty things completely alien to me, like hiking in El Yunque and kayaking in bioluminescent bays. "Anyway, it was really nice, but I missed these losers," she says, hooking one arm around my neck and the other around Lydia's.

"Well, I *thought* I missed you too, but." I stick out my tongue, but I can't help grinning; it's so damn good to all be back together again, especially now that "all" includes Elly. We exchange more hugs, gush over one another's outfits, and take a million pictures and videos, because tonight, all is right with the world.

At least until Isaac suggests we go dance.

"Actually, Tal." Elly squeezes my hand. "Can we talk for a minute?"

"Well, that doesn't sound good," I say, but I let her pull me into a quiet corner while everyone shoots me looks ranging from sympathetic to sympathetic-but-aiming-for-neutral. "What's up? Everything okay?"

"Everything is kind of great, actually," she says, tracing her thumb over the palm of my hand, "but also a little bit not." She takes a deep breath, meeting my gaze with her honey-brown one. "My parents are going on tour together for the first time in like five years—my mom's doing the concert photography for the Clerical Errors for the European leg of their tour, and my dad's playing guitar for the opening band—and they want me to come join them. It's ten cities in two weeks, and I know these are our last two weeks together before I start school, but—"

"But you absolutely cannot pass up an opportunity like that," I fill in, my heart sinking even while I fervently mean the words coming out of my mouth. "That sounds absolutely amazing, El. Of course you should go. Writing that up would be a guaranteed feature somewhere, and I know how much it means to have your parents include you in their work and in their time."

"I wish you could come with me, though." She clasps our hands together and swings them lightly. "I had plans for us. I *still* have plans for us," she amends, "but they might need to be temporarily on hold. Is that okay? Do you think you can wait for me?"

"Eleanor." I bring her hand to my lips and kiss her knuckles. "I waited for you for over a year. Yes, I can wait two stupid weeks. As long as you text or call or FaceTime me every day."

"Obviously. And there *will* be gifts."

"Tell me more."

"Cheesy shot glasses," she says, and I kiss her.

"Obnoxious magnets," she says, and I kiss her again.

"Romantic postcards with mysterious one-word notes and no return address, leaving you to ponder whether it's me or a truly secret admirer," she says. I tip my head to the side in consideration, but she kisses me anyway.

"It's two weeks."

"That's nothing," I say, even though it feels like everything, because after those two weeks, everything will be changing and

I don't know what anything will look like. For the past year and beyond, I'd looked forward to potential sightings of the Redhead everywhere I went on the Upper West Side, and now she won't *be* on the Upper West Side anymore. My local bookstores are no longer her local bookstores and my local drugstore is no longer her local drugstore and my top three favorite bodegas will no longer overlap with hers. She'll have her own versions of all of these things down in the Village, where she'll bump into other girls—college girls—and I'll be that high school girl she dated once upon a time, before Paris and Amsterdam and Prague and wherever else this tour will take her.

"You don't look like you think it's nothing, but I promise you, it's *nothing*, Foxy. Look, let's make a date." She pulls her phone from her black lace clutch and nods toward my little round crossbody bag to get me to do the same. "The day after I get back, I'm picking you up, and we're going out. Put it in your calendar."

So that's what we do. We schedule our reunion date and we kiss and then we head off to dance with my friends and spend a night living in the past before we kick off the future.

Chapter Twenty-Two,

in Which Nat Says Goodbye . . . for Now

*T*o Nat!"

I blush as the entire food truck gang, including Jaime and Cass, lifts their tacos in the air. It's an amazing homage, and Evan has absolutely outdone himself, complete with an inspired new "NYC taco" that contains homemade pastrami, fresh coleslaw, kosher pickle salsa, and an avocado-mustard crema that shouldn't work but somehow does, wrapped in a caraway seed–dotted tortilla. (Mateo initially declared it sacrilege, but if I'm counting correctly, he's currently on his third.)

"Please, *I'm* not the one totally uprooting myself and starting a new adventure three thousand miles away," I remind them, fiddling with the cap on my water bottle. "Mateo, Evan, and Adam are the ones you guys should be cheering."

"Oh, they will," Mateo assures me, swiping a bit of crema from his lip. "The next two weeks are going to be nothing but celebrating us, aren't they?"

The rest of the crowd groans, until Evan says, "And taste-testing a few more recipes," to which everyone cheers. "But you're the one responsible for the fabulous new logo we'll be using for the brand-new Bros over Tacos shop *and* our whole social media rebrand, so tonight, tacos are in your honor. Plus," he adds, hooking his arm around Adam's neck, "you make this loser pretty happy."

Everyone "awww"s and I scrunch up my face in embarrassment, but when I catch Adam's sheepish grin, I can't help melting. It's like he's this entire group's little brother, and they love him so much, and *he* loves (or at least quite likes) me. On the one hand, this must be how five-year-olds feel when grown-ups ooh and aah at their pretend weddings. On the other, having never had any siblings—older or otherwise—it feels surprisingly nice to be the target of their teasing.

God, two months here have turned me into a massive sap.

But truly, it's been the perfect last night in LA. My mom and I went to get sushi, then I met up with Adam at the beach to walk in the waves and make an endless list of plans for New York. (Top of my list: him meeting my friends. Top of his list: eating at Le Bernardin. One of us clearly needs to work on his priorities.) And after, the dinner rush over, we met up with this crew and stuffed our faces with Evan's tacos, Isaiah's deliciously spicy dinich wot, and, also in homage to NYC, Grace's recreation of Four & Twenty Blackbirds' Salty Honey Pie, all while watching the sun set over the Pacific.

I'm obscenely full, my hair and skin are sticky with sand and salt water, and I don't know that I've ever been this happy.

I can't believe this is my last day here.

Adam makes his way back to me and squeezes my hand, and I know he's thinking the same thing. This life would be over regardless of our choices, regardless of whether I stayed, regardless of whether he did. It feels like the waves continue to move and we just have to move with them and hope that when everything lands, we've still got solid footing. It's scary and exhilarating and it makes me want to stay here forever but also skip forward two weeks to make sure everything turns out okay.

"I don't want this night to be over," I mumble into his shoulder. "I just want to stop time right now."

"I know." He drops a light kiss on top of my head and wraps his arms around me as we watch the last of the sun disappear below the horizon. "But there's so much good ahead of us, Nat. And so many pastrami tacos in our future."

"Mmm, you're saying the magic words."

"For what it's worth, I can't believe you're going home tomorrow. I can't believe we've had our last day as deskmates. That as of tomorrow, we won't be seeing each other every day."

"For two weeks," I remind him, even though I can't stop feeling that same sense of finality. Two weeks is nothing. I *know* two weeks is nothing. But when you think of all the minutes in two weeks, how many chances that is for things to fall apart, for Adam to change his mind, for a million unforeseen things . . . two weeks feels like infinity.

"For two weeks," he echoes, smiling against my hair. "I cannot believe how much my life is gonna change in two weeks. It'll be nice to have this very excellent thing be the same."

"Hey, you'll still be living with your brother. You'll still be living in a big city. You'll even still be sleeping on a pull-out couch. Not that much is changing, except that you'll actually be living your dream."

"With my dream girl," he adds, and winces. "Sorry, that was awful. It was supposed to sound romantic."

"Cooking for me is romantic," I tell him, placing a hand on his chest as if I can memorize the feel of his heartbeat. "Stick with that."

"Deal. And speaking of which." He releases me to yank over his backpack. "I made you a couple of things for your flight tomorrow," he says, pulling out several bags. "Thought you could use something that was at least a slight improvement over airline food. There's one experimental recipe, one extremely safe batch of the best mint chocolate brownies you will ever eat in your life, and one toffee cookie from Life Is Buttercream, just in case I'm wrong about the brownies. But I'm not wrong."

"I believe you. But I question the whole 'gentile' thing. You both feed and prepare like a Jew, especially in quantity."

He shrugs. "Never say never. What time's your flight again?"

Okay, so I guess we're just gonna gloss over those three little words that are dangerously close—if not actually bigger—than those other three little words. Not that I'm thinking about stuff like that at this age, but . . . it's not the worst thing to know he's thought about a future for us that goes beyond two weeks from now.

I guess having an unsettled childhood makes you *really* wanna settle down.

I don't hate it.

"Four. Planning to get home just in time to pass out and hope it gets me back on East Coast time a little faster."

"You sure you don't want me to drive you?"

"No, I'm sure I *do* want you to drive me, but my mom really wants us to have this time, and honestly, I'd like to have it too. Besides, I'm seeing *you* in two weeks, but I don't know when I'm seeing her again." It's weird to think about, after spending two whole months with her. My room is going back to being a guest room, and my mother is going back to being my long-distance parent. It feels like a lot of change for what's actually my life returning to what it already was.

Except it isn't that. Not really.

"So do I get to see you in the morning, at least? Or for lunch?"

"Both, if you want 'em."

"I want 'em," he says, his mouth finding mine in the growing dark, one kiss multiplying into a thousand as we fall back onto our blanket on the sand. "I always want 'em."

"I feel like we're no longer talking about meals."

His lips curve against mine, and then we're no longer talking at all.

❁ ❁ ❁

"Does your dad know what time to come pick you up?"

I hoist my carry-on higher onto my shoulder. "We still don't have a car, so no, he will not be picking me up, but yes, Dad has my flight information and I will text him the medallion number as soon as I get into a cab."

"Do you have your passport?"

"Domestic flight, Mom. No passport."

"A book for the flight?"

I pull my phone out of my back pocket and wiggle it. "I have about ten in here."

"I'm not great at the preflight inquiry, am I."

I want to laugh, but the way her shoulders slump when she asks it, I know it's not the move. Instead, I pull her in for a hug. "I had a great summer with you, Mom. Thank you."

"Let's do it again sometime," she mumbles into my shoulder, and at least one of our faces is growing wet. Then she holds me at arm's length. "I know things are going to be different when you go back, but maybe they could be . . . less different. I really want to know how college applications go, and things with Adam, and just . . . your *life*. I even want to know if you end up ever talking to that redheaded girl."

At that, I *have* to laugh. I'd forgotten all about the Redhead, though I guess I must've mentioned her to my mom during one heart-to-heart or other. It's weird to think now how occupied I was by a silly fantasy when the reality I found here is a thousand times better.

"Deal," I promise. "Since we won't be doing Shabbat dinner together anymore, maybe we could commit to pre-Shabbat phone calls or something?"

"I love that idea. I—"

A car horn drowns out the rest of her sentence, and then there's yelling and more horns, and of course there are because this is LAX and we've overstayed our welcome. Instead of trying to talk over it, we just exchange another hug. "I'll text you when I land," I promise. "And we'll talk Friday."

"Friday," she says, as if she's committing it to her already-packed agenda. And then she gets in her car, and with one last wave, she's gone.

Here's the thing I'm thinking about as I roll my suitcase into Departures. I know she's gonna miss a lot of those calls. And maybe I will too. And it isn't gonna be the same as sharing a home, sharing a table, sharing a life. But this summer didn't change the fact that we live a country apart; it just helped us understand that we can connect anyway. And that's no small thing.

Chapter Twenty-Three,

in Which Natalya Has a Visitor

*I*f someone were to count how many times I've checked the clock on my phone in the last three hours, we would all finally learn how high infinity goes.

"Well, don't you look nice. Are you expecting someone special?" my dad asks, glancing up from where he's working on his laptop at the dining room table.

"Ha ha. You know I am." Still, it's nice to hear a compliment. It's hardly a first date, but after two weeks apart, it almost feels like one. The butterflies are fluttering, my heart is beating at time and a half, and I'm wearing my favorite flowered sundress that I only save for special occasions.

My phone buzzes in my hand, and I immediately check it again, and smile when I see the text from my mom. **Are you ready?**

So, so ready, I write back, marveling at the very fact that I've shared enough about my social life with my mom this summer for her to ask that question. Things have definitely changed.

She sends back a string of emojis that have me rolling my eyes out of my skull, and also smiling again.

"Will you be home before midnight?"

"Dad, seriously. We're shopping for stuff like towels and bedding, not hitting up a club." And yet, it feels like it's going to be the best "date" I've ever been on, though maybe that's because the anticipation is killing me. "We'll probably go out for dinner afterward, but yes, I'll be home before midnight."

"Maybe you shouldn't be, given how much time you've been spending here while you mope around waiting," he says dryly.

"I have not been *moping*." Anyway, I can hardly be blamed for holing up in my apartment. Lydia and Leona have been in Italy, Camelio has been inseparable since Cam got back from PR, and I didn't wanna miss a single FaceTime or phone call, especially given the time difference. "And anyway, there's no more moping for me, because the time has come!" As if on cue, there's a buzz on the intercom, and I dance over to it to respond to our doorman, Eddie. "Send up, please!" I declare, no explanation of my visitor necessary.

All my nervous energy has me dancing around the room, but I stop when I catch my dad laughing at me. Or just smiling, really, which somehow feels even more unsettling; mockery, I'm used to. "What? You're giving proud-dad face, and it's weird."

"I *am* proud of you, though, sweetheart. We said at the beginning of the summer that you should try new things, meet

new people, and have some actual adventures, and you're doing it. It's nice to see you so happy."

Well, this is about a thousand times more sentimental than
any other conversation I've ever had with my dad, so I just sort
of mumble in response, and he smirks and goes back to his
laptop.

And then, the doorbell rings, and it feels like a new phase
of my life is somehow beginning with it, like *I'm* the one who
needs towels and bedding for my new home. Of course, I'm
just living vicariously through someone who's *actually* starting
on a new adventure, but in a way, it's my adventure too, sort of.

I certainly hope to be spending plenty of nights on that new
bedding, anyway.

I take a deep breath, open the door, and feel my heart
thump in the very best way. "Hey, you."

-The End-

(Or is it?)

If you want Adam to be behind the door, turn to page (308).

If you want Elly to be behind the door, turn to page (315).

Chapter Twenty-Four,

in Which Adam Has Arrived

*H*ey, yourself," Adam says with a slow smile, and that's about all the playing it cool I can take before I launch myself into his arms.

"You showed up," I mumble into his shoulder, the familiar smell of his skin and deodorant bringing actual tears to my eyes.

He laughs gently into my hair but holds me tightly enough that I know a part of him finds this as surreal as I do. After all, this is a city we've never been in together. This is a home of mine in which he's never watched a movie or made Shabbat dinner or lain on the couch to scroll through food blogs on his phone while I draw. He's never even seen my bedroom here. . . .

A loud cough breaks up my reverie, and Adam jumps away

from me like someone just fired a shotgun in his general direction. "You must be Adam."

He's never met my dad.

Adam wipes his palms on his shorts, and I swear a slight sheen of sweat breaks out on his tanned forehead. You'd think that after all the time he spent with my mom in LA, a parental meeting would be a piece of cake, but! "And you must be Professor Fox," he says, extending a hand and magically turning into a middle-aged man right in front of my eyes.

I roll my eyes when Dad doesn't correct him, but at least he nods approvingly before saying, "And what are your intentions with my daughter?"

"Okay." I rescue Adam's hand from Dad's grip and pull him at least three feet away. "That's enough of that. Adam Rose, Professor Ezra Fox. Dad, this is Adam. He enjoys cooking, horror movies, and long walks on the beach, which he probably won't be taking much anymore because New York City. My dad enjoys reminiscing about his grad school days, doing the crossword puzzle, a good Scotch, Bob Dylan, and general math nerdery. Are we good now?"

"What's the Pythagorean theorem?"

"A-squared plus B-squared equals C-squared."

Dad strokes his chin as if his beard is a foot longer than it actually is. "I hear you'll be cooking us Shabbat dinner one of these weeks."

"I'd be honored to."

"I look forward to it. Okay, you two kids go have fun."

We don't need to be told twice to GTFO.

✽ ✽ ✽

"So, your dad's kinda intense," Adam says when we're safely out of the building, our hands clasped together and lightly swinging as we head to the subway, my mouth tingling from when we positively mauled each other in the elevator.

"It's all bluster except for the math question. Once you get that right, you're in." I squeeze his hand and watch him take in the sights, looking very much the tourist and walking at a pace that's going to get him a nasty side-eye. "How was the flight?"

"Terrifying and exciting, in the way that all of this is terrifying and exciting. But they had TV on the flight, so I literally just watched five hours of the Food Network. Guy Fieri is surprisingly calming. And, of course," he adds, lifting my hand to his lips, "I kept reminding myself that you were at the end of the trip. That helped more than anything."

"Smooth." I lead him down the subway stairs and show him how to pay for the subway, delighted that I get to be the city expert this time around. We're only going a couple of stops, so I instinctively grab a pole and ignore the many open seats, which absolutely perplexes him. "You'll become a New Yorker eventually," I assure him as I relent and take a seat next to him. "You'll see."

"Well, I have a job interview tomorrow for a work study, and hopefully today we'll get me settled in to Evan's apartment, so that's a start."

"And you have successfully paid for the subway!"

"And I have successfully paid for the subway." He looks around. "Good public transportation. What a concept."

"See? This is why I'm a shitty driver."

He fills me in on the past two weeks in LA—leaving work, having one last meal from each of the food trucks, saying good-bye to the beach, and, horrifyingly, having a goodbye lunch with my mom—for the rest of the quick ride and the walk to the houseware store, and then I flip the switch to all-business. I want Adam to feel settled, and he's not gonna do that if he has scratchy towels or a crappy blanket.

The Dinner Party crew chipped in to get him a gift card for houseware, and he texted me immediately after to ask if we could go on a home shopping date as soon as he settled into Evan's. It feels wildly grown up, walking among aisles of toasters and coffee makers, fingers interlaced, talking about whether it really makes a difference to have king-size pillows rather than standard. But before I can make my case, Adam stops us in a corner by the toothbrush holders and says, "Okay, I have to tell you something, and I wanted to do it in person."

"You met another girl," I say immediately.

"Jesus Christ, no." He rolls his eyes. "I'm *towel shopping* with you, Nat. I almost came directly to your apartment from the airport because I couldn't stand waiting to see you any longer. It is not even close. It's not even *my* news."

"Oh?"

"I'm gonna tell you, but you get no more than three 'I told you so's, and then you have to give it a rest, okay?"

I cock my head, trying to decipher what he's starting to tell me, and then it hits. "Oh. My God. Evan and Mateo."

"Evan and Mateo," he confirms with a nod, laughing sheepishly. "Turns out you do recognize your people, even when they don't. He told me I could tell you when I saw you, and also to tell you that he wasn't lying, he just didn't really know *what* he was feeling until you called him out. Then I guess he couldn't get it out of his head, and it made a lot of shit make sense, and he finally confessed his feelings the night before Teo's flight earlier this week."

"I knew it!" I squeal, whacking Adam on the arm. "I told you so, I told you so, I—" I break off, remembering the limit. "I'll save my last one for when I see Evan in person."

"Perhaps also maybe less physical violence," he suggests, rubbing his shoulder.

"You know nonviolence never solves anything."

I'll admit I deserve the impatient exhale. "Can we go pick out towels now?"

"I suppose."

We move on toward the towels, rows of plush terry cloth in sea-glass blue and buttery yellow providing a dizzying array of options. I'm trying to decide which of two feels fluffier when suddenly I spot a familiar flash of red hair not more than six feet away.

Oh my God. Of all places to run into the Redhead. Of all *times*.

I can't help it—the laughter bursts out of me and I have to smother my mouth in Adam's shoulder to keep it quiet. He looks down at me, eyebrows shooting up to space. "What the hell did I miss?"

"Just a blast from the past," I say, rising up on my toes to kiss him. "Trust me, you did not miss a thing. Now, hurry up and pick a color because we have about a thousand other things to get after this."

"I am definitely gonna need to take a nap on one of those mattresses at some point," he mutters, tugging out a hunter green bath towel and matching hand towel and washcloth. "But I'm guessing you have tonight all planned."

"Not too much," I assure him, squeezing his selected bath items to confirm their softness. "Very casual dinner gathering at Lydia and Leona's apartment."

"Would that be the massive and insanely fancy duplex apartment you always talk about?"

"It would."

"And when you say gathering, how many people would that be?"

"Just me and the girls. And the guys. So . . . nine, including us? Unless Leona and Dylan are back together this week, in which case ten."

"Hmm." He furrows his thick brows, tucking the towels under his arm and leading me to bedding. "And how many of them have to like me?"

"As long as you can get Camila and one of the twins—honestly, either one is fine—you're golden. No one cares what the boys think about anything. Although, if you wear any of Isaac's fashion pet peeves, prepare for the worst night of your life."

"So socks and Crocs are out?"

I narrow my eyes into slits. "Adam. You *just* got here. Don't make me dump your ass immediately."

His lips curve into a smile and he puts the towels to the side and wraps me in his arms. "I'm excited to meet your friends," he says into my hair before dropping a kiss on the top of my head. I look at him, silently inviting him to kiss me right there among the soap dishes and curtain rods, and he does, if only for a few seconds, before resting his forehead on mine. "And I'm so fucking happy to be here with you."

"Even if my friends are pains in the ass?"

"Even then."

"Even if my dad gives you math quizzes every time you see him?"

"Even then."

"Even if—"

"Even then, Nat." And he shuts me up with another kiss, and another, and then we pay for the towels and get out of there because a subway ride away is an empty apartment and a pull-out couch with our names on it.

The rest can wait for another day.

Chapter Twenty-Four, Again,

in Which Elly Has Returned

*B*onjour, mi amor." The corner of Elly's mouth quirks up as we drink each other in for the first time in two weeks, her pale skin glowing and hair glinting with fire.

"I think you might have just combined two languages there." I don't know where to rest my eyes or my hands; all I want is to consume her entirely.

She rolls those honey-brown eyes. "Shut up and kiss me already."

I don't need to be told twice. My hand shoots out before I can even formulate a thought, grabbing the few inches of white T-shirt that peek out above her leather corset. She's definitely leaving a mile of telltale red lipstick traces on my mouth right now and I don't even care, because how can I possibly give a shit about anything other than that Elly's back and here and mine?

The sound of a book hitting the floor with a slam jolts us apart with the reminder that my dad is in the apartment, and knowing him, that drop wasn't an accident. We have just enough time to smooth out our clothes and wipe off excess lipstick before he strolls into the foyer.

"Elly! Welcome back."

"Why, thank you, Professor Fox." She holds up the large tote bag I hadn't even noticed was in her hand. "I come bearing gifts."

His eyebrows rise. Elly's just won the Girlfriend of the Year award. He'll never admit it in a million years, but there's nothing my dad loves more than a random present from somewhere out in the world. Unless she got him liquor, in which case, I'm just going to hide in a closet until the awkwardness ends. (Not that my dad doesn't love Scotch, but he will not love a teenager who happens to be dating his daughter getting their hands on it.)

"There happened to be some kinds of art and mathematics conferences happening in Vienna, and there was a fair where you could buy art based on the gallery pieces, and I thought this one was cool." She pulls out a carving designed to look like an intricate window. "This was from an exhibit on Islamic geometric patterns."

"That *is* really cool," I say.

"It is," Dad says, a little awe in his voice. "Thank you, Elly. This will look wonderful in my office."

Elly's not one to beam, but her smirk leans far enough into a genuine smile for me to see that she's thrilled he likes her gift. "And for you," she says, turning to me, "a cheesy shot glass and obnoxious magnet, as promised, *and* a ridiculous snow globe."

"They are *perfect*." The snow globe truly is ridiculous, a reproduction of a sculpture of two men peeing in a pond that she told me about when she FaceTimed me from Prague. The magnet is actually a really cute facade of a gay bar from Amsterdam, and the shot glass is from Paris, cobalt glass with a white etching of the Louvre on one side and the Eiffel Tower on the other. "And I got the centaur postcard from Brussels, thank you. I loved it."

She laughs. "I'm so glad. So, ready to do some dorm-room shopping? Jaya's waiting in their car with the rest of my stuff."

"Am I ever!" We say goodbye to my dad, and off we go, ready to start the next step.

❊ ❊ ❊

Two hours of shopping for sheets, towels, hangers, a hamper, and God only knows what else, we're finally in the room Elly's gonna be calling home for the next year, a totally unremarkable space with two extra-long twin beds and an equally nondescript bathroom. It's hard to imagine my girlfriend living somewhere so colorless, but once we toss red throw pillows onto the newsprint-themed bedding and hang up a bunch of vintage concert posters, print a few little pictures on Jaya's photo printer to tape to her new desk, and string up fairy lights, the room completely transforms.

Or at least half of it does; the other half is still awaiting the arrival of one Virany Chow from Atherton, Florida. "I don't know how you can handle living with a complete stranger," I say as I flounce onto Elly's bare mattress and admire our handiwork. "What if she's an extreme weirdo?"

"First of all, *I'm* an extreme weirdo," Elly reminds me, hopping on next to me while Jaya takes the desk chair. "Second of all, she's not a *complete* stranger. We FaceTimed a couple of times. She's going premed, so she'll probably be in the library five thousand hours a week, and I've confirmed she's not a raging homophobe—apparently the captain of her cheerleading squad is queer and dating the female quarterback of their school's football team. So we'll be just fine."

"Okay, I want to hear a lot more about that," Jaya says, eyes widening, and I nod emphatically. Before I can say anything, though, a knock sounds at the door.

"Must be the rest of the party; Virany's not coming until tomorrow. Come in!" Elly calls.

Sure enough, Nicki, Jasmine, and Lara pile into the room, and we immediately get to chatting about Nicki and Jasmine's new apartment, all the events going on this week, all the hot people we passed on the street and in the halls, and a million more things that make me wish I was joining the rest of them (sans Jaya, who's taking a year off to travel) in college life immediately. My face must give me away, because Elly's arm snakes around my waist and she pulls me close, the leather cuff and silver chains on her wrist digging into my skin just enough to be comforting. "I'll come up and you'll come down," she murmurs in my ear. "And you'll be sending out your own applications soon enough."

I will, and thanks to Elly and my mom *and* Elly's mom, I won't just be throwing shit at the wall and hoping something sticks. And, of course, there's Jasmine, whose business—well, I guess it's *our* business now—has kept me plenty busy over the past couple of weeks, especially after Lara's friend Kiki asked me to draw up some marketing materials for her massive podcast.

All in all, I have faith this is going somewhere, that *I'm* going somewhere.

And speaking of going somewhere . . . The way Elly's fingertips are stroking the skin just above the waistband of my cutoffs, I'm starting to lose the ability to focus on anything anyone else is saying. Then her thigh presses against mine, and things start to go a little hazy.

I mean. It's been two weeks. Two weeks of absolutely nothing but solo activity and some text messages that are definitely not for public consumption. And now we're in her dorm room, knowing that her roommate won't be coming until tomorrow?

"Should I tell everyone to get the fuck out?" she murmurs in my ear.

"I thought you'd never ask."

Turns out, she doesn't need to, because Lara happens to glance our way right at that moment, bites her lip to tamp down a smile, and says, "Okay, I know that look. Everybody out."

"Wha?" Nicki, who must've been midsentence, looks back and forth between Jasmine and Lara. "What'd I say?" Then she follows Lara's eyeline and laughs while Jaya says, "Yikes," and they do, indeed, get the fuck out. "We're still doing dinner, and *some* of us would like to check out the hot guys setting up the new taqueria in Union Square, so don't even think of skipping out!" Nicki calls, right before she slams the door behind her.

"Like I'm thinking of anything at all right now." Elly smothers her laugh in my shoulder, and everywhere a tendril of red hair's escaped from its tied-up knot feels like a firework where it grazes my skin. "Well, except . . ."

"I hear you have brand-new sheets," I tease, hopping up and holding out my hands.

"Totally unused," she confirms as we move from Virany's bed to hers, pulling off our dusty, sweaty shirts as we go. "Honestly, this bed looks way, way too neat." She climbs on top, rising on her knees and cupping a hand around the back of my neck. "I'm gonna need some help messing it up."

"And here I thought we were done exchanging souvenirs for the day," I murmur as I lean in for a kiss so deep, I can feel myself drowning. "But maybe I should leave you something to remember me by."

She laughs breathlessly as I leave a trail of kisses with teeth down her collarbone and up her throat. "I feel like I should be warning you not to give me any hickeys, but who's gonna care about that now?"

"My thoughts exactly." Now, *that* one will definitely leave a mark. "I know I'm not here yet, but I really think I love college already."

"You'll get here," she says, pulling me down on top of her

and twining her legs with mine. "No need to rush. Took us forever to get the nerve to talk to each other, and look at us."

"Ah, yes, moving so slowly that all your best friends just fled because we were literally radiating horniness."

"Oh, shut up." And she kisses me, and I do. There'll be plenty of time to talk and other things to move slowly on later.

It can wait for another day.

Acknowledgments

This was an extremely fun book to write, not least because I pulled from so many different things and people I love as influences on so many elements of Natalya's story—well, stories—both big and small. Like just about everyone's, my teen years and beyond had their ups and downs, but this book was borne in part of a million of my favorite moments, and it goes out to every concert buddy, frequent host, and anyone with whom I ever did anything remotely cool in high school—Tani, Dani (and, frankly, the entire Leeds clan), Talia, Rachel, Ricki, Barrie, Hannah, Lea, Sasha, Graber, Liz, Ilana, Jon, Harry, Avi, Savage, Ami, Noah, Jason, Faber, Aliza, Jess, Erin, Zevi, Sara, Goldie, and so many others. (I'm using "remotely cool" extremely loosely, in case that's not clear.)

For various other inspirations, thank you in no particular order to *Degrassi* (especially Stacey Farber/Ellie Nash), the late Chris Cornell, Foo Fighters, Vitamin String Quartet, Me First and the Gimme Gimmes, the late Edgar Allan Poe, indie bookstores, the Taïm truck, and the entire Failure is an Option crew for inspiring Dinner Party just enough to make Jessica proud but not enough to make Michelle kill me for sharing our secrets.

Of course, huge thanks are owed to the team that's been crushing it for *three* books now, including my agent, Patricia Nelson; editor, Vicki Lame; editorial assistant, Vanessa Aguirre; publicist, Meghan Harrington; marketing pros, Alexis Neuville and Brant Janeway; designer, Devan Norman; and cover designer extraordinaire Kerri Resnick for making every single book look, read, and jump out into the world like a dream. I'm so grateful to you all and to everyone else at Wednesday and beyond for all their amazing work in production, managing editorial, sales, and creative services, including Carla Benton, Diane Dilluvio, Marinda Valenti, Eric Smith, Rebecca Schmidt, Sofrina Hinton, Jennifer Edwards, Jennifer Golding, Jaime Bode, Jennifer Medina, Julia Metzger, D'Kela Duncan, Isaac Loewen, Alexa Rosenberg, Britta Saghi, Kim Ludlam, Tom Thompson, and Dylan Helstien. And to Petra Braun, thank you for delivering cover art that absolutely knocks my socks off every time I see it.

I also must send so much love and thanks to my audio publisher, OrangeSky, especially Kate Dilyard and Bethany Strout, for yet another wonderful collaboration. I feel so lucky to have you as such a huge part of my publishing life.

I'm also extremely grateful for the expert eyes and opinions of Elle Grenier, David Nino, and Brianna Shrum; to Naz Kutub, for the LA help in a pinch; and to Becca Podos and Katherine Locke, because I can't remember which of you introduced me to "Red Sea pedestrians," but fortunately, I like you both.

Speaking of authors I like, I'm so thankful for all the company, commiseration, advice, texts, and Slack/Discord chats along the way. I'll spare everyone repeating the same wonderful people from book to book, but given the sheer volume of communication, I do have to give special shout-outs to Katie (again), Marieke Nijkamp, Jennifer Dugan, Tess Sharpe, Lev Rosen, and Jennifer Iacopelli. And of course, to the whole Springer math team, past and present (even you, Leach): I hope you feel my love for all that time together in these pages.

Second-to-last, but never least, thank you to my family. Between graphic design (thank you for the research help, Dad!), having a way with kids, being stellar in the kitchen, and temporarily embracing LA, I hope you see yourselves in all the good ways in this book. (And none of the bad ways! Let the record show that Technion and blond hair aside, Natalya's parents were based on exactly zero family members.) I know there are a lot of paths life could've taken, and I am eminently grateful that ours happen to have brought us all together. (Like, one-hour radius together.)

Finally, while I want to express endless love and gratitude for all the Bookstagrammers, bloggers, BookTokers, and everyone else out there who spreads the word about my books, this particularly goes out to those who wholeheartedly and enthusiastically embraced the Sapphic Jewish rep of *Cool for the Summer*. You impacted this book way more than you know, and I hope it does you proud.